Perchance to Dream

JoAnn Durgin

Cover Photographer: Cammi Macy O'Teter

Cover Model: Maci O'Teter Hindman

Cover Design: MaxCovers
www.fiverr.com/maxcovers

About the Author

~~♥~~

In addition to *Perchance to Dream*, JoAnn Durgin is the author of the beloved Lewis Legacy Series of contemporary Christian romantic adventures: *Awakening, Second Time Around, Twin Hearts, Daydreams, Moonbeams,* and *Enchantment,* as well as *Prelude,* the prequel to The Lewis Legacy Series. JoAnn's stand-alone novels include *Catching Serenity* and *Heart's Design.* Her novellas and short novels include *Love So Amazing* (The Wondrous Love Series, Book 1), *Echoes of Edinburgh,* and the popular Starlight Christmas Series: *Meet Me Under the Mistletoe, Starlight, Star Bright, Sleigh Ride Together with You,* and *Starlight in Her Eyes.*

A former estate administration paralegal, JoAnn now enjoys writing full-time and lives with her husband, Jim, three children and first grandbaby, Amelia Grace, in her native southern Indiana.

JoAnn loves to hear from her readers. Please feel free to contact her:

WEBSITE:
www.joanndurgin.com

FACEBOOK:
www.facebook.com/authorjoanndurgin

Author's Note
~♥~

Dear Readers,

Ellie Franklin and Ryan Sullivan could be your neighbors down the street or a young couple in your church. Two kids who grew up together and fell in love. Their story is one filled with faith, love, family, and hope as the Lord works in the lives of Ellie and Ryan to bring about His perfect will.

This book is respectfully dedicated to the men and women who have given their time, their energies—and many the ultimate sacrifice—to valiantly defend and protect the freedoms we hold so dear. I honor and commend you for your willingness to serve your country. For those waging the battle on the home front, you have my prayers and deepest admiration.

Special thanks to my very special reader, Cammi Macy O'Teter, for the use of her lovely photograph used for the cover of **Perchance to Dream**. My deepest gratitude goes to the beautiful bride and cover model—Cammi's daughter, Maci O'Teter Hindman—for graciously granting her permission to use the enchanting bridal image captured on her wedding day.

Perchance to Dream is first and foremost a love story, but it is also a story of leaning on one's faith and trusting in the precious promises of the Lord. The setting is small-town Ohio during the Christmas season, but its message is timeless and enduring. Just as Ellie claims those promises to bring about her own Christmas miracle with Ryan, may you seek our precious Savior in every season of your life, and fall in love with Him all over again.

Blessings Always,
JoAnn Durgin
Matthew 5:16

Perchance to Dream
Book Description
~~♥~~

Ellie Franklin has known Ryan Sullivan her entire life. As their Christmas wedding approaches, Ryan is expected home from his second deployment to Afghanistan. Excitement is in the air as Ellie prepares for his homecoming, and the citizens of Cade's Corner, Ohio, anxiously await the wedding of their hometown sweethearts.

When an unforeseen event occurs, will Ellie's plans be postponed or will they come to a screeching halt? With her faith and family to sustain her, as well as the support of an entire town, will this bride's prayers for a holiday miracle be answered?

A heartwarming novel of unfailing love, family, never giving up hope, and claiming the precious promises of God. And, through it all, discovering a true Christmas miracle.

Theme Scripture Verses
~~♥~~

Deuteronomy 20:4
For the Lord your God is the one who goes with you, to fight for you against your enemies, to save you.

Ecclesiastes 3:1-8
[1]There is an appointed time for everything. And there is a time for every event under heaven—
[2]A time to give birth and a time to die;
A time to plant and a time to uproot what is planted.
[3]A time to kill and a time to heal;
A time to tear down and a time to build up.
[4]A time to weep and a time to laugh;
A time to mourn and a time to dance.
[5]A time to throw stones and a time to gather stones;
A time to embrace and a time to shun embracing.
[6]A time to search and a time to give up as lost;
A time to keep and a time to throw away.
[7]A time to tear apart and a time to sew together;
A time to be silent and a time to speak.
[8]A time to love and a time to hate;
A time for war and a time for peace.

Jeremiah 29:11
'For I know the plans that I have for you,' declares the Lord, 'plans for welfare and not for calamity to give you a future and a hope.'

Matthew 21:21-22
[21]And Jesus answered and said to them, "Truly I say to you, if you have faith and do not doubt, you will not only do what was done to the fig tree, but even if you say to this mountain, 'Be taken up and cast into the sea,' it will happen. [22]And all things you ask in prayer, believing, you will receive."

Romans 8:28

And we know that God causes all things to work together for good to those who love God, to those who are called according to His purpose.

Ephesians 2:8-9

[8]For by grace you have been saved through faith; and that not of yourselves, it is the gift of God; [9]not as a result of works, so that no one may boast.

1 Timothy 1:5

But the goal of our instruction is love from a pure heart and a good conscience and a sincere faith.

1 John 3:17

But whoever has the world's goods, and sees his brother in need and closes his heart against him, how does the love of God abide in him?

Chapter 1
~~♥~~

After Ryan Joseph Sullivan dropped a frog down the back of my shirt, I figured I'd hate him for the rest of my life.

At the time, Ryan was six, and I—Eleanor "Ellie" Rose Franklin—was five. While I wriggled around and screamed bloody murder, Ryan had the nerve to laugh. Laugh! I should have suspected as much. He was, after all, a boy, that most dreaded of subspecies. Boys were gross. They smelled stinky, did dumb stuff, and the things they talked about were disgusting.

Still, there was something about that boy.

Turning my back to Ryan, I flapped my shirt up and down in an attempt to dislodge the pesky amphibian. When he finally hopped to the ground, I pivoted in a half-circle and glared at Ryan.

"We're in the same Sunday school," I hissed with all the righteous indignation I could muster. "God says we should love our neighbor. Why do you hate me so much?"

"You are such a girl." Ryan crossed his arms and assumed a battle stance. "I don't hate you, but I can't go to the game this Saturday because of you." He didn't even need to tell me which game. Ryan loves the Cleveland Cavaliers more than just about anything in life.

"Huh?" I shook my head in disbelief at the big old pouter. "That's not my fault!" Boys thought girls could be such sissies, but they were just as bad. Sometimes more.

"Our moms have to go to some stupid ladies tea at the church with your sisters, so that means your dad has to stay home and babysit you."

"So? Your dad could still take you," I said.

"Yeah, but it's not happening. He says we're not going now."

Mirroring Ryan, I planted my feet apart and crossed my arms. "Still soooo not my fault." I lifted my chin to meet his gaze.

"Is too your fault." His expression spelled d-i-s-g-u-s-t.

"Is not." I stuck out my tongue. That standoff happened on a Wednesday, and we didn't see each other again until Sunday morning at church. As it happens, we were studying the Ten Commandments. Ryan sat across the table from me, engrossed in a conversation about superheroes with Trevor King before our class started.

"Ryan, what does 'love thy neighbor' mean to you?" I slapped my hand over my mouth to stifle my giggles while Ryan ignored me (although he did the eye-dart thing in my direction).

Our teacher, Mrs. Sappenfield, couldn't possibly have known anything about the frog incident. I don't think even our mothers knew about it. If I'd told Mom that Ryan had dropped a frog down my shirt, she might not have allowed me to play with him anymore. As annoying as he could be, Ryan wasn't all bad.

Ryan straightened in his chair and twiddled his thumbs on top of the table while Mrs. Sappenfield waited for his response. After a few seconds, he brightened. I recognized that look—he'd been seized by a burst of inspiration.

"It, uh, means you don't blame them for things that aren't their fault." Although Ryan didn't look at me for the rest of the lesson, I never forgot his words. I knew he couldn't really hate me all that much, and I definitely appreciated God's timing and sense of humor.

Ryan grew up four doors down from me on the opposite side of Juniper Street in Cade's Corner, a small town just outside of Cleveland, Ohio. He was born on May 8th— Mother's Day the year he was born—and I was born on May 15th of the following year. The Sullivan family's house is slightly bigger than ours. Both are traditional red brick, middle-class homes with two-car garages and well-maintained lawns (in the months we're not buried in snow from the effects of Lake Erie).

Our mothers are close friends. By virtue of their friendship alone, I suppose Ryan and I were destined to tolerate one another. Our fathers belonged to a few mutual business organizations and attended sporting events together so my dad could escape the "House of Women."

Ryan and I spent a lot of time together during our "formative years" as my Grandma Franklin used to say. Sure, we played with the other kids on our street, but we were the closest in age. In the summer, we'd throw handfuls of sand at each other in our turtle sandbox, make mud pies, catch fireflies, go to birthday parties, play on the teeter-totter at the playground, and splash in the aboveground pool behind Ryan's house. Almost without exception, we'd be the last two playing outside until our mothers called for us to come home.

The cold temperatures and snow forced us to stay inside a lot during the winter months, which both Ryan and I found torturous. For the short periods every day when our mothers allowed us outside to play, we took full advantage. We made snowmen and snow angels, pelted each other with snowballs, zoomed around Dead Man's Curve on sleds, and then we'd gulp down warm cocoa with gooey, melting marshmallows in either his family's kitchen or mine.

For whatever reason, Ryan took it upon himself to tease me. Ryan's list of "crimes" (more like minor offenses) was already lengthy by the time he dropped that aforesaid frog down my shirt. Even after his admission in Sunday school, he continued to pester and annoy me. Ryan probably took pity on me since I don't have a brother to do the honors, only two older sisters who ignored me most of the time. They hung around more with his only sibling, his brother, Nick, four years Ryan's senior.

My oldest sister, Kara, was ten when I was born, so she qualified as the Planned Child. Then along came Staci, who is seven years older. She was the Wanted Child. Since Dad hoped for a boy (according to Kara), I wasn't the

Afterthought, not the Disappointment, but the Third Child. Period. That's it.

We don't look much alike, either, since my sisters are both blonde and blue-eyed like Mom, and I'm dark-haired and hazel-eyed like Dad. The one physical trait I inherited from my mother is my petite stature while Kara and Staci got their height from Dad's side of the family. Total injustice, but it's the way God made me, so I've finally come to terms with being the runt of the family and can appreciate its finer points (there are a few). I have a long neck, and I'm fairly well-proportioned, so I'm not entirely lacking, genetically speaking.

As far as I can tell, I haven't suffered any lasting psychological or emotional damage from knowing my father wanted a boy the third time around. If anything, I was closer to Dad than Kara or Staci. My sisters were always more interested in boys, makeup, boys, clothes, shoes, purses, boys—anything girly that involved frills or fashion. And, oh yes, boys. Kara and Staci's influence was more in the form of "don't do this" or "don't touch that" instead of giving me useful, helpful advice. Every now and then I'd share a special moment with each of them, but for a long time, we moved in entirely different realms of being.

As it always does, the reminder of Dad makes me smile. Losing my father when I was 16 was the hardest thing I've ever endured. Not a day passes that I don't miss him, but a certain sweetness has now mollified my sadness.

Dad was my first love, my first hero.

And then along came Ryan.

My cell phone chimed with an incoming text, startling me from my musing. I seized the phone from my desktop. *Ryan.*

HEY, SASS. BACK AT HOME BASE NOW. MISS MY BEAUTIFUL GIRL.

I couldn't move my fingers fast enough. RYAN! SO GREAT TO HEAR FROM YOU. MISS YOU, TOO. STILL ON TO SKYPE TONIGHT?

YOU KNOW IT. 10 P.M. CLEVELAND TIME. LOVE YOU, ELLIE.

CAN'T WAIT. LOVE YOU BACK, RYAN. XOXOXO

My sparkling engagement ring with its modest round diamond caught my eye as I lowered my phone to the desk. I've proudly worn Ryan's ring for a year-and-a-half, and it shines brighter than ever (I'd also just had it cleaned professionally). My gaze moved to the picture of the two of us taken during the summer before Ryan's second and (hopefully) final deployment. Laughing, so in love, sharing the day at Cedar Point Amusement Park, the "Roller Coaster Capital of the World" in Sandusky.

I picked up the frame and sat back in my chair, studying the photo. I ran my finger over the image of my fiancé—Ryan Joseph Sullivan, E-3 Private First Class, U.S. Army.

Ryan stands at six foot two (nearly a foot taller than me), with thick, dark wavy hair (until he had to shave it off—a travesty if not for the most noble of reasons), a tiny dimple (not really a cleft) in his chin, strong features and smooth skin, a slightly sharp nose (I tell him it makes him look aristocratic) and ears bigger than he'd like (they're adorable), and deep-set, gorgeous eyes the color of light sapphires with a hint of gray.

He works out and takes care of himself. Ryan has always been athletic, but I think it's ingrained in him because of his Army training. The reward? Broad shoulders, a firm chest, and muscles in all the best places.

If I listen closely, I can hear his laughter. See how the right side of his mouth lifts higher than the left when he smiles. Remember the warmth of his hand in mine. Witness how the blue in his eyes darkens and intensifies right before he presses his lips to mine.

Oh, how I love Ryan's smile.

How I've missed his touch.

I long for his kiss.

I ache for my best friend.

With a deep sigh, I replaced the photo on my desk. I can't look at anything, do anything, or say anything, without thoughts of Ryan constantly popping into my mind. I haven't seen him in almost 14 months. The closer the time draws near for his return stateside on December 20, 2006, the more excited and anxious I become. Anything to serve as a distraction and to pass the time, especially in these final days before his return, is a relief and a blessing.

Now I need to turn my attention back to Perchance to Dream.

The first thing I do every afternoon when I come to the Perchance to Dream headquarters—a small space in a quaint, historic storefront in downtown Cade's Corner—is flip the calendar to the current date.

I turned the page and smiled. The verse for today is from 1 John 3:17: *But whoever has the world's goods, and sees his brother in need and closes his heart against him, how does the love of God abide in him?* What a perfect verse for the nonprofit, charitable organization Ryan and I co-founded three years ago.

"Ellie?"

Maura Hennessey, my closest girlfriend, maid of honor, and faithful assistant at Perchance to Dream, stood in the doorway of my office.

"Sorry to interrupt. You look deep in thought."

"Just thinking about Ryan. Come on in." When I motioned to her, Maura approached my desk. Tall, with Nordic good looks and impossibly slender, she was still dressed in her dark gray suit jacket, pencil skirt, and crisp white blouse from her day job as a paralegal in Nick Sullivan's law office. In my old jeans and holiday sweater, my long hair pulled back in a ponytail, I feel casual and underdressed by comparison.

Maura's sole concession to working after hours was the one button undone at her neckline. As usual, her long, straight blonde hair is pulled back into a rather severe bun— Maura calls it a chic "chignon"—that emphasizes her model-worthy cheekbones. Fancy French word or not, it's still an old-fashioned spinster bun.

"People take me more seriously when I wear my hair this way," Maura insisted when I suggested she wear her hair down every now and then. In some ways, she and Nick were two of a kind. Beneath all that professionalism were the kindest, most compassionate individuals I'm honored to know and count as my dear friends.

"I have the finalized letter to Senator Hardin for your signature and the updated list you wanted." She handed them over and tucked an escaping strand of hair behind one ear.

"Thanks." I scanned the sheet with at least ten new names and requests—a surprising number considering we typically wind down the Perchance to Dream project by the middle of December. "Looks like we have some more gifts to buy. I'll start working on it right away."

"Those are the last ones that trickled in after the deadline. This is it for the year."

I shook my head. "I really hate enforcing a deadline for something like this." The needs are ongoing throughout the year, but that doesn't make me feel any better.

Maura waited until I glanced up from the list and then fixed her compassionate, blue-eyed gaze on me. "Perchance to Dream is making a difference, Ellie. One child at a time. You're giving kids hope. You're showing them that someone cares, and no one can put a high enough value on something like that."

I gave her a grateful smile. "Thanks. That was our goal when Ryan and I started Perchance."

Maura tapped her fist on the desk. "If you need extra help with anything, let me know."

"Will do. I'd like to get everything wrapped up, so to speak, by the end of the week. Could you pick up some rolls of oversized wrapping paper?" I glanced at the list again. "Some of these toys come in large boxes."

"Got it covered," Maura assured me. "On another bright note, tonight's your big reunion Skype session with Ryan, right?"

"Sure is." I glanced at my watch. I've lost count of how many times I'd checked the time throughout the day. "At exactly ten p.m. tonight. Fourteen days, six hours, three minutes, and thirteen seconds—give or take—since we last Skyped." I am immensely grateful to the brainiac responsible for creating the technology that makes it possible for me to talk with Ryan across the globe in Afghanistan.

"Enjoy your chat, and give Ryan my best. I was at Keeley's Market the other day, and Isabelle Sanders called your wedding *the* social event of the decade. Two hometown kids who've known each other their whole lives. Your story has captured the imagination of everyone in town."

"I just want Ryan home again so we can write the next chapter of our lives." I laughed under my breath and crossed my eyes. "Corny is my middle name these days. I can't seem to help myself."

"You're entitled. I'd feel the same way if I had a handsome soldier coming home to marry me on Christmas Day. I'll be here for another couple of hours. If you need me, holler." Maura departed with a wave over one shoulder.

I retrieved the letter for Senator Hardin and read through it one final time. The big-hearted politician was one of our best supporters. Satisfied my words to the state senator sounded appropriately formal yet also personal, I signed the letter and placed it in the basket on my desk.

Next I concentrated on the list of names and made a few shopping notes. During the Christmas season, I devour the weekly sale flyers every Sunday afternoon. A number of the wished-for toys had been prominently featured this week. Due to their popularity, I pray I can still find them. Because of the toy shopping I do for Perchance to Dream, I've become somewhat of an aficionado on the best places to buy certain items, cost comparisons, and price matching. The young mothers at church routinely come to me for advice and recommendations.

An hour later, I tucked the list and my notes inside my purse and grabbed my things. With the signed letter and my tote bag in hand, I walked into the outer office and stopped beside Maura's desk.

"I've signed the letter. And now I'm armed with my list and ready to fight the crazed shoppers to fulfill these Christmas wishes."

"Let's hope it doesn't come to that although I hear shopping for holiday toys can be a competitive sport." Maura took the letter from me. "I'll take care of mailing this first thing tomorrow morning on my way to the law office."

"Thanks." I pushed my arms through the sleeves of my coat. "I'll bring the other toys in by the end of the week so we can get them wrapped. I'm glad we ordered extra Bibles this year since it looks like we're going to need most of them. Ditto the pink and blue notecards."

She nodded. "Based on the increase since we started three years ago, we're going to need even more next year."

I smiled as I buttoned my coat. "Thanks for all you do, Maura. Ryan and I couldn't operate Perchance to Dream without you, Nick, and our volunteers."

"Right back at you, my friend." Maura leaned against her desk and crossed her arms. "You may not realize this, but I look forward to this project. In some ways, it's my sanity."

"How so?" I pulled my purple knit scarf from my tote bag and began to wrap it around my neck.

Maura gave me a weary smile that sent sparks of guilt shooting through me.

"Things have been tense at the law office lately. I feel like I'm spinning my wheels with some of our current cases. Coming here in the evenings has been a God-send for me. I know it's been the same for Nick, too. So, in some ways, I'm sorry to see Perchance come to an end for this year."

Her mention of Nick gave me pause. I've suspected for the last three months—since we'd begun our work in earnest with Perchance to Dream this year—that Maura harbored a secret affection for Ryan's older brother. I'm certain Maura considers it inappropriate to have a crush on her boss much less to consider dating him. Granted, it could get complicated, but my two favorite people are meant for each other. Now to convince *them*.

A thought popped into my mind.

"Maura, can you come to dinner at the house on Friday night? Say seven o'clock?" After tugging my gloves out of my coat pocket, I slipped them on and wiggled my fingers. When she hesitated, I hastened to plead my case. "It's the holiday season. Live a little." I arched a brow. "Time to let your hair down for a change."

Maura's smile brightened. "I'd love to come. Let me guess. You're still working through those recipes for Ryan and need a guinea pig?"

"Of course. It's my other project besides what we're doing here. I've made all the recipes from his mother except for three I've been avoiding due to suspect ingredients. I'm hoping Ryan will be amazed by my improved cooking skills."

"I'm sure he'll love you for it. Even more than he already does," Maura said. "I'm happy to be your guinea pig. What can I bring?"

"Some sparkling cider might be nice. Pick a flavor. Anything's fine."

"I can do that."

"Oh, and Maura?" I tucked the ends of my scarf into the front of my wool coat. "One more thing?"

Headed back to her chair, Maura paused. "Sure thing. What do you need?"

"Bring Nick with you to dinner."

I caught Maura's surprise but tugged on my purple knit hat and darted out the front door before she could respond. I might be sneaky in my methods, but I prayed Maura would take my less-than-subtle suggestion.

Chapter 2
~~♥~~

On the way home, I stopped by Mom's for a quick visit to discuss wedding details. We've finally transitioned into the active preparation phase. Afterwards, I darted into Keeley's Market to pick up a few ingredients I'd need for the dinner on Friday night. I'd already planned which recipe I'd try next and—call it providence—I'd written the items on an index card and slipped it inside my purse earlier in the week.

While I was in the whole foods section at the market, Ryan texted again.

CAN'T WAIT TO SEE YOU TONIGHT, BABY.

My heart jumped. Resting my arms on the shopping cart, I quickly punched in my response.

MY FIANCÉ IS THE JEALOUS TYPE. WE MUST BE CAREFUL.

☺ LOVE MY GIRL. TALK TO YOU TONIGHT, ELLIE. NOT LONG NOW UNTIL I'M HOME TO STAY.

CAN'T WAIT. COUNTING THE DAYS AND HOURS. ALL MY LOVE.

♥ ELLIE. BYE.

BYE RYAN. UNTIL TONIGHT. XOXOXO XOXOXO

As I pocketed my phone, I wondered how Ryan expected me to function effectively when he kept texting me. Not that I'm complaining.

Ryan's mom, Mary, had given me my husband-to-be's favorite recipes over a year ago. A couple of days each week, I'd make one of the dishes and then I'd choose a new recipe from a cookbook I'd checked out from the library, found online, or spotted in a magazine. The chicken dishes and casseroles are relatively uncomplicated. They tasted fine, but under no circumstances will I ever make anything with beets (much to my dismay, I'd discovered one among Mary's recipes). I teased Ryan that I was going to write a "No Beets" clause into our wedding vows.

"Face it, you'll never be a chef, Ellie," Ryan told me once (thankfully, he's since revised his opinion). I was twelve at the time, and I'd made an awful, gag-inducing concoction with broccoli and carrots (his favorite vegetables, as it turns out, a fact I did *not* know beforehand) and mushroom soup for our church social. Mistake number one: not using a recipe and believing that because I'd successfully made a green bean casserole, I could improvise like a pro.

Kara had informed me that cooking vegetables "beyond recognition" negated their nutritional value. So, afraid of that, I undercooked them. Out of desperation, I tossed a butter-flavored cracker topping and grated cheddar cheese over the so-called casserole since that was Mom's quick fix for any questionable dish. I'd hoped it would also detract from the ugly grayish/brown color of the soup. It seriously looked like mud. Still, I packed up my mud and quietly added it to the buffet line at church. And hoped for the best.

Unfortunately, the crunchy mess tasted as unappetizing as it looked.

As if things couldn't get any worse, my dad's business partner, Eldridge Gray, cracked a tooth at that church supper. I wanted to run and hide for fear he'd cracked his tooth by biting into an undercooked broccoli floret or baby carrot. No accusations were ever made, but I suffered a guilt complex over that cracked tooth for years.

Fully aware it was one of my first attempts at cooking (another lesson learned—never make an untested dish for a crowd), Ryan forced down every bite and proclaimed it was one of the best casseroles he'd ever tasted. In spite of his earlier offensive remark about my future cooking skills (as if he could possibly know such a thing), I considered him quite the sport for lying through his teeth on my behalf. What a guy. Then he marched back to the buffet line for seconds. Not to worry since there was plenty left over.

I'm fairly certain that's when I began to fall in love with Ryan.

In the past few months, especially, I've bounced around town with a goofy, besotted smile. I'm sure I've been annoyingly upbeat and perky. "I'm getting married on Christmas," I'd sing under my breath to a no-name tune like some deliriously happy animated character. Deranged might be more like it. Even the frigid temperatures and unrelenting snow cannot dampen my mood. Instead of wet and bone-chilling, the snow is light, fluffy, and romantic.

Love colors my world happy.

Billy Crandall darted behind a produce display at Keeley's Market last week in a clear attempt to avoid me. I'd heard the poor kid got dumped by his girlfriend, so my blatant reminder of premarital bliss must have offended his sensibilities. Of course, I feel bad for him, but Billy's only sixteen, a mere babe in terms of romantic relationships.

Not even crotchety Marvin Kinderson in the town library can deter my enthusiasm. That codger has been admonishing me to be quiet for years, but he isn't about to stop me now. If I wasn't mistaken, the corners of his lips curled the last time I was in the library browsing through the cookbook section.

You'd think for someone who's known her fiancé her entire life, I wouldn't be so giddy and obnoxious. If anything, knowing Ryan and I would be joined as man and wife soon made me more excited. Instead of the phone calls, texts, emails, and Skype sessions we'd shared for the past 14 months, we'd finally share the home we'd picked out, fought over (the little stuff), and prayed over before he left for Afghanistan. Ryan will be right beside me to try out new recipes, plant a garden, snuggle together and watch movies, do our devotions, and share everything. Maybe get a puppy. Start a family in a couple of years (we'd like at least two or three children).

Ryan plans to finish his senior year at Ohio State (the extension in Cleveland) after his return from the military, looking to a career in business management. I'm sure my future husband will also be active in the local military recruiting office while I plan on a career in marketing and public relations. I'd decided to wait to finish my education until Ryan returns, although he has not endorsed that decision. For now, I work part-time at The Beckett Agency, a small but prestigious advertising agency in Cade's Corner. For one thing, temporarily postponing my education gives me more time to devote to Perchance to Dream.

I quickened my steps as the small, one-story Cape Cod style cottage came into view when I turned the corner onto Dream Street. Yes, Dream Street. I was convinced the good Lord Himself had a hand in that one. Our future address wasn't the reason we'd put the bid on the house, but it hadn't hurt.

Reaching into my purse, I fumbled for the keys. I rushed into the house, pushed the door closed behind me, shed my coat, and plopped onto the sofa.

I'd taken my time decorating and furnishing this cozy home. Until recently, I divided my nights between the family homestead with Mom and the new house. I wanted everything to be perfect since we'd be getting married, honeymooning, and then settling in here right away.

I'd referred to our house as our "future love nest" when I'd Skyped with Ryan two months ago. I should have known he would not be amused.

"We're not birds," he said. "Nests are for birds."

"But it will be filled with love," I'd insisted like the eternal optimist I am. He hadn't argued that point.

Ryan's not perfect, by any means, and I'm definitely far from perfect. Yet he loves me in spite of my many faults. For one thing, Ryan gets grumpy when he's tired and sometimes gets fired up about things over which he has no control (then again, so do I). We've both learned when to shut up and give in. Not that we can finish each other's sentences (why would we want to?).

As I see it, here's the most important thing: by the grace of God, we've settled into the grooves of life, and we know how to repair the fissures before they crack and become irreparable.

I understand marriage can be difficult—even in the *best* of circumstances—and that it's not all sunshine and roses. My parents had some pretty fierce arguments, but they always took their words to another room of the house. Ditto Ryan's parents (from what he's told me although I've never witnessed a cross word between them). My older sisters and their husbands are always involved in some tiff or other. No one is immune from disagreements because of the basic differences in human nature. If we agreed all the time, life would be incredibly boring.

Tugging off one snow boot and then the other, I made small grunting sounds. Then I checked my watch and ran into the bathroom to brush my teeth and gargle. Silly to gargle for a Skype session, I know, but it was my routine. I ran a cleansing cloth over my face and then dusted light color over my pale winter cheeks. Much better.

Ryan likes it best when I'm fresh-faced without makeup. He claims to love the light smattering of freckles dotting my upper cheeks. When we're alone, Ryan often traces his finger over the patterns of my freckles and then kisses them, one by one (as best he can). That's the type of tender, romantic memory that carries me through my roughest moments, especially when he's deployed, and I'm missing him the most. This second deployment has been much harder on both Ryan and me.

After releasing my hair from the ponytail, I ran a comb through it and then arranged it around my shoulders. Then I applied a light coat of mascara and pale pink gloss. Checking my smile in the mirror, I slicked my tongue over my teeth. "Thank you, Dr. Melton." I'd worn braces from the age of nine until I was almost eleven.

Ryan told me once that he could tell I "might be cute" when my braces were removed. The day they came off, I marched down to Ryan's house to show off my new smile. All he said was, "Good job, Doc Melton." I ran straight home, buried my head under my pillow, and shed a few tears. Why should I care what Ryan Sullivan thought? Realistically, what had I expected him to do? I dried my tears and vowed never to shed another tear over that boy.

Ryan was one of those blessed kids who didn't need braces, only a retainer. He kept flicking that gross thing in and out of his mouth to get a rise out of me (another one of Grandma Franklin's sayings). Once he dropped his retainer in my cup in the school cafeteria without my knowledge. When I started to take a sip, Ryan grabbed the cup from my hand, spilling the contents all over me and the floor. Then he confessed his crime and vowed to get me into the middle school football games free for the entire season. Being a first-stringer was an advantage, so it's not like it cost him anything. Still, his regret was obvious, and I considered his efforts to make things right an admirable gesture.

My gaze darted to the clock on the bathroom wall. "Ten minutes to showtime."

I took one last glimpse of my appearance in the mirror. No, this wouldn't work. The sweater had to go. This occasion definitely calls for my light blue silk blouse. I ran into the bedroom and scanned the contents of the closet. With Nick's help, I'd already moved most of Ryan's "civilian" clothes into the closet. They currently resided on the left side with mine on the right.

Now, where is that blouse? I shuffled through a few hangers on the rack.

Bingo!

After pulling it out, I carefully tugged the sweater over my head and then slipped into the blouse. I loved the silky softness of the fabric against my skin. Ryan loves this color on me, and the blouse is much more feminine than my holiday sweater. I want to be alluring when he sees me, not remind the man of his grandmother.

I fluffed my hair again and checked my appearance in the full-length mirror. No cockeyed buttons. Good. As a last-minute impulse, I unfastened the top two buttons. The last few times I'd talked with Ryan, I'd worn a turtleneck. Not that I'm trying to show myself off—far from it—but what does it hurt to remind my fiancé that I actually *have* a neck and smooth skin buried beneath my multiple layers of clothing?

Cade's Corner is home, so bundling up in heavy clothes is a given. We make our concessions in life.

Hawaii sounded better with each passing minute.

Marriage sounded better with each passing second.

Ducking into the closet one last time, I rummaged through my collection of shoes and pulled out a pair of black, high-heeled pumps. "It's been too long, my friends." I hopped on one foot and then the other as I peeled off my thick wool socks and slipped on the heels. Maybe I was silly, but Skype conversation or not, I wanted to dress the part. The shoes made me feel prettier and more like a flesh-and-blood woman.

Satisfied that I looked presentable, I darted into the kitchen and grabbed a cold water bottle from the fridge. Then I hurried down the hallway to the small second bedroom which doubled as the study (until the day when it would be transformed into a pretty, pastel-colored nursery).

My heart pounded—hard—and I moved my hand over my chest as though that action could somehow slow it down. Fat chance. T-minus 30 seconds to Skype time.

Dropping into the chair, I switched on the computer. I drummed my fingers on the desk as I waited for the computer to boot up and grinned at the sight of Ryan's weights, baseball bats, and golf clubs in the corner. Then my gaze traveled to the bookshelf stuffed full of his various sports trophies and ribbons.

Ryan's dedication to physical fitness made me ponder how many hours I could spend in the gym before the wedding. Starvation wasn't an option to lose weight. I'd never make it past the third day. Besides, Ryan fell in love with me just the way I am. I hadn't gained any weight since he deployed, and in fact, I'd lost ten pounds. If I thought I wouldn't risk straining an important muscle, I might try lifting some of those weights. Nope. Bad idea.

The last few times we've Skyped, I've noticed how Ryan's skin is bronzed a gorgeous golden color in stark contrast to my oh-so-pale winter white skin. When Mom showed her sister, Susan, a recent photo of Ryan, my aunt thought I was marrying a Mediterranean man, and that I'd ditched "that cute boy from down the street."

Should I hit the tanning booth before the wedding? No, that idea had *catastrophe* written all over it. I tan fairly well, but I'm reminded of the misadventures of the best man in a wedding of good friends. The poor guy visited a tanning booth the day before the ceremony and was red-faced, literally, in all the photos. The bride told me he'd also singed an area of his body not visible in the photos. That explained why he'd preferred to stand, even during dinner.

When I heard the telltale beep, I turned my attention back to the computer. Unexpected things can happen at the base, and there have been a few times when Ryan hasn't been able to talk at the appointed time. If I couldn't talk to him tonight, I might just let out a small scream, but not loud enough to alert the neighbors.

I *needed* my "Ryan fix" tonight.

"Please God, let him be there."

Chapter 3

~~♥~~

After several heart-palpitating, pulse-racing moments, we were connected.

I blinked hard as I drank in the sight of Ryan. *My* Ryan. Gorgeous as ever and wearing a bright smile and an olive green T-shirt that showed those well-developed upper arm muscles and chest to great advantage.

I touched the screen and spread out my fingers. As was our custom, Ryan mirrored my actions by placing his right hand against the screen, palm flat with fanned fingers that extended beyond mine. We drank in the sight of one another.

"Hey, Ellie. You look beautiful, baby."

I breathed out a sigh. "Thanks. You look great, too, Ryan." Tired, but handsome as ever. "Your hair's getting a little long for the Army, isn't it?" My teasing often disguises my true emotions, and Ryan understands that about me. Although longer than the regulation buzz cut, his hair is still short by civilian standards.

"Yes, but there's no one around to cut it on a special mission." He laughed under his breath. "I don't trust the other guys to do it if I don't want a whack job."

His smile sobered. Ryan's admiring gaze swept over my face. My future husband loved me with his eyes, making me feel heated even though he's a world away.

"I've missed you a lot, Sass. Knowing I'd be talking to you tonight has been the most exciting thing in the last two weeks." I don't remember when or why Ryan started calling me Sass. He's the only one who's ever used that nickname, and I like it.

I knew Ryan wasn't allowed to reveal anything about his missions, so I'd given up asking him a long time ago. I also knew enough to read between-the-lines. He was telling me his last mission had been uneventful. He appeared healthy, so that's all I needed to know. Ryan's always been more of a service-oriented man than a battle-focused soldier. Whatever he's doing in Afghanistan must be to help others in some capacity.

"You say the sweetest things." I twirled a lock of my hair around my index finger. "If your two weeks haven't been exciting, that's actually a good thing, considering where you are. Right?"

"You got it." He watched me for a moment. "You've done that twisty thing with your hair since you were a toddler." His voice held an edge of huskiness.

"I've only *had* hair long enough to twist since I was five. You know I was bald until I was almost three." My mouth was dry, and I took a quick swig from my water bottle.

Ryan's grin emerged, twisting my insides in a marvelous way. "I remember, but I thought that was the kind of thing I'm not *supposed* to remember." As a kid, his laughter was infectious and fun. Now it's deep and sexy, especially from my rugged soldier. There really *is* something about a military man, especially a man in uniform whom I happen to love madly.

"So, I'm making headway at The Beckett Agency," I said. Beckett Larsen, the owner of the agency and my boss, is 70 years old and possesses one of the sharpest minds of anyone I've ever known. He consistently creates and executes highly successful advertising and marketing campaigns for clients all around the globe. A man who could sell the citizens of Cade's Corner on a Vietnamese restaurant in the middle of the town square? Brilliant!

"That's great to hear." Ryan didn't sound surprised. "Tell me more." After twisting the cap off his water bottle, he took a long drink.

"You know how I told you he always thinks old school? That strategy works extremely well for him, but I think Beckett is catching on that I might actually have some valid ideas, even though I'm only a part-timer and a young pup."

"And you thought you'd be fired before your second week. You've been there what—nine months? You're obviously doing something right."

"Almost ten months, actually. I make Beckett's coffee the way he likes, so that's in my favor. And he likes my shoes. Not in a perverted way, but he said his late wife, Babs, always loved her bright-colored high heels, too. So, knowing I have something in common with a dead woman is weirdly comforting in terms of job security."

"You're right, but I can see how it might be a positive career move." Ryan raised his water bottle in a salute. "To Beckett and his beloved Babs. Great names, by the way."

"Aren't they? Maybe someday we'll have little Sullivans running around with those names."

"Beckett's kind of cool and might grow on me, but I'm not sure about Babs."

"Stands for Barbara. And until I'm chasing kiddos around all over the place, I love my heels. You know that."

"I do. Just be careful in this cold weather."

I smirked. "Don't remind me. I've accepted my snow boots as a fact of life, and I'm being smart. No way am I hobbling down the aisle of the church on crutches to marry you." I considered raising my foot to show him my heels but then decided against it.

After taking another drink from his water bottle, Ryan grinned. "I remember a pair of particularly memorable turquoise shoes you wore the night of Marnie Wilson's wedding."

Oh, yes. Those raw silk shoes, dyed to match my bridesmaid's gown, had rubbed painful blisters on both my heels. The only reason I'd kept them on for the whole shindig was because Ryan said he loved them. That observation guaranteed I'd suffer to please my guy.

By the end of the evening, the burning on my heels was so painful, I could barely walk. Ryan swept me into his strong arms like a romance novel hero and carried me back to his truck, giving me a mini-lecture the entire way. Didn't he understand I'd left on The Shoes of Torture for him? Men could be so clueless.

"That was the first foot massage you ever gave me." Hmm. Maybe Ryan wasn't so clueless after all, and I shouldn't be quick to judge. Leaning my elbow on the desk, I rested my head on my propped fist. "I miss them." Being on the receiving end of one of Ryan's foot rubs ranked high on my list of favorite things in life.

"No more than I do," Ryan said. "Soon. Not much longer."

"I know. Can't wait. You've always been very good at distracting me, be it foot massages or other things."

Warmth rose in my cheeks as I pushed myself farther up in the chair. "You know, Ryan, Susie Martin was telling me about what she and Peter do when they Skype since he travels a lot for his job. What they...talk about." I traced my finger in circles on the desk while I waited for him to respond.

In the middle of taking another long drink, Ryan grunted and twisted the cap back on his water bottle. "I can imagine. I hear it all the time around here."

"It's harmless, don't you think? Susie didn't give me any specifics, of course. I'm not talking about anything that crosses the line."

Ryan leaned closer to the screen and beckoned with one finger. "Come here, baby. Closer to the screen."

I did as he asked. "I'm listening."

"Repeat after me. I will make the commitment. Say it, please," he insisted when I said nothing.

"I will make the commitment." I shook my head and sat back in the chair. "Shouldn't I know what I'm committing to before I say those words?"

"I want us to pledge to one another that we won't do—or say—anything that doesn't glorify the Lord. First of all, Susie and Peter are married. That's my point. Once *we're* married, there will be plenty of time for that kind of talk. And other things."

"Oh. Okay."

Ryan's shoulders lifted with his sigh. "It's almost impossible for a guy to stop the thought process once he allows his mind to start down that path, Sass. Let's not or we'll both end up going crazy by the end of this conversation." His tone had grown quiet with his last words.

How I admired the firm conviction in this man.

"You are such a good man, Ryan Joseph. Better a man than I am a woman." I laughed when he winked. "You know what I mean."

"I do. You're a gorgeous woman, Eleanor Rose, and there's nothing I want more than to marry you. But, like I said, until we're married, I can't go there and keep my sanity. It's hard enough not being able to see you in person, not being able to touch you, and hold you."

"I'm sorry. I didn't mean to upset you." His words thrilled me, but now I regretted bringing up the subject. My cheeks warmed and I squirmed on the chair, wondering if I should button my blouse to my neck. Good thing I *hadn't* shown him my shoes.

"You haven't upset me." Ryan stared directly into the camera, his blue eyes luminous. "If anything, it makes me love you more. Now, I don't think you finished what you wanted to tell me about your work at the ad agency. That seems like a safe topic. How about we go with that?"

I sat up straighter. "I proposed an idea for a new advertising campaign, and I think he liked it."

"How could he not?" Ryan's smile illuminated his entire face. It's not just sweat or the heat in Afghanistan, either, but happiness and pride. In me. What have I done to deserve this man's love?

After I told him about the campaign, Ryan proclaimed I was the most brilliant advertising whiz he knew. Then I brought the conversation around to the dinner on Friday night.

"I told Maura to bring Nick."

As I knew it would, that comment got Ryan's full attention. "Really? Good for you. Sounds like a plan. I've been suggesting the same thing to Nick for a few months now. Let me know how that goes. I'll be curious to hear."

"Of course. I hope you don't mind that I'm not waiting until you come home. The holidays seemed the right time. You know how busy Nick and Maura are at the law office."

"I don't mind. You're right. The holiday season puts people in a more festive frame of mind," Ryan said. "Seize the moment." He raised his water bottle again. "*Carpe diem.*"

"I'm doing my best." Then I told Ryan about some of the happenings around town. Normal everyday stuff. The kinds of mundane things he told me he needed to hear because they helped establish his connection with home away from the harsh reality of war. Even though he hasn't been involved in active combat from what I know—I shivered at the thought of it—Ryan has known a couple of guys killed in Afghanistan.

Next, I filled him in on the status of Perchance to Dream and told him about the last-minute wishes this year. We always end our Skype sessions by talking about our project. A bittersweet feeling overtakes me, knowing our conversation will soon end.

"I wish I could be there with you, Sass. To help with Perchance to Dream and everything else." The regret in Ryan's tone made my heart ache. But I also knew this: given a choice, Ryan would choose a hundred times over to be exactly where he was at that moment.

As we always do, we bowed our heads.

When Ryan closed our time of prayer a short time later, tears filled my eyes. "You're exactly where you need to be right now, Ryan. Where you're meant to be, serving God and others. You're always with me. Right *here*." I rested my hand over my heart.

"As you're in mine, Ellie. Always." Ryan's smile fills me with longing.

"There will be many more years ahead for us to fulfill those children's wishes together," I said. "You know what my wish right now is, don't you?"

"An Easy Bake Oven?"

Oh, yes. Ryan can always make me laugh.

Chapter 4

~~♥~~

Thursday, December 14

After leaving The Beckett Agency for the day, I greeted the staff at the only nursing home in Cade's Corner. Some in town insisted on calling it a senior *living* center, a term I consider a misnomer. The woman I'd come to see—Cora Brown, my 93-year-old former neighbor (who lived on the street behind our house)—certainly isn't enjoying much quality of life.

Cora suffered a stroke last year, and she's been in a semi-conscious state ever since. The staff does the best they can for someone in her condition. Since Ryan's deployment, I've visited Cora twice a week, if not more often. Usually, I stop by after work, but this afternoon and evening, I need to go on a shopping expedition in Cleveland to find the remaining toys and other items. I have my detailed list, along with store circulars, tucked inside my oversized tote bag.

"Hi, Ellie. Not long now until the wedding!" one of the ladies called from the hallway of Cora's wing as I swung around the corner. "Have you talked with Ryan lately?"

"Last night as a matter of fact." Stopping at the staff station, I placed a festive holiday tin on the counter. "We had a Skype session."

"The technology you kids use these days boggles my old brain." Trudy the Dietician's brown eyes grew wide as she spied the tin. "What's this?" A handful of other staffers gathered around her.

"Some cookies and fudge I made last night. To say thank you for all you do for Cora and the other residents here." I enjoyed their enthusiasm as Trudy peeled away the wax paper separating the layers of sweets and sighed with appreciation. I always need to come down from the "high" of my Skype sessions with Ryan, and my restlessness often leads me into the kitchen to make something sweet.

"Ellie, you're an angel of mercy," one of the newer, younger workers said. "Just this morning, I was saying how I'd kill for some homemade frosted Christmas cookies." Selecting a snowflake sugar cookie with light blue frosting and sprinkles, she bit into it and gave me a thumbs-up.

"And we told Carole that's not the most advisable thing to say considering her line of work, not to mention *where* she works." Trudy winked at the girl.

I smiled. "I'm sure you get a lot of holiday goodies at this time of year."

"Not as many as you might think. These aren't slice and bake cookies, either, but the real thing. I didn't realize some of you young gals still bake from scratch." That comment came from Patsy, one of the aides who regularly attended to Cora, as she reached into the tin. "Oh, ladies, she made both chocolate and peanut butter fudge. Thanks so much, Ellie."

"You're welcome, ladies. Enjoy in good health!" With a small wave, I headed down the immaculately clean, highly polished hallway to Room 365.

As I walked into Cora's room, I lamented that my sweet, elderly friend couldn't enjoy a piece of peanut butter fudge. That's always been her favorite. My mom used to send me around the neighborhood with similar tins of holiday treats.

Cora is now fed through tubes. To my knowledge, she hasn't left her bed since the stroke. Sometimes her eyes are open, but more often than not, they're closed. On occasion, Cora will turn her head slightly or move her hand during my visits. In those moments, I'm almost convinced she hears me speaking to her.

"How are you today, Miss Cora?" I go through the same routine each time. After slipping my coat from my shoulders, I draped it over a chair and then pulled the other chair close to the bed.

"You've got a bit more color in your cheeks today." That wasn't exactly true, but on the off-chance she could hear me, I wanted to pay Cora a compliment. I figured God would forgive me for a white lie.

"Ryan's coming home soon. Have I ever told you my Amelia Earhart story? No? Then I think that'll be my story for today."

No answer except for the hum of the machines. The sun peeked through filtered blinds, and I could hear the sounds of instrumental Christmas songs from the room across the hall. One of the staff members had strung up a strand of colorful twinkling lights on the side wall. A wedding photo of Cora and her husband, Ronnie, sat on top of a small bureau. A second photo showed Cora holding their only child, a daughter named Beatrice. A daughter who lived in another state—Minnesota, I think—and only sent the occasional card.

Everyone deserves to be loved. Everyone deserves to be valued.

Even if Beatrice never contacted her mother, I would be here for Cora.

And with that thought, I began today's story.

Not long after I turned twelve, Ryan rode his bike past my house one day in mid-June. I sat on the front step, reading. Because of all the time spent inside during the cold months, I'd developed a love of reading that carried over into the warmer months. I had my nose stuck in a book more often than not and enjoyed the different worlds it opened to me.

Ryan raised his hand as he sped past my house. That boy always rode too fast. At the end of the street, he did a one-eighty and speed-pedaled back to our front yard. Jumping off his bike, he lowered it to the ground with care.

"Hey." He plopped down on the step beside me. "What are you reading?"

"Hey, yourself. A biography of Amelia Earhart. She's a personal heroine of mine."

"Yeah. Sad what happened to her, though." He shrugged. "Adds to the mystery, I guess."

"Like your fascination with the *Titanic*." Setting my book aside, I propped my knees on the front step and wrapped my arms around them. "Think of all Amelia accomplished, Ryan. She had such a sense of adventure and was a pioneer in aviation. Ahead of her time, they say. She wrote books and was independent and super intelligent. Not that I ever hope to be famous, but I want to do something—even if it's just one little thing—to impact someone else's life for good. Make a difference, you know?"

Ryan stretched out his legs. "I'm sure you will, Sass."

"Thanks." I felt warmth rise in my cheeks at his unexpected compliment. "Do you think it's something about the tragic nature of Amelia's story that makes it so appealing?"

He shrugged. "I don't know. You mean like the element of the unknown, something like that?"

"Right. Sad stories get people's attention, I know that much."

"It's like that wreck over on Main Street last year," Ryan said. "Remember how everybody came running outside to see what happened? It was exciting in a weird way since things are always so quiet here."

Cade's Corner rarely had anything more than a fender bender, but that accident had been pretty serious. No one died, thankfully, but the townspeople blamed it on the folks from out-of-town speeding through the center of town. They'd narrowly avoided hitting Manfred Jones, one of the town's citizens and one-time mayor, as he'd crossed the street against the light, as usual. Everyone in town knew of Manfred's penchant for jaywalking, but the ones passing through swerved to avoid him and crashed into a lamppost, bringing it crashing down on their car, shattering their windshield. People still claimed they found tiny shards of glass on the street.

I shot Ryan a sharp glance. "Are you saying Cade's Corner is boring?"

"No. I don't think it is, but you know what I mean. It gives them something to talk about."

"I suppose so." I blew out a sigh. "When bad things happen to people, I'd like to rewrite their stories. Give them their happy ending."

Ryan shook his head. "You and your fairy tales." Then he winked. I don't think he'd ever done that before. Maybe his older brother taught him how since Nick was dating now.

"They're not fairy tales, and I'm not talking about rewriting history." I could hear the defensiveness in my tone. "Kara says Amelia Earhart's story is romantic. And Staci thinks the whole *Titanic* saga is, too. Go figure." I cleared my throat. "Anyway, in the book, it talks about how Amelia made a homemade ramp. Then she attached it to the roof of her family's toolshed. Her version of a runway, I suppose. She climbed in a wooden box and then…" I made a soaring gesture and then dipped my hand in a downward spiral.

"No way!" When Ryan gave me a broad grin, I knew we were thinking of the same thing—the time we strapped cardboard "wings" to our arms with belts and tried to fly off the roof of his house. With Nick's help, we'd hauled several old mattresses (their mom had quite conveniently placed them beside the curb for pickup) and positioned them for a soft landing.

Thank the Lord we survived our own foolishness.

"What happened next? Was she hurt?" Ryan twisted around on the step to face me.

"The wooden box broke apart during the flight. She got a bruised lip out of the deal, and her dress was torn, but she had a blast and said it felt like flying. Amelia considered that experience her first documented flight." The corners of my mouth curled and I nudged Ryan's arm. "I'm glad we've stuck to safer pursuits since *our* flying experiment."

"Me, too," Ryan said. "And I'm glad Mom put those old mattresses out for pickup. Hey, remember when we slid around my basement floor in our socks? That was way better than a skating rink."

"Sure. That was pure genius." Ryan's mom had asked him to clean their basement, including polishing the bookcases. Some of the polish got on the linoleum floor by accident. Ryan discovered it when he fell and hit his elbow hard on the ground, but the idea was born. He used a whole can of lemon furniture polish on that basement floor.

I couldn't stop my grin. "You are so weird, genius or not. I remember how your mom made us scrub and mop the entire floor the next day to make up for it."

"Yep, and totally worth it. We had fun." He winked again. What was up with that?

I nodded. "Without a doubt."

"Well, I'd better get moving," Ryan said. "I promised Mom I'd ride over to Keeley's and get a carton of eggs. Grade A Extra Large. She's making a cake for the church supper tomorrow night. I made an egg sandwich earlier and used all the eggs, so I owe her." The boy did love his fried egg sandwiches with mayonnaise and a slice of American cheese.

"You might want to slow it down on the bike if you want to keep the eggs intact," I cautioned. "Cakes don't taste the same without eggs. Trust me. I tried it once."

"I remember that cake but speed has nothing to do with it. Hey, are you making anything for the church supper, Sass?" If he dared to wink again, I might have to bop him.

"I learned my lesson," I assured him. "Don't change the subject. You know what I mean."

"I do, but no promises."

I rolled my eyes. "When you start driving a car, at least promise you'll be careful. I'm sure even an Indy 500 race car driver would tell you the same thing."

"Fine, Mom. I promise to think about it, okay? Just remember—I might be fast, but I'm careful." Ryan jumped to his feet and then hopped down from the stair. Standing on the sidewalk, he watched me for a long moment. "You know that thing you said about making a difference?"

"Yeah?"

"Well, I think you've already touched more people than you know. Bye Ellie." He ducked his head as though he was embarrassed.

I stared at him, my mouth hanging open, as Ryan took off on his bicycle.

Almost a year later to the day, I sat on my front step reading when I heard squealing tires. Then nothing. Within seconds, there was shouting. "Somebody help! Call 9-1-1!" a woman screamed. Sounded like it came from Poplar Street, the street behind ours.

With sickening clarity, I knew it was Ryan.

Chapter 5

~~♥~~

"What happened next?"

I turned in my chair beside Cora's bed to find two of the nursing aides—Krista and Pam—standing in the doorway.

"Sorry, Ellie," Krista said. "I hope you're not mad, but we were passing by in the hallway and couldn't help but overhear."

Pam nodded but said nothing although her cheeks colored a pale pink. She lowered her gaze from mine.

"I'm not mad," I reassured them. "Talking about Ryan is therapeutic for me. Even if I start talking about something else, it seems my thoughts always come back around to Ryan."

"Of course. That's only natural since he's uppermost in your mind right now." Krista's expression was kind. "Please go on and forget we're here. I'd like to hear what happened if you don't mind."

My phone signaled an incoming text message. I held up one finger. "Hold on a second. It's Ryan."

"By all means," Krista said. "We'll leave and give you some privacy."

"No, you can stay. This won't take long."

I STARTED PACKING TODAY.

I smiled and typed my response. A LITTLE EARLY, ISN'T IT? ☺

NOT SOON ENOUGH, SASS. WHERE ARE YOU?

IN CORA'S ROOM. TALKING ABOUT YOU. ARE YOUR EARS BURNING?

THAT EXPLAINS WHY THEY'RE WARM. LOVE YOU, ELLIE.

YOU, TOO. ISN'T IT LATE THERE? OR EARLY? Glancing at the clock on the wall, I calculated the 8-1/2 hour time difference between Cleveland and Afghanistan. Since I never knew where he was at any given time, we'd agreed that—at least for now—Ryan would be the one to initiate the text messages.

YEAH, BUT I'M AWAKE AND THINKING OF YOU. NOTHING NEW.

BYE, MY LOVE.

BYE, ELLIE. ♥

"Ryan doing okay?" Pam said. "Judging by your smile, I'd say so."

"He's great, thanks." I slipped the cell phone back into my purse. "Now, on with the story."

Ryan always cut through his backyard on his bike to get to Poplar Street. With my heart pounding in my chest, I ran as fast as I could. Rounding the bend, my eyes welled with tears at the sight. Ryan was sprawled in the middle of the road, writhing in pain, his right leg twisted at an odd angle.

Thank you, Jesus. At least he was alive and conscious. Ryan loved his new bike, but the red metal was twisted, scraped, and bent beyond repair.

A big white car sat in the middle of the street. The driver's door was open, the engine idling, and a middle-aged woman leaned over him. "I'm so sorry," she repeated over and over, her voice thick with apparent regret as she wrung her hands. "I didn't mean to hit him. He came out of nowhere and swerved in front of me. By the time I saw him, it was too late."

The woman gave me a quick glance as I crouched on the opposite side of Ryan. "Should I touch him? I don't know what to do."

"No, better not. Not his leg, anyway." I prayed under my breath that she wouldn't hyperventilate. Her skin was very pale, almost white, and her lips were tight and drained of color.

"Ma'am, do you have a phone?"

"No, sorry. I hate cell phones." She tilted her head and surveyed me. "How old are you?"

"Just turned thirteen." I leaned close to Ryan and gently brushed his dark bangs to one side of his forehead, away from his eyes. They'd grown long over the summer. "Ryan, can you hear me?"

He stared at me as though in a daze. "Yeah, Sass. I hear you," he rasped between groans. The right side of his face was scraped and bleeding as well as his right elbow. Thank goodness they only looked like surface wounds.

"Is your mom home?"

"Nah." He groaned and shook his head. "She's at the library."

My mind raced. Should I run back home to use the phone? Surely one of the neighbors was home. I couldn't believe no one else had come running outside with the commotion, but it was mid-morning on a summer day. Other than birds chirping, the only sounds came from air conditioning units up and down the quiet residential street.

"I'll be right back," I said to Ryan and then fixed my gaze on the woman. "Stay with him and I'll go get help. Don't you dare leave."

She nodded, and I could see her swallow. "Okay."

I hated to leave Ryan in the middle of the street, but someone had to take charge and she didn't seem so inclined. I took off at a run, praying the whole time that Cora was home.

"Mrs. Brown!" I rang the doorbell several times in succession since she was somewhat hard of hearing and didn't wear her hearing aid like she should. Using my fists, I pummeled them on the front door loud enough so she could hear, especially if she was out back on her sun porch watching her "stories" (her term for soap operas).

Within a minute, Cora answered my insistent knocking and peeked out the front door. "How nice to see you, Ellie." As soon as I explained what had happened and asked to use her phone, she opened the door wide.

"Oh my! That sweet Sullivan boy. By all means, dear, come right on inside."

A couple of minutes later, after I ended my conversation with the emergency operator, Cora pressed a folded, damp paper towel into my hand. "Here you go, honey. You let me know if you need anything else."

Thanking her, I flew back down the street again. The woman who'd hit Ryan sat on the curb, absently chewing on a fingernail, staring into space.

Ryan groaned and bit down on his lip so hard it started to bleed. He struggled to sit up, but I placed one hand on his chest and told him to breathe deep, in and out.

"Try and stay still," I said, attempting to keep my voice calm. "Your leg is probably broken, and if you keep squirming, you're only going to make it worse." I had no idea what I was saying, but I figured it couldn't hurt. I hated to see my friend in such agony.

"I think you're right." He grimaced and then winced as I cleaned his wounds using as gentle a touch as I could. Then he gripped my arm, not in an attempt to stop me, but because he was gritting his teeth in pain. I stopped my ministrations and cradled his head in my lap.

"Thanks, Sass. You're...a...great nurse." I'd never seen Ryan's eyes so full of pain. His dark lashes fanned across his tanned cheeks as he closed his eyes and moaned again. Perspiration dotted his forehead and he panted.

"Welcome. Just rest. Help is coming." I leaned my head against his and began to pray as I heard the siren of an emergency vehicle in the distance. The woman rose to her feet and moved to the center of the street. At least she'd finally snapped out of her near-catatonic state. I felt sorry for her, but my primary concern was Ryan.

"Dear Jesus, please be with Ryan and ease his pain," I said. "Be with the EMTs and"—I darted a glance at the woman who was now blathering nonstop as the workers jumped out of the ambulance—"be with the lady who hit him. Give her comfort, Lord. Most of all," I said, the hard lump in my throat making it difficult to speak, "thank you that Ryan is okay. I ask these things in the name of our precious Savior, Jesus."

I don't know why, but I kissed his forehead.

"Amen," Ryan murmured, and he opened his eyes. After gently releasing my hold on him, I backed away so the EMTs could move beside Ryan. They lowered a stretcher to the ground and then crouched beside him to assess his injuries. After answering their questions, Ryan reached for me. I stepped forward again and grabbed hold of his hand.

"Stay with me, Sass. Please."

"Okay, but I need to call your Mom."

"Yeah," he murmured. "Hope she doesn't freak."

I answered questions about the name, address, and telephone number of the "victim" from the first EMT—KENT based on the embroidered name on his shirt. I hated hearing Ryan called a victim, true or not.

"Can I use your phone or walkie-talkie or whatever?" I said to the EMTs. "I need to call my friend's mom to let her know what's happening. She can get kind of high-strung sometimes, so it might be better if I'm the one to tell her."

Kent stared and me and then nodded to the second guy. "Give her your phone."

Pulling it from his pocket, the man—the embroidered name on his shirt read TONY—asked me for the number. "How old are you?"

"Thirteen. How old are you?" Why did people keep asking me that question? Still, it was no reason to be rude. "Sorry," I mumbled.

"You're okay," he said with a grin. "I'm twenty-four. You got an older sister?"

"Yes. Two of them." That question seemed even creepier.

"I like your spunk, kiddo." After punching in the phone number I gave him, Tony handed me his phone as both EMTs attended to Ryan. They positioned boards on either side of his right leg to stabilize it. Yep, it was broken all right.

I watched as they tied long strips of cloth around the boards to keep them in place.

Ryan's mom, Mary, took the news better than I thought. I tried to keep my voice steady as I relayed the basic facts about what happened in as few words as possible. Then I handed the phone back to Tony. "She's three minutes away."

Tony spoke with Mary and, sure enough, Ryan's mom arrived a few minutes later. She talked with the woman who'd hit Ryan. The poor lady still appeared pretty upset. I was impressed by how Mary stayed calm and consoled her. I'm sure she was mad or upset, but Ryan's mom demonstrated remarkable grace that day. I'll never forget it.

I stood in the middle of the street, watching, not sure what to do next. A police officer arrived—Bobby Mercer's dad—to take an incident report. He asked me a couple of questions, and I answered them as best I could even though I hadn't been an eye witness to the accident.

Trying not to cry, I watched as they loaded Ryan onto the stretcher and then lifted him into the back of the ambulance.

"Ever consider a career in emergency medicine, little lady?" Kent asked me as he closed the back doors.

"No," I said with a touch of defiance mixed with sadness. Ryan hadn't wanted me to leave him, but the guys wouldn't let me ride in the ambulance because I wasn't family. Besides that, I was a minor. I made Tony promise to tell Ryan that I'd *wanted* to go with him in the ambulance but they'd told me it was against the rules.

Tony saluted. "You got it, kiddo."

"Ellie." Mary put both hands on my shoulders. "You are so smart and brave. The men and Mrs. Rogers"—she angled her head to the woman—"told me how you took charge of the situation. Thank you, sweetie. Come and visit Ryan when he's out of the hospital. You can keep him company."

"Okay," I mumbled.

Mary gave me a quick hug and then climbed into her car, prepared to follow the ambulance to the hospital.

Sergeant Mercer finished taking his report and asked Mrs. Rogers if she was okay to drive. After assuring the police officer she could, she glanced at me and mouthed *Thank you.*

I nodded and forced a small smile. Then I slowly walked home, feeling oddly bereft.

Although I was thankful I'd been able to help Ryan, and I was glad he would be okay, I still felt...helpless. And helplessness is one of the things I hate more than anything.

Chapter 6

~~♥~~

Stopping my story, I glanced at Cora in her bed. The only sound in the room was the steady hum of the machine hooked up to her, keeping her alive. "I'm so glad you were home that day."

I couldn't imagine being confined to a bed for a day much less a year. Ryan and I had agreed that we didn't want to be kept alive by artificial means if it ever came to a quality of life issue. Nick had drawn up our wills before Ryan left for Afghanistan this last time. We'd signed them along with other estate planning documents. We'd also taken out universal life insurance policies and opened a joint checking and savings account. And we co-owned the house.

Since Ryan wasn't coming home until a few days before the wedding, we wanted to have as many details as possible handled in advance. I planned to change my name on all the legal documents after we returned from the honeymoon.

Since we're getting married during the holiday season (you never know when our local courthouse staff will close up shop if they're not busy, or have to walk the dog, or need to visit the beauty parlor), Ryan had signed a power of attorney to Nick. Having a future brother-in-law who is a respected lawyer in town is a definite advantage. He'd researched the legalities of getting a marriage license while Ryan is stationed overseas. So, when Nick accompanied me to the courthouse, that process thankfully went off without a hitch.

I breathed a big sigh of relief on the courthouse steps once that was crossed off my list.

"You've loved your fiancé a long time, haven't you?"

I glanced up to see Krista standing in the doorway, her eyes damp. Pam was nowhere to be found. Krista had moved to the area within the past year with her husband and three kids, so she couldn't know my long history with Ryan.

I smiled. "For as long as I can remember. But don't tell Ryan that. It'll swell his head."

Krista dabbed beneath her eyes with a tissue. "It'll be our secret. And you've known Cora a long time, too, I'm guessing?"

"Yes. Cora's been a widow for a long time, and she was home most of the time. She had her routine of going to the church service every Sunday morning and prayer meetings on Wednesday nights. Her husband had been a cabinet maker, and when we entered first grade, she presented the kids in the church with a small cedar chest. She told us to call it our Prayer Box, Wish Box, Hope Box, Remembrance Box, or whatever we wanted. And then she encouraged us to put things inside the chest that meant something deeply personal to us."

"Let me guess," Krista said, stepping farther into Cora's room. "You filled your box with things that remind you of Ryan?"

"Yes, but not all of them." Her comment resonated with me. "I called it my Dream Box." At first, I'd called it my Dream Chest until my sisters set me straight. I knew exactly where the box was in the new house, but I hadn't opened it in years. I should take a peek at my collection of items in the box to see just how many things in that chest *were* connected in some way—no matter how large or small—to Ryan.

Krista motioned to the other chair in the room. "Do you mind if I sit a bit and listen? I'm on my break, and I'm fascinated by your story. I don't want to intrude, but I'd love to hear the rest."

"Ryan and I are just two regular, ordinary kids." I watched as Krista removed my coat and scarf from the other chair and laid them across the foot of Cora's bed.

"Yes, in some ways. But your story is also incredibly special," Krista said as she settled in the chair beside me. "I hear the love in your voice when you mention his name. Do you even realize how your eyes light up like the Christmas lights when you're telling your stories? You've known each other since you were kids and started out as friends first. I think that's significant to the bond you share. And, if you don't mind my saying, I think the foundation of deep friendship you've built together over the years is helping to carry you through now while Ryan's on deployment."

"I hadn't thought of it that way, but I'm sure you're right." Hearing the perspective of someone who hasn't known Ryan and me as a couple is refreshing.

"There's something to be said for whirlwind romances, but a romance that's grown over time? That's a beautiful thing, Ellie. True love like you and Ryan share is rare. That's not ordinary at all, sweetie. It's really quite *extraordinary*. And it's a true gift from God."

"I count my blessings every day. My story with Ryan is simple, really. A small-town girl who loves a small-town boy. And he loves her back. But you know what?"

"What?" She watched me with an air of quiet expectation.

"I wouldn't trade what we have for anything else in the world. Not riches, not fame…nothing." I twisted my hands together in my lap and watched the light snow falling outside the window. "The only thing I wish is for Ryan's safe return. Then I can breathe again and finally get my life back to normal."

Krista squeezed my hand. "You're a model of strength. Ryan would be proud."

"Thanks. The hardest part of waiting is my own impatience. The closer the time comes, the more anxious I'm becoming. I keep repeating the *be anxious for nothing* verse." I laughed under my breath. "If you hear me talking to myself in the hallways, it's only Crazy Ellie Franklin giving herself a pep talk."

"We understand, sweetie. Most of us around here do the same thing. Ryan will be home again before you know it."

My gaze moved to dear Cora lying in the bed beside me, the rhythmic sounds of the machine connected to her loud in the quiet room. I squeezed her warm, delicate hand. The blue veins appeared more prominent than ever as I ran my thumb lightly over her diamond ring. Such a unique design in an intricate platinum setting.

"Cora used to invite me to share a glass of homemade peach iced tea on her back porch," I told Krista. "She liked the company, and I found her stories fascinating. Cora's husband, Ronnie, was in the military, and they'd lived all over the world."

I glanced down at Cora's ring again. "She told me this ring once belonged to her mother-in-law. Cora married Ronnie when she was eighteen, and she's never had to replace the diamond. I remember she said, 'Quality craftsmanship stands the test of time. Like a good man. My Ronnie stood the test of time until the good Lord called him home.' She talked about Ronnie a lot, about how much she missed him."

I heaved a heavy sigh. "And now, here I sit beside Cora, telling her about my love for Ryan, and how much I miss him."

Two women in love. Each longing to be reunited with her beloved. Different in many ways and yet the same.

"Do you think that somehow Cora…knew…about you and Ryan?" Krista's voice was quiet. "I mean, that you'd eventually end up together?"

My smile held sadness as well as hope. "Hard to say. Maybe? I'll say one thing. She demonstrated her love in many tangible ways to the community, and especially to the kids."

"Then I guess you could say Cora helped to inspire the idea for Perchance to Dream?" Kristi said. "That's the name of the charity I've heard about, right?"

"Yes, that's the one. I think you might be right. Cora, as well as other members of Cade's Corner…they all helped to inspire our project."

"Sounds like a story for another day." Krista rose from her chair. "Thank you for sharing your stories, Ellie. I've enjoyed hearing more about your memories with Ryan."

I met Krista's gaze. "I'm the one who should be thanking you."

"I have one more completely random question," Krista said. "Did Tony ever meet your sisters?"

That made me laugh. "Funny you should ask. He married one of them."

Krista's eyes widened and she shook her head with a smile. "Seriously? I was only kidding."

I shrugged. "What can I say? It's a small town. Tony still calls me kiddo, too. He and my oldest sister, Kara, have two daughters. And my sister Staci married an accountant who apprenticed as a teenager in our dad's accounting firm. They have one son."

"Sounds like you have a special family."

"We have our moments, like everyone does, but family is everything."

"You can say that again." I could tell my sentiment touched Krista in a special way when she moved her hand over her heart in a seemingly unconscious move.

I lowered Cora's hand to the covers. Bending close, I planted a soft kiss on her lined forehead. "Sleep well, Cora. I'll see you again soon."

I retrieved my coat and then pulled my purse over one shoulder. As I headed out of the room, I pressed my hand on Krista's arm and gave her a light squeeze. "I'll be back to see her again tomorrow."

I enjoyed the brisk air as I walked home. Large snowflakes fell around me, and I lifted my head to catch them on my tongue. I've loved doing this since I was a little girl. A fresh snowflake was straight from Heaven. Pure. Beautiful and unique.

I loved taking walks with my father in any season of the year, but especially when it was cold outside. He'd hold me by the hand. Sometimes he'd put one arm around me and snuggle me tight against him. Sometimes he'd unbutton his long overcoat and pull it around me, making me feel warm and loved.

Dad wasn't a man to speak of trivial things. He was an accountant with a methodical, analytical mind. Even so, he seemed very in-tune with me in terms of being able to express his love. From what I understand, his father had never been openly demonstrative. In some ways, I'm sure that influenced how my father treated my mother and "his girls" as he called my sisters and me. We never lacked for his affection.

Dad's every word seemed measured and weighted with purpose. He knew how to make others feel important, and without fail, he made me feel special—not just to him, but also to God.

"Each snowflake is unique and perfect. Just like you," Dad observed as we walked home from church together one snowy night in late February when I was ten.

I looked up into the sky and marveled at His awesome handiwork in the bright stars.

"You think I'm perfect?"

"In some ways, yes," Dad said. I could hear the smile in his deep voice. "When you were born, I counted every little finger and toe. You were pink and had a very healthy cry. But none of us are perfect, Ellie. We're made in the image of God, and we need to strive to be perfect, but only Jesus was perfect in every way. But you're an extraordinary person."

"You mean to you and Mom?"

He nodded as we walked. "Yes, but to many others, as well."

"Daddy, what makes me extraordinary? To you, I mean." Extraordinary was such a big word, and it sounded impressive. I loved that he'd used it to describe me.

Taking my hand in his, Dad swung my mitten-covered hand between us as we walked. "You ask a lot of questions," he said. "That's good, and it shows your inquisitive, compassionate nature. You want to know why God made some of us tall and some of us short. You want to know why some people get cancer, and some don't. You're not the type of person to sit on the sidelines. You jump right in there, take charge, and get things done. You're smart and, if you don't know how to do something, you ask your questions and then keep trying. You never give up."

As I absorbed his words, Dad squeezed my hand. "You're going to do important things in your lifetime, Eleanor Rose Franklin."

"You really think so?"

"Without a doubt." The firm conviction in his voice was unmistakable.

After opening his coat, Dad wrapped me in it for the last block we walked to the house. I shuffled beside him, protected in a warm cocoon-of-sorts, and he slowed his much longer strides to keep pace with me. It became a game of sorts, a special closeness shared only between my daddy and me. The church bells rang for the final time of the evening. I took great comfort in the sound, and I'd always associated the sound with the walks with my father.

"Dad," I said after a few seconds of companionable silence, "what important things do you think I might do when I grow up?"

"That's easy." His smile was tender, reflected in the lights from the lampposts lining our street.

I grinned. "Are you going to tell me? Or are you going to make me wait to grow up first?"

With a chuckle, Dad opened the side door and ushered me inside our warm house. The scent of Mom's pot roast we'd enjoyed for Wednesday night supper lingered in the kitchen. From the front of the house, I heard Mom coming in with Staci (they didn't share our love for walking in the snow and had driven the few blocks home from the church).

Planting both big hands on my shoulders, Dad turned me around to face him and looked me straight in the eye. "You are an encourager, Ellie. That's a special gift God gave to you. You're the kind of person other people will come to when everything else is falling down around them. You're strong, and you understand that God is always in control. And that, my girl"—he tapped my nose—"makes you the best kind of friend, sister, and daughter—anyone could be blessed to have."

After another hug, he released me. "One day you'll make a fine young man an excellent wife."

"Eww." I scrunched my nose. "That's not going to happen for a long time. Maybe when I'm really old." Laughing and teasing, we took turns peeling each other's gloves off our cold fingers. I love my memories of the little moments in life such as that one which—long term—are actually quite significant. The memories, both large *and* small, that have enriched my life and shaped my future.

I miss you, Dad. I'm blessed for having loved you.

I breathed in deeply of the fresh, clean air, a reminder of why I've always loved small town living, free from the exhaust fumes, the busyness, and the noise.

My boots crunched lightly on the newest layer of snow as I walked. I glanced at the winter wonderland surrounding me. How I wish that for one last time, I could see my father's big footprints next to my much smaller ones.

I'll love him always, miss him forever. But tonight, no tears come as a quiet joy swells my heart, bringing with it my smile. I'm a better person for the man God gave me for a father. If only every kid could be so blessed. His legacy has also fueled my desire to help as many children as possible through Perchance to Dream.

Reaching the front walkway to the house, I raised my face to the sky, still smiling. On a whim, I stretched out my arms and twirled in a slow circle. And then I caught a few more snowflakes on my tongue. My father's faith in my abilities and talents meant the world to me when I was ten, and it means even more now. I attribute a lot of who I am as an adult to the confidence he instilled in me all those years ago.

He was extraordinary.

I paused outside the front door as I heard the church bells ringing at Cade's Corner Community Church a short distance away. As always, the sound makes me smile.

"I hope you're having a good night, Daddy," I whispered as I unlocked the front door and stepped inside my warm little house.

"Thank you for teaching me *how* to love."

Chapter 7

~~♥~~

Friday, December 15

The next morning, I sat at my kitchen table, thinking about Ryan. What else is new?

"Just bring him home safely, Lord." Ryan loved to play the hero. I wanted him to play it safe. Only five more days and he'd come home to me. Maybe that's selfish to think that way, but I couldn't help it. The Army could no longer claim him. He'd be a veteran and no longer on active duty.

As I took a bite of my hot, maple pecan oatmeal, my thoughts wandered to the time immediately following Ryan's bicycle accident. He'd apparently thought he was invincible. In some ways, I think Ryan still believes in that idea.

I'd nicknamed him the "Impatient Patient." After his release from the hospital, Ryan's right leg was in a full cast. He moped around his house for weeks, and "Cranky" became his new middle name.

"I can't do anything with this dumb thing on my leg," he complained one day in the first week. He slapped his cast with the back of one hand. "It's like a stupid straitjacket."

"You probably don't even know what a straitjacket is," I teased.

"Sure I do. From the movies. It restrains a person so they can't do anything."

I smirked. "A straitjacket's for crazy people so they can't hurt themselves. And you're not crazy. You're just bored out of your mind."

Ryan's blue eyes bore into mine. Sometimes he left me to wonder what he was thinking since—unlike me—he didn't always blurt out his thoughts. "Just say it, Sass."

"Say what?" I shook my head, confused.

"I've been waiting for you to say, 'I told you so.' You warned me to be careful." He ran his hand through his hair.

Plopping back on the sofa, he crossed his arms behind his head. "Might as well get it out of your system. Have at it."

"At least you're okay. I'm definitely glad about that. Besides, I don't think anything I can say will change the way you are, Ryan. Not that I'd ever want you to change."

A slight grin creased his lips. "Yeah? Thanks. Have to say, I wasn't expecting that."

"It won't stop me from telling you to be careful in the future."

He laughed. "I wouldn't expect anything less."

I got in the habit of grabbing a book and walking down to Ryan's house every afternoon. He never asked me to come, and I never said anything—I'd just show up, and he didn't send me away. If he ever said anything ornery about my visits, I was armed with his mother's invitation the day of his accident. He'd never admit it, but Ryan secretly liked my company. I know he did.

I read mystery stories to him—his favorite—and we'd play Monopoly. That ended the time I bought the high-end properties and bankrupted him. After that humiliation, he swore never to play Monopoly with me again. I called him a sore loser, and we compromised by playing Battleship. He usually skunked me, but unlike Ryan, I didn't mind losing to keep the peace.

"Don't you have anything better to do with your time than babysit me?" he said one miserably hot and humid afternoon.

"Nope. I'd rather spend my time listening to you bellyache."

Ryan balked. "Ah, come on, Ellie. I'm not that bad a patient, am I?"

"No, you're the worst patient ever. You've now entered the red zone of the Grump-O-Meter. That's the zone that screams danger is imminent."

We talked about all kinds of things—school, sports (he was surprised I knew so much about the Cavaliers, and I could tell it pleased him), movies, and books. We both liked action movies and detested mushy romantic comedies. Ryan's mom would float in and out of the room now and then with a little smile. She'd dust, check on us, or bring us something cold to drink. At first, she brought us snacks, but then Ryan told her he was getting fat from all the sitting around.

Sometimes his friends would come over to the house. When I saw their bikes out front, I'd turn around and head back home. I figured they'd tease Ryan if they saw me coming.

"I'm tired of this," he complained one rainy afternoon. For some unknown reason, he seemed particularly sensitive to the changes in the weather.

I elbowed him as we sat together on the sofa watching a movie about a talking dog that went into outer space. Or something like that. "Who are you kidding? You're just sorry your accident didn't happen during the school year so you could milk your injury with all the girls." For the first time that I could remember, I was more focused on Ryan than the silly movie.

He grinned, but we both knew I was right. The girls noticed Ryan, and he noticed them. Sitting there with him that day, it smacked me in the face: I liked Ryan Joseph Sullivan. As a friend, yes, but I'd also developed a massive crush on him. My first, honest-to-goodness crush on a boy. I was determined Ryan would never know.

It became clear early on in his recuperation period that Ryan desperately needed to get out of the house. I'd caught him trying to scratch his itchy leg beneath the cast with a wire coat hanger and was afraid he'd hurt himself. All the kids in the youth group had signed his cast, but he'd played connect the dots on it to the point where the names were blurred and illegible.

Maybe it wasn't the best motivation, but I persuaded our youth pastor to take a group of the teenagers to a recreation center in Cleveland for underprivileged kids.

"I don't want to go," Ryan announced the day of the event. "If I can't play basketball, what good am I?"

I stared at him, surprised by his whining. I'm sure he could tell by my expression that his question was one of the dumbest things I'd ever heard him say. "Well, you can play board games or astound them with your amazing conversational skills and scintillating personality."

"Do you always have to be so sarcastic?" he groused.

I laughed. "Yep. I've assumed that's why you've called me Sass all these years. Only living up to the reputation, my friend." I smacked his cast with my hand but didn't know it was so solid. Ouch. "Okay, I've had enough out of you, Ryan Joseph. Time to get over your little pity party."

Inhaling a deep breath, I needed to keep going. "Things could be a whole lot worse, you know. You could be dead or in a coma or something." My eyes welled with sudden, unexpected tears. "And you need to be careful and not do reckless things. There are people who care a lot about you, and we—*they*—don't want to be worrying about you all the time."

Ryan's soulful eyes grew rounder. "Are you one of those people, Ellie?" His words were quiet. "You care about me?"

"Don't be silly. I hate you. That's why I'm over here every day." A few tears spilled over onto my cheeks, and I impatiently brushed them away. "Come on. Let's get moving. Pastor Jon's outside in the van and you're going to make us all late."

I stomped over to the corner of the family room and grabbed his crutches. "Now, haul yourself off that sofa and get these things positioned. It's time to go to the youth center and bless someone."

"Yes, ma'am."

Once we boarded the church van, Ryan settled across the aisle with his crutches propped against the adjacent seat.

"Ryan?"

He glanced over at me and raised a brow. "Yeah, Sass?"

"Don't ever call me ma'am again. Even when I'm old and gray. Promise me."

Ryan's grin made my stomach turn over in a good way. Then I heard him mumble, "Yes, ma'am."

I turned toward the window to hide my smile.

Startled, I sat up straighter in the kitchen chair. Was that my cell phone ringing? Goodness, I'd left it in the bedroom! I dashed out of the kitchen and down the hall, sliding in my stocking feet on the hardwood floor as I rounded the corner into the bedroom. In my haste, I'd narrowly missed banging my hip on the door jamb. That was close. I'd prefer not to have a nasty looking bruise on my honeymoon.

"You are ridiculous," I muttered under my breath. Still, it *was* a valid thought even though Ryan wouldn't care. I grabbed my cell phone from the night table and read the text message.

GOOD MORNING, BEAUTIFUL. DREAMING OF ME? ☺

I laughed. I'VE BEEN UP FOR HOURS. MY SOLDIER IS COMING HOME SOON, AND I HAVE VERY IMPORTANT, LIFE-CHANGING THINGS TO DO.

"Take that, funny man." Still smiling, I sent the text. While I waited, I inspected the bedroom ceiling. Then I sat up on the bed, cross-legged, impatient as ever. It's amazing I've been able to accomplish much of anything these past few days.

Within seconds, I heard Ryan's incoming text and then focused on the screen.

I'M EXCITED TO SEE WHAT YOU'VE DONE WITH OUR HOUSE.

YOU SHOULD BE. IT'S A PLACE YOU'LL BE PROUD TO CALL HOME.

I KNOW THAT. ALL I NEED IS YOU TO CALL IT HOME. ♥

YOU'RE BEING INCREDIBLY SWEET AND ROMANTIC, RYAN. DID YOU DO SOMETHING WRONG?

Haha. No. If loving you is wrong, Ellie, I don't wanna be right.

Hold on a second while I groan. Okay, I need to scoot now. Someone keeps texting me, and I'm getting behind.

Tell him to leave you alone. You're MY woman.

I'll be sure and do that. Be careful Ryan. ♥

I love you, Sass. Guess I'll go pack some more. And I'll be careful. Promise.

Chapter 8

~~♥~~

Mid-December through the end of January was the slowest time of the year at the ad agency. Which meant Beckett more or less ordered me to leave before lunch. He handed me a plain white envelope with my name handwritten on the front and told me not to come back to the office until after my honeymoon. Subtlety isn't an attribute of an ad man, I've learned.

Beckett watched as I gathered my coat and prepared to leave, making me feel rather self-conscious, as if I'd done something wrong. Then he advised me not to open the envelope until I left the office. His tone of voice made it sound like I was Nancy Drew in The Case of the Mysterious Envelope. Or it could be that my overactive imagination was taking over again. Wouldn't be the first time.

So, although it was difficult, I stuffed the envelope deep into my tote bag and tried to forget about it. For now. Surely my boss wouldn't hand me a pink slip inside that envelope. Feeling somewhat befuddled, I paused by the front door. "Will I see you at the wedding?"

"I wouldn't miss it." A rare smile creased the older man's face. That smile alleviated my concerns a bit.

"Thank you for whatever is in the envelope. I appreciate your thinking of me."

The corners of Beckett's eyes crinkled. "You're very welcome, Ellie."

I began to walk the few short blocks from The Beckett Agency to the nursing facility. The wind was especially biting, and I burrowed my chin into my thick scarf. As I hastened my steps, I heard townspeople calling out holiday greetings to one another. Merilee Jenkins rang the red Salvation Army bell in front of Keeley's Market while Cody Tucker—the local 14-year-old trumpet phenomenon who some claimed could be the next Miles Davis—played his heart out in an impassioned version of "Silver Bells" in front of the Cade's Corner courthouse.

Squinting in the bright sunlight, wishing it provided more warmth, I caught sight of the huge Christmas wreath—flanked by candy canes—swaying on wires strung across the middle of Main Street. An enormous inflatable snowman with a somewhat demonic smile waved and bobbed up and down in the town square.

Nat King Cole crooned "The Christmas Song (Chestnuts Roasting On An Open Fire)" when the door to Cade's Corner Hardware opened and Luther Nelson stepped outside.

"Hey, Ellie." He stopped and drew in a deep breath as though it were a beautiful spring day instead of one with below-freezing temperatures. In his wool overcoat, Luther wore a hat but no gloves. I couldn't imagine.

"Hi, Luther. Don't stay out too long. Mighty cold today."

"Yeah, but I love it. Grew up with this kind of cold in Minnesota." He tapped his fist on his chest a few times. "Keeps a man well-preserved."

"Only because you're frozen," I mumbled under my breath. Or maybe those chest thumps jump-started his heart. I needed to keep moving. "I'll talk to you soon!"

"Yep. At the big wedding if not before."

The warmth of the nursing facility welcomed me as I stepped inside. Still shivering, I hurried down the hallway into the center of the building.

"You sure have been faithful in coming to see Cora in the last few weeks," Trudy said as I approached the station closest to Room 365. "Not that you weren't before."

"I'm antsy these days and need to stay occupied." I shrugged. "All the wedding plans are in place, the house is all set up, and now Beckett doesn't want me back at the agency until after the honeymoon." I raised my hands. "So, what's a girl to do? I'm playing the waiting game."

"Well, have a cookie. That should kill a few seconds. And don't tell me you can't afford the calories." Trudy pushed the familiar white box, decorated with holiday motifs, across the counter. "Saundra from The Bakery Shelf brought these to us this morning."

"How sweet." I caught my pun and grinned before selecting a bell-shaped sugar cookie with red frosting and those hard little silver beads that were supposedly edible. Not wanting to risk anything this close to the wedding, I picked the beads off the cookie and deposited them in the trash can at the end of the counter.

"The Bakery Shelf's cookies are good, but they're too doughy for my taste. And the frosting's not as rich and decadent as yours." That comment came from Krista as she walked toward the counter with a clipboard and a smile. "How are you today, Ellie?" She pulled me into a quick hug.

"Peachy, thanks. Trying to stay off the streets and out of trouble."

The ladies all laughed.

Patsy spoke up next. "We're wondering if you could tell us how you and Ryan came up with the idea for Perchance to Dream. That's a story we haven't heard."

"Sure, why not? I take requests." I was surprised they hadn't heard the story since our project had been written up in the local paper in the past and again a few weeks ago. Of course, not everyone takes the time to read the weekly paper in Cade's Corner. I grabbed another cookie *sans* silver beads. "Follow me."

Five minutes later, I sat beside Cora, holding her hand. The group of ladies gathered in the room was larger than usual. I smiled. "Is today a slow day?"

Trudy nodded. "Yes, thank the Lord. You won't hear us complain. Before you start your story, the staff collected a little something for you." She handed me another envelope.

Wow. Must be the day for envelope-giving. I am so blessed.

"Thank you so much. You shouldn't have—"

"Use it for whatever you want," one of the aides—Trish, I think—told me. "There's a couple of gift cards in there for you and Ryan, too."

"You ladies are the best. The unsung heroes."

"Thanks, but you're *our* hero," Patsy said.

"How do you figure that?" I tucked the envelope in my tote bag. "Ryan's the hero, not me."

"Of course he is, but so are you, Ellie. People forget about the ones left behind on the home front," Trudy said. "Ryan might be fighting a physical war, but you've had your own battle to fight right here at home."

Not much more I could say to that. Trudy was right although I didn't consider it a fight, as such. "If you would, I'd appreciate your prayers," I said. "That's the most important thing. Pray that Ryan will return home safely. And that, until he does, the Lord will keep my nerves calm. Not to mention his mom, dad, and brother. Keep them calm, I mean." I rolled my eyes at my stammering.

"You've got them." That sentiment came from Krista and several of the ladies nodded in agreement.

"Thank you." I took a quick breath. "Now, since I know you probably need to work at some point today, I'd better begin my story."

Chapter 9

~~♥~~

Ryan and I first discussed the idea for Perchance to Dream over a hot fudge sundae at The Soda Shoppe almost four years ago. The Soda Shoppe has always been one of our favorite places with its tile floor, gleaming chrome fixtures, vintage straw dispensers and a jukebox that plays classic 50s and 60s music. We'd both had birthday parties there. Stopped here for burgers and cheese fries after ballgames on weekend nights. Then we'd shared early dates as moony-eyed kids trying to navigate a relationship—that awkward yet sweet period when we weren't sure what to say or do as we transitioned from "just friends" to friends who could freely kiss one another on the lips.

The servers are outfitted in retro uniforms, and many of them have worked at The Soda Shoppe since they were teenagers when the place opened 35 years ago. Tradition and family are what Cade's Corner has always been about, and it's one of the best aspects of small-town living.

"I think we should do something lasting together," I said to Ryan.

He stopped his spoon halfway to his mouth. "Okay. You don't think we will?"

I grinned. Best not to dwell on the ramifications of his question. "I'm talking about in the grand scheme of things. Something bigger than you and me as a couple."

That hadn't come out right based on Ryan's quick frown.

He took a bite. "Before I say anything else, maybe you'd better explain."

"I want to make a difference. I know that sounds cliché, but I'm talking about here in town, not globally. As much as I want to save the world, I've come to terms with the fact that it's simply not possible." I scooped the cherry from the top of the ice cream with my long-handled spoon before Ryan could claim it. Plopping it in my mouth, I made a big show of savoring it.

Ryan waved his spoon at me. "Let me guess. You want to name a charity after Amelia Earhart. I remember you said something about wanting to make a difference the day you were reading the book about her."

"Good memory. I did, as a matter of fact. You're thinking along the right lines, though."

"Okay. I think it's becoming clearer now. You're talking about a nonprofit to help people. And we"—he motioned between us—"would be co-founders. How am I doing?"

I nodded with enthusiasm. "Now you're catching on."

Ryan took another bite and appeared to consider the idea. "Actually, you never know how far-reaching your efforts could be. Whether saving souls or doing good deeds, one person at a time, like Pastor Derek says."

Ryan waved across the restaurant to the high school girl standing behind the counter. "Rachelle, can I get some more cherries? Ellie's hogging them over here." He fed me another plump cherry.

"Sure thing, Ryan." Goodness, Rachelle's voice practically dripped with sugary-sweet syrup. Who could blame her? I wasn't blind. Half the girls in town were in love with Ryan.

Leaning across the table, Ryan opened his mouth and caught the cherry I flung at him in a moment of juvenile silliness.

"No fair sweet talking the server," I said. I indulged in another bite of the delicious sundae, this time with an extra dollop of hot fudge. Nothing like warm hot fudge.

"You're the only one I sweet talk, and you know it," Ryan said. "Tell me what's on your mind, Sass. I'm sure you have a plan. You always do."

I quirked a brow. "Is that a complaint?"

"No. It's a sincere compliment." Ryan took a bite of the sundae and when he met my gaze, I nearly forgot my name much less my last thought. I've known Ryan my whole life, and he still has that effect on me. Always will.

"I'm thinking about starting an organization to help people who can't meet a need on their own for whatever reason. We could start it, and head it up, but we'd need to recruit volunteers to help carry out the work."

"Goodwill and The Salvation Army take care of the basic needs—food, clothing, shelter. Stuff like that." Ryan took the bite I offered him from my spoon and then licked his lips. "Let's start by narrowing it down to a focus group."

Thankfully, he hadn't questioned my sanity and seemed more than willing to discuss the idea.

"Well, we both love kids," I said. "Let's start there. We can provide help with their wishes or something. Like the Make-A-Wish Foundation. I've always admired what they do."

Ryan's handsome face sobered and his brow creased. "No dying kids, Sass. Please. I couldn't handle that." My big strong soldier and he can't handle the idea of a child being sick or worse. Makes me love him even more.

"How about granting Christmas wishes?" he said. "We both love Christmas, and every kid should get a gift or two. I know they have the angel trees at churches and other community groups to meet needs, but from what I know, there are always more than enough requests to go around. Maybe we can work in conjunction with them, if needed, and fill in some gaps. I'll make some calls."

"Sounds like a great place to start," I said. "Thanks for jumping onboard."

"Sure thing." Ryan appeared thoughtful. "We need to do something besides buy gifts."

"Like what?" I scooped another bite of the ice cream. "Hold on a second." Abandoning the spoon, I massaged my temples. "Brain freeze."

"Want something warm to drink?"

"I'm not sure that'll help."

Ryan shifted in his chair and touched my arm with a concerned expression. "Here's what you do. Before your next bite, roll your tongue into a ball and press the bottom of your tongue against the soft palate at the back of your mouth."

"I know where the soft palate it is, smart man."

"Seriously. It will warm up your mouth and help the ice cream go down easier."

"Or make me seriously gag." I frowned.

"Okay, as a last resort, you could press your thumb to your palate."

"I've never sucked my thumb, even when I was a kid, and I refuse to start now," I said with feigned indignation. "How do you know all this stuff, anyway?"

"I'm a certified brain freeze expert. Observe and learn." Ryan spooned another bite of ice cream into his mouth and sucked in his cheeks. "Warming it on my tongue first," he said through pursed lips.

I shook my head. "Back to the topic of conversation, please."

"We could write a personal note to encourage each kid and tuck it inside a children's Bible," he said. "If we buy the Bibles in bulk, we could get a decent discount. Or maybe the Gideons will donate some to us."

I pondered his suggestion while Rachelle brought him the bowl of cherries, at least a dozen. I eyed them with a quirked brow. "You're going to get a massive sugar rush from all those cherries."

"No more than you with all that hot fudge you're eating, Miss Brain Freeze."

"Thanks for the sympathy." I licked the rich, luscious chocolate off the spoon. "So you caught me. You know I go weak in the knees for hot fudge."

"That's not all." Ryan's brows lifted up and down. I grinned and felt my blush down to my toes. Even though he was only referring to kissing, our kisses had grown better with time. That's quite a feat when they've been great from the start. Ryan's kisses always seem new. He's a very creative man.

I cleared my throat, needing to concentrate. "I think your idea has definite merit although discussing a discount on Bibles sounds somehow disrespectful."

"Not at all," Ryan said. "We still need to be financially responsible. I'll check on the legalities with Nick and get him to help us set it up." A slow-moving grin creased his face. "I can see your mind working over there. You already have a name picked out for our project, don't you?"

"You know me too well. A good thing, I suppose." I dared to take another slow bite of ice cream and pointed to my mouth to indicate I was warming it on my tongue. "I'm thinking Perchance to Dream might be good."

"Shakespeare?"

"Right. It's part of *Hamlet's* "To be or not to be" soliloquy, although that has no bearing on my reasoning."

Ryan tilted his head with a bemused expression. "Wait a second. Isn't Hamlet thinking about *suicide* in that speech?"

"Well, yes. I was hoping you wouldn't remember that aspect." Putting down my spoon for a final time, I paused to gather my thoughts. "After Hamlet's uncle murdered his father and married his mother, Hamlet started going crazy and wanted revenge. At the same time, he desired the escape of death, but he was afraid there would be no peace in death."

"Because of the dreams that may come." Ryan dropped his spoon in the empty sundae dish. "That's all I remember from high school English class. Although, now that I think of it, do we dream when we're dead?"

Going off on tangents is nothing new with us.

"I'm sure if you're not in Heaven, the nightmare becomes reality, but we digress. I gave up trying to figure out Shakespeare a long time ago. My point being that Hamlet's speech is the emotional centerpiece of the play, but our purpose in using the name will be much different. I'm referring to dreams as being wishes. The wishes of children, in this case. Not to discount The Bard, but I want to bring hope to kids and lift their spirits." I shrugged. "Bottom line, I think the name sounds elegant and classy."

"So do I," Ryan said with a definitive nod. "Let's do this, Ellie."

"You're on." I gave him a brilliant smile as he offered me the last two cherries on his spoon to seal the deal.

I stopped my story and glanced at the staff members in the room. "So, there you have it, ladies. It's not an exciting story, but that's how the idea for Perchance to Dream began." I smiled. "Four years later, here we are. We've been operational for three years and we're hoping to continue for many more years. Every child receives at least one toy, a Bible, and a handwritten note."

"I think it's a fabulous thing you and Ryan are doing," Trudy said.

"It's a collaborative effort between our volunteers and sponsors."

"How many gifts are you giving to the kids this year, Ellie?" Patsy asked.

That question stumped me. "I've honestly lost count. I think about 350, including this last group of gifts. We had some last-minute requests. The number keeps growing," I told them. "In a way, it's a sad commentary, but on the other hand, I'm thankful we have the means and volunteers to help."

I rose to my feet and gathered my things. "I need to take off for today. I have to scoot over to the office to wrap the last few gifts."

I held my tongue not to let it slip that I was also playing matchmaker tonight between Maura and Nick. Ryan's older brother was considered one of the most eligible bachelors in Cade's Corner. Once certain individuals (who shall not be named) finally accepted the fact that Maura hadn't been born and raised here in town, they'd grown to love her as I do. People could be so ridiculous sometimes. I'm sure many in town were speculating about a possible match between those two, but in case this dinner crashed and burned like the *Hindenburg*, I'd be better off not to say anything.

"I know Perchance to Dream will keep flourishing. Thanks for coming by today." Trudy walked beside me as Krista and Patsy waved and headed in the opposite direction.

"I wouldn't miss it." My smile sobered. "Trudy, do you think Cora has any idea I'm here? That maybe somewhere in her subconscious she knows?"

Trudy's dark eyes softened. "I like to believe she does, sweetie. I know something else."

"What's that?"

"You've blessed the staff here. Your visits always brighten our days. Your optimism and your deep love for Ryan reminds us old married ladies what it's like to be young and in love. Matter of fact, you've inspired me. I'm thinking of doing something special for my David tonight."

A smile upturned my lips. "I hope you and David have a terrific evening, Trudy. I'll see you again tomorrow."

Chapter 10

~~♥~~

Friday Evening—Chez Ellie

"Very nice," I said under my breath as I surveyed the table set for three. Mom used to watch those home decorating/cooking shows, and she'd ingrained it in me that *presentation is everything, darling.*

Reaching behind me, I untied my apron. After whisking it off, I hung it on the hook in the kitchen. Right on schedule. Maura, and hopefully Nick, should arrive within the next five minutes. I wore my nicest pair of jeans and a pretty blouse (not the blue satin since that's only begging for trouble if I'm serving food). And yes, my beloved high heels (electric blue this time) since I'm not planning on leaving the house. Kara tells me I'll give up wearing my heels after marriage—definitely when children come along—but I have my doubts.

The flames from two tapered candles dance in the middle of the immaculately set table. I'd used my best white linen tablecloth and some of the fine china we'd received as a wedding gift. I know Ryan won't mind. This dinner is all about promoting the cause of true love, after all.

I lowered the setting on the chandelier dimmer switch. Installing that switch without electrocuting myself had been my biggest achievement to-date in the house.

"Ambiance. Check."

Soft jazz played in the background. "Romantic music. Check."

The doorbell rang. "And here we go."

With a welcoming smile, I floated across the living room with the grace and elegance befitting a New York socialite. After I opened the door, my face fell when I spied Maura standing solo on the front doorstep.

"Hi. You didn't bring Nick?" I tried not to make it sound like an accusation as I ducked my head out the door, glancing from side to side.

"Good evening to you, too." Maura's smile belied the sarcasm in her words.

"Forgive me. Please, come in." I swung the door wide as she stepped past me and stamped her feet on the mat.

"Relax, Ellie. Nick's here. He's parking the car. These are for you." From behind her back, Maura pulled out a bouquet of a dozen deep pink roses and offered them to me. They were partially wrapped in cellophane with the signature Keeley's Market gold oval sticker bearing their logo. "Nick talked with Ryan earlier, and your fiancé practically ordered him to bring these. Sorry, but we didn't take the time to write out a mushy sentiment on a card."

"That's okay. Thank you." My eyes misted as I accepted the gorgeous bouquet and inhaled their lovely fragrance. "For these *and* for bringing Nick."

Putting the flowers on a side table for the moment, I took Maura's coat and couldn't miss her slight frown as I hung it in the small front closet. I was in for a scolding.

"Seriously, Ellie? Candlelight? And since when did Barry White sing Christmas tunes?"

I suppressed my grin. "It's instrumental jazz. No deep-voiced soul singers here tonight."

Maura shook her head. "You couldn't be subtle if you tried. Don't you dare rush off in the middle of dinner with some flimsy excuse about having to dart home. No convenient emergencies tonight. Promise me."

"Wouldn't think of it. You're the one hearing Barry White in your overactive imagination, so maybe I *should* leave. Never mind the fact that I can think of a lot worse things in life than being left alone with—gasp!—Nick Sullivan."

My gaze took in my friend's dark dress jeans and pretty light pink sweater. "You look gorgeous tonight, by the way. I'm glad you finally took my suggestion to leave your hair down. The man is nuts if he doesn't fall madly, deeply, completely in love with you by the end of the evening."

Maura laughed. "Pouring it on a bit thick with the adverbs, aren't you?"

Nick always knows when to make a timely appearance, and he darted inside the house as if on cue. Physically, Nick is quite different from Ryan—shorter, stockier, with light brown hair and chestnut-colored eyes. Handsome in a nontraditional way. Nick is much more serious than Ryan, and in my opinion, he could stand to laugh more often and give his sense of humor free rein. It's buried in there somewhere, but it's been submerged and needs to come out and play. In terms of character, Nick is much like Ryan in his steadfast faith, inherent honesty, and loyalty. Both would do anything to ease someone's pain or suffering.

"Man, it's wicked cold out there." Nick closed the front door firmly behind him. Without hesitation, he kissed my cheek and then handed me a bottle of chilled, sparkling white grape cider. "Thanks for the invitation, Ellie. Ryan's a blessed man."

Nick is polite almost to a fault. Not a bad quality in a family law attorney.

"Wicked, indeed. Your years spent in New England are showing. I'm glad you could come. Thanks for the roses from Ryan and the sparkling cider." I gestured for him to remove his coat. Maura had walked into the kitchen with the bouquet of roses, so as I hung Nick's coat beside hers, I leaned close and lowered my voice. "Please tell me you got Maura flowers, too."

His brows arched. "Why would I do that?"

I frowned. "Because you're one of the most polite gentlemen I know. Try that on for starters. You earned a law degree at Yale. That proves you're not entirely clueless. Although, on second thought, you might be a little short in the common sense department."

Nick laughed like I'd said the funniest thing he'd heard in years. "Let's see how tonight goes first. Sorry to tell you, Ellie, but this isn't a date, no matter how much *you* might want it to be."

I tilted my head as if considering his words. "Fair enough, but I can't say I'm not disappointed."

"You'll get over it." He stopped when I stared at him. "What? Did I say something wrong?"

"No. What you just said...Ryan said the same thing once." In a different context, of course, but the delivery was eerily similar.

Nick stepped closer and put one hand on my arm. "You okay, Ellie?"

I raised my chin. "I'll be fine. You just witnessed a sentimental moment, that's all. I've been having a lot of those lately."

"Understandable. Mom's the same way."

Yes, it's obviously a *female* condition.

Nick rubbed his hands together. "Not to change the subject, but something smells great in here. What's on the menu tonight at *Chez Ellie*?"

That made me smile. With men, it's all about the food. "Everything's ready. Come to the table and let's feast."

Maura came out of the kitchen with the roses in a vase and carefully set them in the middle of the table. It's nice to have a good friend who knows where I keep everything.

As we prayed and then began our meal, I appreciated the fact that Nick didn't tease me about my former lack of cooking skills. Maura had grown up in Cleveland, so she only knew what I *wanted* her to know although I'm sure she's heard the rumors. Doesn't matter. I've triumphed over the adversity.

An hour later, we enjoyed coffee with slices of pecan pie and vanilla ice cream, warm for Maura and me but room temperature for Nick. In many regards, his food preferences are similar to Ryan's. My dinner of tossed salad, chicken cacciatore, and homemade three-cheese dinner rolls—my newest recipe find I know Ryan will love—had gone exceedingly well based on how Nick scarfed down two generous helpings. I hope Maura doesn't think he's a pig since I've never seen him eat so fast. For her part, Maura—normally a picky eater—seemed to enjoy the meal but she had gone a wee bit overboard with her effusive compliments.

"You don't have to exaggerate to make me feel better," I protested.

Maura took a sip of her coffee and lowered her cup to the table. "I'm not exaggerating. Why would you think that?"

"Sorry. I don't know why I said that." Embarrassed, I focused on smoothing my napkin across my lap beneath the table. Made from white linen, they matched my tablecloth.

"I think I know." Seems Nick can't stop being an attorney even after leaving his office. While it can be annoying, I appreciate his frankness most of the time.

"Number one, you still can't get over that casserole you made for the church social all those years ago." Okay, so maybe he wanted to play psychologist tonight instead.

I opened my mouth to protest but Nick raised his hand to stop me.

"Number two, you think people feel sorry for you because Ryan's been gone for such a long deployment this time and you've had to make all the wedding arrangements on your own."

"Do you have a little checklist written on your hand over there?" I smiled to let him know I was teasing. "Look. Even if Ryan *were* here, I'd still be learning how to make his favorite dishes. And handling all the last-minute details. I'm more than happy to take care of everything."

I needed to put in a plug for Maura. I'd been making comments here and there throughout our meal about how I couldn't do half of what I do without her expert assistance. In many ways, that wouldn't be stretching the truth. "With Maura's help, and my mom and sisters, we've managed to get it all done. As long as Ryan shows up at the altar, we're good."

Nick chuckled. "I'm sure that won't be a problem. Great pie, by the way. Throw in a few chocolate chips for Ryan and you're golden." He took another hefty bite.

"Thanks for the tip."

"Have Kara and Staci been helping more?" Maura sounded genuinely surprised.

"Depends on your definition of more, but yes, they're doing what they can. With kids and busy families, and the fact that they live forty minutes away on a low-traffic day, their time is limited. I'm just thankful they didn't balk at the cranberry color I chose for their gowns."

"It goes beautifully with their coloring," Maura said. "And I absolutely love my gown."

I gave my maid-of-honor a grateful smile. Her tea-length gown was just a shade lighter than the dresses Kara and Staci would wear.

In many aspects, Maura is like a sister to me. She's the one who helps me in the church nursery once a month. She sits with Mom and me in church every Sunday morning while my sisters attend churches in Cleveland closer to their homes. Maura is also the one who dries my occasional tears when I miss Ryan so much I'm not sure I can endure another day.

Maura is my encourager, my prayer partner, my confidante, my closest female friend. Everyone should be so blessed as to have a Maura in their lives. If only I could infuse that idea directly into Nick the Attorney's thick skull.

Actually, Maura and Ryan's older brother appear to be getting along famously. Maybe this evening is going even better than I'd realized. They'd managed to put aside the "boss" and "assistant" hats and didn't seem in the least bit awkward with one another. Three years older than me, Maura is only two years younger than Nick. That's a good age difference.

I'd caught Nick sneaking glances at Maura during dinner, studying her profile. For her part, Maura laughed at his attempts to make a joke and seemed to appreciate Nick's dry sense of humor, such as it was.

I quietly observed them for a minute. Maybe Maura's suggestion for me to dart out of the house—at least out of the *room*—might not be such a bad idea. But, no, these two were grown-ups. They were more than capable of handling their relationship on their own. I'd poured the foundation but it was up to them to build upon it.

Wow. I sound rather full of myself.

The ring tone on my cell phone sounded. I smiled to the beginning strains of "It Had to Be You." *Perfect timing, Ryan.*

I pulled the phone from the pocket of my jeans and rose to my feet. "If you'll excuse me."

"Give Ryan our best," Nick said. "Tell my little brother I can't wait to see his ugly mug."

"Will do," I called over my shoulder as I stepped into the kitchen. "Hi, Ryan."

"Hey, Sass."

I glanced at the clock on the wall. "It's the middle of the night over there. Why are you up?"

"Couldn't sleep, as usual, so I thought I'd call and see if my favorite matchmaker's efforts are working."

"Sorry you're not sleeping, and I know the feeling. So far, so good with the matchmaking. You'd be very proud of me, Ryan. I let Nick and Maura do most of the talking during dinner, and they seem to be getting along well. Maura's hearing Barry White in her head and Nick's stealing glances."

Ryan's laughter rang through the phone, making me smile.

"No one can tell a story like you, Sass."

"That's what they tell me."

"Have you been talking about me again in the town square?"

"Only on alternate Wednesdays during Happy Hour. Two-for-one special. Silly man, I'm always talking about you. Don't let it swell your handsome head, but you're my primary topic of conversation these days and you know it."

"I get it. Same here about you, baby. The guys think you're a combination of Superwoman and Miss Universe. So, did you crank up Barry White and encourage them to work off your dinner by shaking a leg?"

Now it was my turn to laugh. "Who says 'shake a leg' anymore? Are you eighty years old?"

"I feel like it. That's what a lack of sleep will do. And I hope you caught my huge compliment in that last speech."

"I did, thanks. Miss Universe, eh?"

"You are to me."

I sighed. "You say the sweetest things sometimes. I'd better make sure to polish my crown so it's not tarnished when you come home." I frowned. Not sure that came out right.

"Tell me what's happening now, baby."

Ryan's adept at keeping me on track. "Okay, then, Maura and Nick are currently having dessert. Which means our conversation needs to last at least a few minutes to give them some privacy. Let's just say your brother might do some pew-hopping and sit with Mom, Maura and me this week instead of with your parents."

"I'm sure my parents would be thrilled."

I agreed and then thanked him for the roses. "They were the perfect centerpiece for the dinner table tonight."

"Terrific. I'm glad Nick was willing to do my bidding for once, but he'll do anything for you, Sass. Was he able to get the dark pink roses you like?"

"He did. Your brother's a keeper, Ryan. And so are you, of course. There's something about you Sullivan men. Your parents definitely raised you well." I leaned my elbow on the table and twirled a long strand of hair around one finger. "I was afraid Maura would resist the idea of dating Nick since they work so closely together."

"They're not dating yet, Ellie, but that's exactly why they *should* be a couple," Ryan said. "They understand each other and have similar interests. Besides, in a small town like Cade's Corner, it doesn't matter to anyone else if they fraternize after working hours. In a way, it's more or less expected."

"Maybe," I mused, "but not always. Speaking of which, Mom has gone out a couple of times with her new boss, Dr. Phillip Bernard. He's a widower and has only been in town a few months. She inadvertently let it slip when I was talking to her earlier today. When I asked her if she was dating him, Mom admitted she is although she's not sure whether the relationship will 'go anywhere,' as she put it."

"Why is that?" From Ryan's tone, I couldn't tell whether or not he was supportive of Mom dating Dr. Bernard.

"Maybe because she's still in love with Dad." That's how I'd feel if anything happened to Ryan. In my heart, I'd always belong to him.

"How do you feel about your mom dating again?"

"Honestly? I'm not sure." I continued to twirl my hair. "Most of all, I want her to be happy. That's my main concern. I guess I should have suspected something was up when the good doctor showed up in church last Sunday, and Mom invited him to sit with us." I can tell she likes this man. Even over the phone, her voice goes soft when she mentions him.

Ryan whistled under his breath. "I'd say that's pretty significant."

"Mom told me she knew Dad would have liked him, so yes, I think something may eventually develop between them if not in the near future."

"I'll look forward to meeting Dr. Bernard when I come home." Ryan paused for a few seconds before speaking again. "You're twirling your hair right now, aren't you?"

I laughed. "Even without seeing me, you can tell? I'm not sure if that's a good or a bad thing."

"It's more the wistfulness in your voice."

Yes, the man knows me so well. He can "read" me simply by the inflections in my voice.

In another couple of minutes, we signed off after making absurd kissing noises (well, more me than Ryan) over the phone that would mortify me if Nick and Maura overheard. When I joined them in the dining room once more, they were deep in conversation, *engrossed* in one another. *Hmm.* If they angled their heads just slightly, they'd almost be kissing. Nick's arm was casually draped over the back of Maura's chair, and I stood in the doorway for a full ten seconds before Maura glanced my way.

"Nick." When he kept talking in low, hushed tones, Maura nudged his elbow with hers.

A slow smile creased Nick's face, reminding me a bit of Ryan. His cheeks colored with a slight flush. "Hey, Ellie." He started to shift his arm away from Maura.

"Hey, yourself. You leave your arm right where it is."

He obeyed. "Okay, we—Maura and I—have a confession." Maura avoided my gaze and busied herself with pouring another glass of sparkling cider for Nick.

I resisted moving one hand to my hip. "I can't wait to hear it." This should be good. I reclaimed my chair and eyed the remains of my pecan pie. I could forego the calories. I had a fantastic new swimsuit for the honeymoon, but even a tummy-tucking, one-piece designed to make my legs appear elongated could reveal things I wish it didn't.

Nick exchanged a smile with Maura and my eyes widened when he placed his hand over hers. "We've actually been dating for a couple of months."

My mouth dropped open as I stared at them. How could I not have known?

"Why, you under-the-radar stinkers!" Balling my napkin, I tossed it across the table at him. Scooting back my chair, I ran around the table to where Maura sat next to Nick. I brought one arm around her neck and moved the other around Nick's shoulder. I hugged and then mock-strangled them both.

"I can't believe you didn't say anything, but I'm absolutely thrilled! Be honest now. If I hadn't invited you to dinner, were you two ever planning on telling me before the wedding? Especially considering you're both *in* said wedding?" I gave Nick a light swat on the back of his head. "Good thing we've already paired you up to walk down the aisle together."

"Yeah, by process of elimination," Nick said. My two brothers-in-law were groomsmen to round out the wedding party and to escort my sisters. Maura was the only one not in the family—yet. After tonight, who knows?

Don't get ahead of yourself, Ellie.

Maura looked at Nick with a smile. "We wanted to make sure things would go well before making our relationship known. If it makes you feel any better, you're the first person we've told."

"It does. Thanks." I moved back to my chair and looked from one to the other of them, marveling over this new development. "You think you're so sly. You've been sitting over there, holding hands beneath the table at every available opportunity, haven't you?"

"Only a few times." Nick shrugged. "We didn't want to rub it in or make you feel bad."

"Why? Because Ryan's not here?" I balked. "Ryan's everywhere in this house." I pointed to the bowl on the coffee table a few feet away. "He made that in high school art class." I nodded to the antique chair in the corner of the living room. "That chair belonged to my Grandpa Nichols. Ryan reupholstered it before leaving on his first tour of duty. Even the clock on the bathroom wall? We picked that up at an antique fair. When I took it to be repaired, I found out it was rare and valuable. That was a shock, and I haven't told Ryan about it yet. I can't wait to see his surprise when he sees the clock on the wall, and I can tell him the story."

"We know Ryan's here with you, Ellie." The compassion in Nick's voice touched me as it always does.

Seated beside Nick, Maura's expression held such love for me that it almost made me cry. "Ryan's not just in this house. He's in your eyes and in your smile."

"You're part of one another," Nick said. "Honey, your support of what Ryan's doing overseas means everything to him."

Something about Nick calling me *honey* made me want to burst into tears. The three of us understood that—if it hadn't been for his time spent in the Army—Ryan and I would have been married by now. All in God's timing.

I swallowed hard. "Thank you, Nick. Coming from you, that means a lot."

"It's only the truth." How I appreciated this man.

"We should discuss our final plans to finish out the season with Perchance to Dream," I said a few minutes later in the kitchen. They'd insisted on helping, so who was I to refuse? "Nick, I need you to come in and write the notes for the boys to put in the Bibles. We have about ten more." He'd taken over that responsibility in Ryan's absence.

"Sure thing. What else do you need?" Nick took the plate I handed him and loaded it into the dishwasher.

"Maura, are you still available to meet me in the office tomorrow at two o'clock to finish wrapping the gifts and write the notes for the girls?"

"I'll be there." Maura stacked more dishes on the counter. "That's everything from the table."

"Wyatt and Justin are coming in at four tomorrow to pick everything up," I told Nick. "If you can stick around, they might need some help loading everything into their vehicles. If you're available afterwards, they're delivering them downtown." From there, we had more volunteers to distribute the toys. What would we do without our faithful volunteers?

Nick nodded. "I'm relatively free tomorrow since it's Saturday. I'll definitely stop by the office mid-afternoon."

A short time later, Nick and Maura thanked me and said their good-byes.

"I'm sorry if you think we deceived you in some way," Maura said after Nick went out to warm up the car. "You know how it is in the beginning of a relationship. It's special but fragile."

"I understand. No worries." I gave her a quick hug. "I really am very happy for you, and I'm praying this relationship works out between my two favorite people."

Maura laughed. "No pressure there. Love you, my friend."

"You, too." I waved and blew a kiss to Nick as he came back to escort Maura to his car.

A few minutes later, as I undressed and pulled on my flannel pajama bottoms with Ryan's Cavaliers T-shirt, I ran through the mental list of things I still wanted to accomplish before Ryan's return. Practical things like organize the linen closet and pair up the sheets. Someone had shared the ingenious tip of putting the folded sheets inside the matching pillowcase. What a great idea! The closets were small enough as it was, so that would be a great space saver.

We've had a few wedding showers, but I'd attended them alone. Ryan would be coming home to so many new things, and it'd be fun showing them all to him.

"Things are nice, and it's generous of people to give them to us, but I don't need fancy sheets to pull over me at night. I just need you," Ryan said during one of our Skype sessions. "Which reminds me, didn't you have one of those showers where the ladies gave you sexy nighties and stuff?"

I laughed. "It's called lingerie, but isn't that getting a little too personal?"

"Yeah, I guess it is. Sorry, baby. After we're married, I hope you'll give me a fashion show."

"That's a given." Secretly, I was glad when he said things like that. Things that got my pulse racing. When he was in a certain frame of mind, Ryan sometimes said the most wonderful, romantic things. If I stopped to think, it was only in the past month when he'd told me we shouldn't say such things. The Lord knew how difficult this was for both of us. All over again, I missed Ryan so much, I physically ached. The evenings and nights are the worst and when I feel the most alone.

After brushing my teeth, I ran into the bedroom and quickly slipped under the covers. Crossing my arms behind my head, I watched the shadows made by the tree branches outside the bedroom window. The glass panes were frosted over, and I shivered and snuggled farther under the blanket as I heard the sounds of the blustery wind. Our planned honeymoon in Hawaii couldn't come soon enough—three days in Oahu, three in Maui, and four in Kauai.

My gaze moved to the new pristine pillow next to me. I smoothed my hand over the Egyptian cotton with a thread count I'd never dreamed of having, a wedding gift courtesy of Beckett Larsen. I found it endearing, but also bittersweet, how my boss had signed the card with both his and his dearly departed wife's names. Like Cora, Beckett missed his spouse terribly. Those two souls had truly been blessed with the love of a lifetime.

And so have I.

With a deep sigh, I shifted onto my side in the queen bed with the beautiful carved maple headboard inherited from Ryan's grandparents. Our small house was filled with antiques as well as newer items. Each and every one had its own story.

"Good night, my love," I whispered in the darkness of the night. "See you soon."

Chapter 11

~~♥~~

Saturday, December 16

I haven't slept much as the date for Ryan's return draws near. I tossed in the bed for over an hour this morning before giving up the idea of more sleep. Finally, I pushed back the covers, slipped my feet into my warm, cozy slippers, and then padded into the kitchen at five a.m.

It was a little chilly in the house, so I turned up the heat and then went through my exercise routine, such as it is. Okay, I cheated a little. All right—a lot. Leg lifts and sit-ups at such an early hour of the morning is pure insanity. Who *does* that?

Saturdays are my "catch up" days.

After gulping down orange juice and swallowing a few bites of granola and fruit, I tackled the mounting pile of laundry.

"Ugh. This won't do," I mumbled as I began to sort the clothes into separate piles. How does one person accumulate so much laundry? Ryan teased me that I go overboard since I normally wash an article of clothing after I'd worn it only once.

As part of our marriage counseling with Pastor Derek, we'd survived a series of Marital Tests shortly before Ryan's deployment. Meaning we were required to do laundry together three times, cook five meals together (at least one breakfast, one lunch, one dinner, one snack—the fifth was optional), and clean the house together. In that order. Apparently, those were the household tasks that could make or break a relationship.

At first, I wasn't sure we'd get past The Laundry Test.

"Three-time rule," Ryan insisted after protesting the fact that I was adding a few of my color-fast, preshrunk tops to the laundry load. "You can get by with wearing something three times. It saves money, water, electricity, and your manpower. Womanpower," he added after catching the look on my face.

"What if you get all sweaty?" I said, shaking my head in disgust. "Sweat breaks down the fibers and then the…smell…gets ingrained in the fabric, thereby diminishing the life of the garment."

"What's a garment?"

I stared at him. "Are you for real? Clothing. Shirts, pants, sweaters. Things you wear."

"Oh, as opposed to a sheet or something?"

"Okay, if that works for you." I didn't bother to bring up the topic of my delicates and his underthings. We'd tackle that another day. I love the man, but I'll wait until I'm wearing his ring to deal with that reality.

"Yeah, sweat is grounds for immediate dismissal to the laundry bin," he said. "I'm talking about something you wear on a normal basis, Sass. What you wear to the office and not something you wear to the gym. The exception to the three-time rule is food stains. If you dribble, spill, pour, splat, blubber, spit, or drool, then you have to spot treat it and wash it right away. That's a mandatory given."

"And your implication with that statement would be?" I shook my head, wondering if I should get a bib for Ryan as a gag gift. "Never mind. You're incredibly weird, but you're also very cute, so I'll keep you."

Next came The Meal-Making Test.

"That's easy," Ryan said. "All you need to know how to make is a fried egg sandwich with American cheese and mayo."

"Been there, done that. *You* need to know how to make that for when you're in the doghouse and need to rely on that four letter cooking technique called F-E-N-D."

As he laughed and reminded me he'd been making those sandwiches almost from the time he could walk, I handed him a selection of recipe cards. "Here you go. Your mother was gracious enough to write down some of your favorites. We're going to learn to make a few of them together."

"Okay, but I'm in charge of the cooked vegetables." I threw a raw carrot at him. I'd never live down that stupid casserole.

All in all, we had a good time together in the kitchen. His mother hadn't taught him as much as I'd assumed. Maybe that wasn't such a bad thing. So, we started with a basic lesson on kitchen items, ingredients, and common cooking terms.

"How can something called 'mince' be a common cooking term?" he said after I handed him an onion and a knife.

"It just is. I didn't make up the term out of thin air, you know."

"Why can't I use that handy little gizmo you keep under the counter and just chop up the onion with that?"

"Because that would be chopping, not mincing."

"It tastes the same." He began to peel the onion in preparation of whatever he was going to do to it. "What's the difference?"

"Just do it, Ryan. I'm tired, and I don't really know. Texture maybe. Overall blend with the rest of the ingredients. And, for future reference, a clove of garlic needs to be minced, or it's way too strong and gag-inducing."

He laughed. "Are you giving me a taste of what marriage will be like? 'I'm sorry, honey. I'm too tired tonight.' To *mince*," he added with a sly wink.

I couldn't help my grin and shook my head. "You are so bad."

"You love it." Ryan finished the task of mincing and then, standing behind me, he wrapped his arms around my waist. Swaying from foot to foot, he dropped a light kiss on my neck. "We're going to have a lot of fun being married, Ellie. How about after we eat, we can talk about the different terms and methods of kissing?"

I turned around and moved my arms around his neck. "Oh, I don't know. Kissing's just kissing, right?" Ryan had a gleam in his eyes that I recognized.

"Well, there's bussing. And then you have macking. Then there's all-out necking. A few others I can think of. I'm sure there's many more we need to explore."

"Sounds dangerous," I said, planting one hand on his firm chest. "We have to be careful, Ryan. I think it's best if we hold off launching the exploration team until after we're man and wife."

With a deep sigh, Ryan rested his forehead on mine. "Agreed. Thanks for keeping me straight, baby."

"We keep each *other* in check," I reminded him. It worked both ways.

The final (premarital) test was what Ryan dubbed The Toilet Test. It's pretty much exactly like it sounds. He had me laughing hysterically when he showed up in the bathroom in scrubs and a face mask, armed with a toilet brush. "Say a prayer. I'm going in."

In the end, so to speak, Ryan taught me a few tricks he'd learned in latrine duty in the Army during his first deployment.

"Trust me, if I could scrub those disgusting things, I can clean anything," he told me. I begged him to spare me the details. In turn, I showed him how to clean around the sink and faucet and how white vinegar could do wonders for cleansing, deodorizing, and controlling mildew.

Who knew scrubbing a bathroom together could be such fun? I try to find the humor in life where I can.

We survived those three Marital Tests and earned our official Certificate of Completion. Only then could I admit they weren't such a bad idea. Not at all.

Chapter 12

~~♥~~

Continuing with my Saturday chores, I dusted the furniture and then vacuumed several rooms of the house. When I finished those housekeeping tasks, my "reward" was revisiting the contents of my Dream Box, the cedar chest Cora had given me when I was a child.

After retrieving the box from the top of the bedroom closet, I sat cross-legged on the bed. Even after all these years, the box made by Cora's husband, Ronnie, still held the scent of cedar.

First, I pulled out and unfolded a piece of paper—my sixth grade Ohio History test on Lake Erie facts. Dad helped me study for this particular test. That must be why I'd saved it. I'd missed two questions—there are 24 Lake Erie islands (I'd said 25), and Lake Erie has a surface area of 9,940 square miles (I couldn't remember and guessed an even thousand).

I scanned over the test, refreshing my memory.

Lake Erie was carved by receding glaciers of the Great Ice Age. The area surrounding Lake Erie was originally inhabited by the *Erie* Native American tribe. Louis Jolliet, a French trader and explorer, was the first European to make a record of Lake Erie in 1669. Finally, Lake Erie played a strategic role during the War of 1812. I'd written "a tragic role" (instead of strategic) on the test. My teacher made a smiley face beside it with her red pen, but she hadn't marked me down.

I put the test paper aside and then pulled out a smooth, flat rock. I'd found it at Huntington Beach among all the broken shells and added it to the sand castle that Ryan, Nick, Staci, and I made on our combined families' annual summer trek to the shore when I was 15 (Kara was 25 and living on our own by that time).

It was a nondescript, brown rock with nothing remarkable about it. I'd kept it because Ryan had written

Ryan & Ellie on it with a magic marker he found on the beach. We hadn't started dating yet, so he probably assumed I'd tossed this rock years ago. I smiled as I thought about showing it to him.

My cell phone rang. Leaning across the bed, I retrieved it from the night table.

NICK FESSED UP ABOUT MAURA. LET'S DOUBLE DATE AND MAKE THEM INCREDIBLY JEALOUS WHEN WE GO HOME TOGETHER.

I giggled. DON'T BE SMUG, MR. COMPETITIVE. ☺ GO PACK SOME MORE AND COME HOME TO ME.

I'M WORKING ON IT. TRUST ME.

HAPPY SATURDAY, RYAN. ♥

SAME TO YOU, ELLIE. HOPE YOU HAVE A FUN DAY.

CHECK IN WITH ME LATER?

ALWAYS. SENDING YOU LOVE, SASS. XOXOXO

Putting aside my cell phone, I pulled out a gold locket from the Dream Box by its chain. This was the first piece of jewelry Ryan ever gave me. I'll never forget the way he looked at me when I came into the living room, and he saw me in the gown for my senior prom. I'd never owned such a gorgeous dress. The pale coral color complemented my lightly tanned skin (Mom had taken me to Florida for spring break).

Ryan must have been in cahoots with Mom because he brought me an orchid corsage that coordinated beautifully with my gown. He was so cute when he presented it to me. After two seconds, he gave up trying to help me pin it to my dress. "Sorry, Sass," he said, throwing his hands in the air. "It's not like they give guys lessons in how to do this."

Mom was more than happy to take over the honors while I blushed furiously.

I couldn't stop staring at how handsome Ryan was in his black tux, the first time I'd ever seen him in formal wear. The "live" version, that is. I'd known he'd gone to a few other proms and dances, but I'd refused to even acknowledge— much less look at—the photos. Every time I went to his house, I avoided those photos (proudly displayed on the wall for all who entered the Sullivan home to see) like they'd strike me down blind if I dared to look directly at them.

Call me jealous…because that's *exactly* what I was. I was shameless and didn't bother to hide my feelings although I never said anything specifically to Ryan. I cried myself to sleep on the nights I knew Ryan was at a prom—dancing with another girl. And who knows what else. He was a Christian boy, but I'd heard from Kara and Staci what even good Christian boys were capable of trying with girls.

Ryan wouldn't. He was different. I wish my sisters had never planted the seeds of doubt in my mind.

By the time of my senior prom, we were a solid couple. Everyone in town knew we were unofficially pledged to one another. I knew how much Ryan loved his truck, and I insisted he drive it to the dance (held at a fancy hotel in downtown Cleveland) and not throw away his hard-earned money for the exorbitant cost of a limousine.

As soon as we reached the end of our street and turned the corner, Ryan pulled his truck over to the curb. He left the engine idling and shifted in his seat to face me.

"Is something wrong?" I said. "Did we forget something?"

Before I could say anything further, Ryan pulled me close and caressed my cheek. "You are the most beautiful girl I've ever seen, especially tonight, Eleanor Rose Franklin." He kissed me tenderly and then presented me with the locket. He was adorably inept—again—when he fumbled with the chain, but he managed to fasten it at the back of my neck. Sweet gestures like that seared this boy further into my heart.

I didn't have many occasions to dance, but dancing with Ryan at my senior prom was like a dream come true. He wasn't a great dancer, but neither was I. We had fun, laughed a lot, and stayed until almost ten. Ryan told me we should leave since he'd promised Mom to have me back home by midnight. So, while many of my classmates left the prom to go "party" (another way of saying they'd booked hotel rooms), Ryan took me back to Cade's Corner to The Soda Shoppe (they stayed open extra late the night of the senior prom).

I could tell he'd prepared a big speech about how he couldn't disrespect me, and how he refused to do what everyone else did just to be considered part of the "in" crowd.

"Ryan, I'm not disappointed," I remember telling him over my chocolate shake and cheeseburger. "I think you're very sweet and honorable, and I love you for it. Besides, I'm the only girl in my senior class who showed up with a college man. That's pretty special in itself. And, by not taking me to the hotel, it shows your maturity."

I'll never forget his smile that night. "I like to believe it shows my *faith*, Ellie. I just want to make sure you know it's not because I don't find you…well, you know…physically attractive." Oh, so cute, that boy. I fell even more in love with him that night.

Now, sitting on the bed with the Dream Box beside me, I opened the locket and gazed at the photos of Ryan inside. His high school senior picture was on the left. On the opposite side was a photo of Ryan in his Army dress uniform. He'd grown from such a cute boy into a handsome, honorable man.

I sorted through the remaining items in the Dream Box: a dried corsage from a Father-Daughter Dance when I was 12, tickets to a Cavaliers game when Ryan and I first started dating, Ryan's high school graduation program, and a newspaper clipping. I put my hand over my mouth when I realized the clipping was my father's obituary. I read through it and, surprisingly, I didn't cry. But then I put it aside before I would be tempted to cry.

I pulled out a valentine from Ryan from when we were kids. I turned it over. Valentine's Day, sixth grade. Then I spied the Valentine's Day card Ryan gave me when I was 18. I opened it in all its gaudy glory and read the sweet poem, short with only four lines, the first he'd ever written. He claimed it was also his *last* attempt at writing poetry, but I thought it would be great as the words to a lullaby we'd sing to our children one day.

> *Sweet like the sunshine after the rain.*
> *Precious like the promise of a rainbow.*
> *You are all these things to me, my baby.*
> *You're all these things and more.*

~~♥~~

Saturday, Late Morning

I needed to jump in the shower and then grab a quick bite for lunch. Before meeting Maura at the Perchance office, I wanted to be sure and stop by the nursing facility.

An hour later, I walked into Cora's room.

"Hi, Cora." I removed my coat and scarf and laid them on the end of the bed. "I hope you're feeling well today." I smoothed one hand over her white hair, still wavy and fairly thick and bent to kiss her forehead.

"I've been thinking a lot about my father lately. Missing him," I said as I sat in my customary chair. "I'm sure you remember him. His name was Curt Franklin, and he died when I was sixteen. It's hard to believe it's already been six years since he passed away."

I waited as if I somehow expected a response. When none came, I continued. "In some ways, my daddy was my first love. And when he died, my heart was broken."

I took Cora's warm hand in mine. I liked that personal connection, that touch. If she ever awakened, I hoped she'd know that I'd been here. "Don't you think that's the way it should be? A little girl should adore her father. He should be the one man who'll always be there for her. He was the best man I've ever known. I realize how blessed I was to have him as my dad, and for as long as I did. Selfishly, I hate like anything that he won't be here to walk me down the aisle at my wedding. I like to think that somehow he knows."

With a sigh, I lowered Cora's hand to the blanket. "Sometimes I think about Heaven and wonder if our loved ones who've gone on before us are watching."

The corners of my mouth upturned slightly. "For all I know, they pull up chairs, make popcorn, and enjoy the show. I'm sure they find us very amusing. I can just hear Dad talking to Grandpa Franklin and saying, 'If only they know what we do.' And then I wonder if they're able to see everything we do and if they can 'hear' all our thoughts. That's when it gets a little weird. But I'm thinking, no. God's the only one who's omniscient, right?"

Shaking my head, I laughed under my breath. "Forgive me. My words sometimes ramble just like my mind."

I sat for a minute without saying anything, listening to the rhythmic sounds of the machine. How I wish I knew whether or not Cora heard my rambling monologues. I glanced over my shoulder. For a change, none of the staffers stood in the doorway today. Considering my reflective mood, perhaps that was for the best.

And so, as always, I began my story.

Chapter 13

~~♥~~

My father's death when I was 16 was one of those things I'd never thought would happen to our family…until it did. Dad died of an undetected heart problem. He keeled over in his recliner, on a bright day in the early fall, in front of the TV in the family room. Mom got to him first, and then me.

On either side of him, we held onto both of his hands. We kissed him, hugged him, and held him close. Mom rocked back and forth with him, clinging to him, her tears soaking his shirt. I told him I'd never forget him. I like to believe Dad heard me. Even if he didn't, he'd known how much I loved him. Small comfort, but it's all I had at the time. Words meant to comfort the ones left behind, not the one slipping out of our grasp. My heart never hurt so much.

"I love you, Daddy," I whispered before kissing his cheek. Then I left Mom with him, so I could go call for help. Neither one of us thought to call earlier. Or maybe we did, but understand his remaining time was precious. In our hearts, it's as though we both *knew* Dad was leaving us, and in those last few moments, it was more important to say our final good-byes.

By the time the paramedics arrived, he was indeed gone.

Ryan came to check on me as soon as he heard the news. He'd been at football practice and practically burst through our front door in his full Fighting Grenadiers uniform (named after the grenadier that was a soldier, not the bottom-dwelling fish). My mom had the presence of mind to make him remove his cleats. He kept his gaze trained on me as he did, and then he rushed across the room and pulled me into his arms. Then he kissed the top of my head and murmured how sorry he was, how my dad was a great guy, and how much he'd miss him.

Through my tears, I saw Mom's eyes widen, but she backed out of the room without saying anything and left us alone.

He didn't say much as he sat with me on the sofa, listening to my memories spill out of me. I appreciated how he let me talk and held my hand. I don't even remember what I said, and half of it was nonsensical stream-of-consciousness rambling.

"Ryan, you shouldn't have left football practice to come," I told him at length. Secretly, I was thrilled in the midst of my overwhelming sense of numbness.

Grief was slowly beginning to seep into my soul.

"I had to come, Ellie. You're my best friend. I'm here for you. Whatever you need." Warmed and comforted by his words, I squeezed his hand and leaned on his shoulder for a long time.

What happened in the next few days was a blur until I sat on the hard wooden pew at Cade's Corner Community Church, staring at my dad in his coffin. Everyone kept saying how "natural" he appeared, but that wasn't my father. My dad was tall, handsome, and strong. With color in his cheeks, a deep voice, and a twinkle in his eye when he looked at my mother. I determined then and there that I would have a closed coffin when it was my time to go. I want people to remember me as I am in *life*, not in death.

I hated to even think about death, but facing it head-on, I couldn't ignore it like it hadn't happened. Like it wasn't a part of our existence. My grandparents were all still alive at the time, and—call me ungrateful—but how could it possibly be that Dad was gone before both his parents? He was only 54 and much too young to pass.

So not fair.

Before the funeral service began, my mom, sisters, grandparents, and other family members stood at the front, shaking hands, accepting condolences, hugging everyone. Maybe I should have been up there with them, but I just couldn't do it. I'd done my part during the calling hours and that had been the hardest thing I've ever done. Kara motioned for me to join them, but I saw Mom put her hand on my sister's arm and shake her head.

Thank you, Mom.

"I never want to die," I said over my shoulder to Ryan, sitting on the pew behind me.

"We all have to die sometime, Sass."

"How come?" I ignored Aunt Sophie's glare as she moved up the center aisle, leaving behind the overpowering scent of her gardenia fragrance. Didn't she understand a lot of people had sensitivities and allergies to perfumes these days? It was my daddy's funeral, and I'd talk with my best friend if I wanted. Following behind Aunt Sophie, her husband—my Uncle Bob—gave me a reassuring nod.

"God's plan."

I frowned. "That's too easy of an answer."

"Maybe, but it's all I've got to offer right now." Crossing his arms on the back of my pew, Ryan leaned forward. "If you're around when I die, don't let them put me in an open casket, especially if I'm all mangled up or something."

"And, if you're around when I die, don't let them cremate me," I whispered. "For the record, I don't want an open casket either."

We were being highly irreverent both to God and my Dad's memory, but Ryan's warped sense of humor in that moment—morbid or not—went a long way toward soothing my frazzled nerves. Most people never talk about death, especially at our age, so it was good information to know although I prayed it wouldn't come into play until we were both old and gray.

I slumped farther down on that uncomfortable pew and resisted the almost overpowering urge to cross my arms. Sometimes being a teenager didn't give me the inherent right to act like a pouty kid. Today, I wished it did. Maybe I could consider it a self-hug. Surely that was allowed.

"I don't understand the mind of God," I said. "I guess that's why He's God, and we're...not."

"True," Ryan said. "I think it's up to us to trust that He's always got our best interests at heart."

"That sounds like something my Dad would have said."

"Sorry." He nudged my arm.

"Don't be. It gives me comfort."

Ryan asked Jesus into his heart when he was seven, and I'd done the same when I was eight. Seemed I was always a year behind Ryan even though it's certainly not a competitive thing.

Sitting on that pew the morning of my daddy's funeral, I'd never felt so alone. What a confused mess I was, spitting mad one second that the most important man in my life was gone, and rejoicing that he was in Heaven the next. At that point, I wasn't sure if I was mad at Dad or God. Or both. Or mad at myself for feeling that way.

God had him now, but I wasn't ready for my father to be gone from my life.

Oh, Daddy. I miss you already.

He'd taught me to ride my tricycle and then my first two-wheeler. Dried my tears after our dog, Buster, died when I was ten. Kissed my boo-boos, made me pancakes on Saturdays, played catch with me in the backyard. The only thing he wouldn't do was play dolls with me. I could understand. Perhaps taking pity on me one particularly cold winter day, he'd once endured a tea party with me, Miss Sassafras and Miss Franny, my two stuffed bears. I'd love him forever for that memory. Did parents know how special those things were for kids?

One more thing—Dad couldn't dance worth a lick. Every time he tried, I howled with laughter, which he did not appreciate. He claimed men aren't supposed to dance, only women. To which my Mom would smile and say, "Sure they are, Curt. Men are made to dance *with* women." That shut him up. I didn't understand the full ramifications of her observation back then, but now it makes perfect sense. And makes me blush every time I think of it.

As the organist played before the service, I felt Ryan's hand on my shoulder. "You okay?"

"I miss my daddy, Ryan." A tear slipped down my cheek and onto my new navy blue dress. Staring at it, I watched as the spot deepened and spread. Then I crossed my arms over my chest in a vain attempt to stop trembling.

Rising to his feet—Ryan had grown three inches in the past year alone—he skirted around the end of the pew and dropped down beside me. When he moved his arm around my shoulders, it felt completely natural. Ryan's presence, his kindness, and his warmth, helped to soothe my emotions and profound sense of loss.

"Ryan, did you know Dad got baptized in the Cuyahoga River when he was twelve?"

"No. If he was brave enough to do that, he's definitely going to Heaven." The Cuyahoga River was polluted with industrial waste and an oil slick caught fire in the river in 1969, bringing a certain amount of infamy and shame to the Cleveland area. I knew Ryan was teasing, but as the men from the funeral home stepped forward, closed the top of the coffin, and then draped an American flag over it, I sat as though in a stupor. More tears welled in my eyes, spilling over onto my cheeks. I let them go.

"Shh." Ryan brushed one gentle finger beneath my right eye and then did the same under the left eye. In my blurry haze, I was vaguely aware when he rubbed his fingers together to absorb the wetness from my tears. Funny the odd things you remember at a time like that.

Lorraine Bennett, the church organist, climbed back onto her bench and began playing "It Is Well with My Soul," my father's favorite hymn, to signal the beginning of the service. My father had a resonant tenor voice, and I'd heard him sing this hymn many times. I softly hummed the tune under my breath.

I tried to imagine where Dad was now, but my finite mind couldn't comprehend what Heaven was like. Kara thought it was paved with gold and jewels. Winged horses carried us wherever we wanted to go.

As hard as it was to accept the reality of Dad's sudden death, it'd have been worse if he'd been diagnosed with slow-moving cancer. If I'd been forced to watch him whittle away, that would have been terrible for all of us. Dad would have hated it most of all. So, in a strange way, the way he died was ultimately a blessing.

"It was his time," so many people said. I hated that expression. I didn't *want* it to be his time.

From what little I heard of the message, Pastor Derek honored my father with a touching, heartfelt service, and eulogy. Then several of Dad's friends and co-workers at his accounting firm spoke and said meaningful and poignant things about him. They'd respected him greatly. Then a few of the church elders and deacons said a few words. I knew they meant every word, and their anecdotes made me smile. Hank Young mentioned how much his daughters meant to Dad, and he even mentioned the walks he took with me.

Eldridge Gray concluded the remarks and winked at me as he passed by my pew. I shrank back in horror. Good grief, he'd never had that cracked tooth fixed? The man knew how to manage money, and I know he made enough to pay a dentist. I'd never understand people. I determined from that point on I'd forever cook the *life* out of broccoli and carrots, so I'd never risk cracking someone's tooth ever again.

Ryan and I sat together, not speaking until Mom told us it was time to come outside. Dad was to be buried in the small cemetery behind the church. Mom's plot was next to his. Dad couldn't have had any idea he'd need his plot so soon, but he'd been prepared.

We stood and watched as the pallbearers carried the casket out of the sanctuary and then followed them down the front steps.

"Please don't let them stumble," I said under my breath.

"They're steady." As if to reinforce his point, Ryan kept his arm around me. I leaned into him, and I appreciated his support more than I could ever express.

At the gravesite, Ryan stood behind us with his family. Because my father had served in the Army, an Honor Guard—in full military dress—attended the service, wearing solemn expressions. Although I didn't know if any of them had personally known my dad, their respect for his service to his country was clear.

Silently, they removed and folded the American flag that had been draped over Dad's coffin and presented it to my mom along with their murmured sympathies. She dabbed at her eyes with a tissue and modeled grace and poise. My sisters wept quietly beside her, and it was all I could do not to break down and bawl. We were happy Dad was in Heaven, of course, but he'd been ripped from our lives so abruptly. Later, we'd rejoice, but not now. For now, we'd go through the motions and put on a brave face in public. Any breakdowns would be suffered in private.

When the officers shot their rifles into the air in a full military salute, I jumped. Stepping closer, Ryan slipped his hand over mine. In front of God, our families, our friends, everyone. And held on tight.

My daddy might be gone, but God had given me another protector. Another hero.

In that moment, I knew—no matter where our lives would take us—I would forever hold this boy close in my heart.

Chapter 14
~~♥~~
Saturday Afternoon—Perchance to Dream Office

The envelope from Beckett!

How could I have forgotten to open it? Reaching for my purse beside my desk, I rummaged through its contents. I'd buried it deep, and I had a lot of papers in there—last Sunday's church bulletin, gift registry printouts, emails, wedding trip confirmations, and other assorted pieces of wedding correspondence.

"Where are you?" I mumbled, frustrated. I didn't want to dump the contents of my purse on my desktop.

Finally locating the plain, business-size envelope with Beckett's small, precise lettering spelling out my name, I pulled it out. I grabbed my letter opener—I couldn't risk a paper cut on my to-be-manicured fingers before the wedding—and slid it beneath the flap.

As usual, Beckett had written the note on a sheet of plain, ruled, white paper. The type kids used in school, but the wide-ruled variety for the younger grades. And senior citizens, too, apparently. Most of his notes to me at the agency had been written on this same ruled paper.

Dear Ellie,

I know you've only been with The Beckett Agency a short time, but in that time, you've proven yourself invaluable. I don't know if you're aware, but my dear wife, Babs, and I were not able to have children. We'd always hoped to have a child who could continue the agency once I retire or move on to greener pastures, shall we say. However, in the absence of our own child, we'd hoped someone would come along who could carry on the legacy I've started.

This may come as a surprise to you, and I realize you have a lot going on in your personal life at the moment, but after you return from your wedding trip, might we sit down and have a chat about your future at Beckett? Not to sound mysterious, and to be more specific, I think you might be the right person to take over for me at The Beckett Agency *in the next few years.*

You have a unique gift for bringing out the good in the people around you, Ellie. You possess a sharp wit and a quick mind that could carry you far in the advertising world.

We can discuss this matter further in the New Year. I look forward to hearing your thoughts.

With utmost admiration for your many talents,
Beckett Larsen

My hand shook almost uncontrollably. I'd noted a check tucked inside the envelope. I pulled it out and stared at the number of zeroes. What I'd thought was a holiday bonus for $50 or thereabouts was more. *Much* more. In the memo line of the check Beckett had written, *Investment in the Future.*

"Miss Franklin?"

I glanced up to see a young woman and a small girl, who looked to be about five years old, standing in the doorway of my office. Tall and thin with short, curly dark hair, the woman was dressed in jeans, a red wool jacket, and she wore a tentative smile. The child wore jeans and bright pink outerwear that surely glows in the dark.

In one hand, the woman held a department store shopping bag.

"That's me. Please, come in." I hastily stuffed the letter and check back inside the envelope and then put them in my desk drawer. I stood and offered my hand. "Please call me Ellie."

The woman appeared slightly ill at ease. "I'm Kate Simms, and this is my daughter, Ellie."

I smiled at the girl. "Hi, Ellie! I love meeting someone else who shares my name. If your mommy says it's okay, would you like a piece of candy?" I had a whole drawer filled with leftover sweets from Halloween.

As expected, my offer brought a light to the little girl's blue eyes and she looked up at her mother for confirmation. "Can I, Mama? Please?"

When Kate nodded, Ellie moved closer to my desk.

"Come around here and you can choose a few pieces." I opened the drawer as she scooted around the corner of the desk.

"You have a lot of candy!"

"Just pick three. That's all," Kate told her daughter. After poking around the drawer, Ellie selected three fruit-flavored candies and then scurried back to her mother's side.

"We don't want to keep you." Kate pulled up the other chair for Ellie and the child scampered onto it.

"That's okay. My time is yours." I returned to my chair and motioned for them to sit.

"My husband, Mike, was a police officer in Cleveland." Ducking her head, Kate avoided my gaze. "He was killed in the line of duty four years ago."

"I'm very sorry." My words sounded so woefully inadequate. "I'm thankful for your husband's service." I couldn't bring myself to use the word "sacrifice."

"Thank you." Kate fiddled with her fingers on her lap. When she raised her head and met my gaze, I could see she was struggling to maintain her composure. "Even though we got a good settlement from the police force, we fell into some hard times." She straightened in the chair. "But that's not why we're here. We're here to thank you, Miss Franklin."

"Thank me?" I shook my head, confused.

"Perchance to Dream helped me out a couple of years ago when things were very tight financially. You provided three wonderful gifts for my daughter. And the Bible we read every night." Ellie had removed her knit cap, and Kate smoothed one hand over the girl's curly blonde hair.

"I got a pretty dolly," Ellie said around a mouthful of candy. Her lips and tongue were now bright red. "Her name is Splendiferous. She has beautiful red hair and a blue sparkly dress, but Mama wouldn't let me bring her on the bus."

"That's a very creative name. I'm sure your Mama wanted to protect…your dolly…so she wouldn't get lost on the trip."

"We wanted to come and thank you in person," Kate said. "Ellie calls you 'the nice lady.'"

I sat back in my chair, overwhelmed by the unexpected sweetness of it all. First the letter from Beckett, and now this? "I'm thankful we could help. Do you…" I faltered, uncertain as to how to phrase my question.

Kate shook her head. "We don't need anything. But we brought you something."

Surprised, I glanced at the girl. "You brought *me* a gift, Ellie?"

"Uh huh." Ellie's feet didn't touch the floor, and she swung her legs back and forth. "It's a Christmas gift, but you can have it now if you want."

"That sounds fine if it's okay with you."

"Are your hands clean, Ellie?" Kate said. "They're not sticky from the candy, are they?"

"No, Mama." The girl held out her hands for inspection.

Satisfied, Kate nodded. "Show Miss Franklin what you've brought for her."

I watched, wide-eyed, as Ellie pulled a plush, soft puppy dog out of the shopping bag. Light brown in color, the stuffed animal resembled a Cocker Spaniel with long hair, floppy ears, and an irresistible grin.

"Here." Ellie plopped the puppy in the middle of my desk. "I picked him out myself."

"For me?" Rising from my chair, I hugged him and relished his softness next to my cheek. I walked around my desk and crouched next to Ellie. "This gift is so special. I will treasure him, especially since you gave him to me. May I give you a hug, too?"

In response, the little girl threw her arms around me and hugged me tight. I needed that hug more than I could have imagined, and I clung to her for a few moments. Over Ellie's shoulder, I caught Kate's gentle smile.

"We know you're getting married soon, and that your fiancé is returning home next week," Kate said. "We should have come earlier in the season, but I couldn't get off work in time to make the trip out here."

Ellie released me from the hug. "Mama doesn't like to take the bus after dark."

"I can't blame her. Ellie, what do you think I should call my puppy?"

She didn't even hesitate. "Ryan."

I looked into the sweet face of this adorable child. "Okay, then. Ryan it is."

Kate smiled, and it relaxed her features. "I tried to tell Ellie you'd have your own Ryan to keep you...company...soon enough. But she seemed determined."

I smiled at the little girl. "I love the name. Thank you so much, Ellie. It means a lot that you came all the way to Cade's Corner to bring Ryan to me."

Ellie's smile lit her cherubic face. The child positively beamed. "Welcome."

Kate rose to her feet. "We need to go now so we can catch the next bus back to the city."

"May I drive you home? I'll be happy to, but I'd just have to run home and get my car." And call Maura and explain.

"That's not necessary. We'll be fine," Kate said. "Merry Christmas."

I returned her smile. "You, too. Thanks again for coming."

When Kate hesitated, I could tell she had something else to say. "I just wanted you to know that your efforts reach a lot of people you'll probably never meet, Miss Franklin. You can't know their stories, but that doesn't matter to you." Her cheeks flushed. "That didn't come out right. I mean you'd do it, anyway, because that's the kind of person you are. You and"—her gaze went to the plush puppy still in my arms— "your Ryan. God bless you both."

"God bless you and Ellie, too," I said.

With that, Kate helped Ellie with her hat and pulled it down over her head.

"Bye, nice lady!" Ellie put her hand in Kate's, and they departed. Stopping outside the front window, they waved.

After waving back, I picked up Ryan and smiled. "Hello there, little guy. Welcome to my world."

Chapter 15

~~♥~~

Tuesday, December 19

"Ellie, can you tell us the story of how you and Ryan got engaged?"

Half-turning in my chair, I saw that a small group of the staff had gathered in the doorway. I'd dropped off another tin of holiday cookies and fudge, and the ladies told me how much they looked forward to my visits with Cora.

"Not just for the baked goods," Trudy assured me. "Some of us are living vicariously through your stories." She took a bite of a snowflake sugar cookie.

"They're nothing special. But they're mine."

"Goodness, girl, you make them interesting. You could be a professional storyteller." Patsy crossed her arms and leaned against the door. "I hope you're writing down or recording your stories. You'll want to share them with your children and grandchildren one day."

I shook my head. "They're only written on my heart at this point."

"Ah, that's so sweet," one of the newer aides said—Jennifer, I think.

Maybe I *should* consider writing them down as a legacy. Good idea. Our children would never know my father. As much as possible, I wanted to preserve his memory. Not to mention Grandpa Franklin and other relatives we've lost. I shelved a mental note to work on that project early in the New Year.

"So," I said, glancing at the ladies gathered in the room, "you want to hear the engagement story? I'll admit that one is quite…different."

"We're all ears," Trudy said.

As it was, I was almost beside myself counting down the final hours. In less than 24 hours, I'd be in Ryan's arms again. In my mind, I've anticipated our glorious reunion over and over again. I hardly slept a wink last night. Nick and his dad, Mark, planned on making the all-day trip to Wright-Patterson Air Force in Dayton tomorrow—a 213-mile, one-way trip— to meet the Army transport bringing Ryan and some of his fellow soldiers home. I was itching to go, and I'd made Nick promise he'd take lots of photos and drive carefully (not to worry since he sometimes drives like an old man). I'd recorded a video on *Nick's* phone welcoming my favorite soldier home.

I hadn't heard from Ryan, but that was to be expected. Although surely he would text. I pushed the thought aside. I knew he was busy and most likely catching up on his sleep.

Mary, Mom, and I planned a private family dinner back at the Sullivan home. The trip would be good for Nick and Ryan to catch up and spend some quality time together.

I couldn't stop my smile as I began to tell the ladies our engagement story.

The summer before his second deployment, Ryan started delivering gifts to me one week in June. One gift a day. Each one was a little more lavish or expensive, beginning with an oversized greeting card. Then a book. Two tickets to a play I'd wanted to see. Then a bracelet. A matching necklace. He either took me to lunch or dinner every day that week, and he had sweets delivered to me or brought them to me himself. He'd never been so attentive, and I could tell he was building up to something special, especially when he asked me to spend the day with him on Saturday.

So, late on Saturday morning, he picked me up in his red truck (at least his third vehicle—always a truck, forever red). I could tell he was nervous, and Ryan is rarely anxious about anything. He'd left a long-stemmed deep pink rose on my seat, and then he drove out to Marblehead State Park. He'd even packed a picnic basket for us. After parking the truck, we started to walk toward the picnic area. Then Ryan realized he'd forgotten to lock the truck. When he clicked the lock and glanced back at the truck, the color drained from his face.

"What's wrong?" I started to look back, but he put his hand on my arm to stop me.

"Don't look. Trust me. It's not pretty. You don't need to see it." Taking my hand, Ryan tried to guide me in the opposite direction.

"Well, now I *have* to look. I'm sure I won't turn into a pillar of salt."

Pulling away from Ryan, I turned and gasped. A bird was stuck in the front grillwork of the truck! Lodged right in there by its beak with its skinny little bird legs hanging out. After exchanging a glance with Ryan, I sprinted back to the truck.

"Oh, no! That poor little guy. What should we do? Try to pull him out or just drive and…hope he falls out?"

"How should I know? Don't touch him!" Ryan put his hand on me as if he thought I'd be so foolish as to handle the bird carcass with my bare hands. We stared at each other for a few moments. "I honestly don't know what to do." A frown creased his forehead, and he planted his hands on his hips. "This isn't something I ever expected to happen. Today of all days."

Determined not to allow this unfortunate incident to spoil our day, my mind swirled with ideas. "This is a state park, so there's bound to be a ranger or two around, right? They'll know what to do and can probably help us."

"You're brilliant. That's why I'm…" Ryan stopped and gave me a quick kiss. "That's why I love you. Let's go find Ranger Bob. Or Joe."

"Or Susan," I said. "Equal opportunity and all that."

A half-hour later, Ranger Randy and Deputy Paul (I don't know if he was a deputy or not, but that was my nickname for him), carried the dearly departed bird in a bag and wished us a good day. Or at least a better day from here on out. The way they nodded at Ryan with knowing smiles tipped me off that he must have shared his plans for the day. He must have mentioned it during the time I'd walked away.

I'm wondering how that conversation might have gone—
"Thanks for helping pull that dead bird out of my truck's
grill. Now I can go propose to my girl."

In any case, I couldn't bear to watch as they'd disengaged
(for lack of a better word) that poor fowl from the grillwork
of Ryan's truck. At least he was already dead.

I shivered at the thought and ran my hands up and down
my arms.

"What a morbid way to start the day," Ryan grumbled as
we waved good-bye to the helpful park rangers, and they
drove off in their official truck.

"Let's go have a nice, romantic picnic," I said. "The day
can only get better, right?"

We spread the blanket on the ground near a shade tree
instead of sitting at a picnic table. Seemed more romantic
somehow. I kicked off my tennis shoes and settled across
from Ryan. I opened the picnic basket and told him how
much I appreciated what he'd done to make this entire week
special. Ryan prayed for our meal, and then we started to eat
the sandwiches and fresh fruit. The little touches he added
were special—he served me a turkey sandwich on a
stoneware plate and poured apple juice into wine glasses.

Ryan raised his glass in the air and then carefully clinked
it against mine. "A toast to the most gorgeous, fantastic girl in
the world. The girl I've loved since…well, pretty much the
beginning of my life."

I smiled at him over the top of my glass as I took a sip of
my juice. "I didn't know you could be so sentimental."

"I have my moments. And, before you say anything, the
reason I said 'pretty much' is because I can't remember things
from when I was under the age of two."

"Selective memory," I teased. "From what I know, most
people don't remember anything earlier than the age of three.
Besides, I didn't like you very much until you tossed that frog
down my shirt."

"Ah-ha! I knew it!" I watched, amused, as Ryan punched
one fist into the air. "The truth comes out. You thought you

hated me, but I knew that frog would sway your opinion. Long-term, at least. It only took a few more years to convince you."

I nudged his leg with my bare foot. "Are you saying you committed frog assault only to get my attention?"

He chuckled and winked. "Subconsciously, I think that might have been the case. You should have seen yourself. I wish I had a tape of it. You were pretty amusing jumping around and flapping your shirt up and down."

"At least I was only five at the time," I said with a sly wink. "Don't even think about doing it ever again."

Ryan gave me a sweet kiss. "Once we're married, I'm sure I can think of more creative ways to get a rise out of you."

"The things you say, Mr. Sullivan."

The day was beautiful with a slight breeze, and I enjoyed the opportunity to relax and be together one-on-one with Ryan. We talked about our plans for the house and landscaping. Building a deck was something we agreed we'd like to do so we can have cookouts and invite our friends over for summer dinners. String up some lanterns and talk late into the night. Dance under the stars in private.

Halfway into eating his sandwich, Ryan wrinkled his nose. "Do you smell something?"

"Like what?" I asked, chewing my second bite of sandwich. From his expression, I could tell it wasn't a pleasant aroma. More like a stench.

"Something funky." He groaned. "If that's what I think it is, maybe we should go home and try this outing again next week."

"Don't be silly. Wait…what *is* that?" I'd caught a whiff. "I think the wind shifted, and it's now wafted my way."

"And now I've lost my appetite." Tossing the uneaten portion of his sandwich on the plate, Ryan retrieved the plastic wrap.

"I thought animals weren't allowed in this part of the park." I'd pinched my nostrils with two fingers, making my words sound nasal.

"No comment. Some kind of animal's been here. That's for sure. Unbelievable." About that time, we spotted an unleashed dog wandering nearby. That explained the source, anyway.

"You know what? I'm not that hungry." I wrapped my sandwich and began to pack up our things.

"I'll take you to dinner someplace special tonight to make up for this disaster, Sass." Shaking his head, Ryan smirked. "At least it'll smell better."

"Ryan, the place doesn't matter. As long as you're with me, I'll be fine." I planted both hands on the blanket and, on my knees, leaned closer to him. "I find it incredibly sweet that you planned this romantic day for us. I'll never forget it."

Speaking of unforgettable, I gave him a kiss he'd always remember. *Good* kiss. As I pulled away, something on the ground—beneath the blanket—made me lose my balance. I nearly hit my chin on the way down and ended up falling on my side.

"Aw, man! I'm sorry. Are you okay, Ellie?" Ryan jumped to his feet and helped me up. "What happened?"

I couldn't help it. I started laughing.

"Well," I said through my giggles, "I think one of us sat on what was beneath the blanket. The warmth from our body heat made it more…pungent…and that's when—"

"I get your point." Laughing with me, Ryan pulled me into his arms. "You are such a good sport about stuff like this." He kissed the tip of my nose. "Let's get out of here." He eyed the blanket. "I'm not sure I even want to look."

"You don't really need that blanket do you?" I said. "It looks kind of old and ratty."

"Nah, I don't need it. Especially now." As I packed up the picnic basket, Ryan carefully lifted the blanket and then carried it over to a large trash receptacle. After dropping it in the can, he walked with me back to the truck, swinging the picnic basket between us.

Hearing laughter behind me, I turned in my chair beside Cora's bed.

"We're sorry to interrupt, Ellie, but that story is priceless!" Krista gave me a wink. "I'm glad you and Ryan could see the humor in it."

A monitor connected to Cora beeped. And kept beeping, sounding more insistent. A light started flashing. Krista and several of the other ladies rushed past me and started speaking in medical terms.

I rose from the chair and quickly left the room. One of the aides called for the doctor.

Please, Lord, be with Cora if this is her time. I knew she was ready, but was *I* ready to let her go? I was overcome by the sense that I shouldn't be the only one in her room. Where was her daughter? Why didn't Beatrice come to visit her mother?

I retreated to the hallway. A staff doctor flew down the hallway and darted into Cora's room, closing the door behind him.

Leaning against the wall, I bowed my head and prayed.

Chapter 16

~~♥~~

I felt a hand on my shoulder a short time later.

Opening my eyes, I met Krista's concerned gaze.

"She's okay, but this type of event is happening more often with Cora."

"Krista, your honest opinion, how long do you think she has?"

"It's difficult to say. She could go at any time. Then again, she could go on in her current state for another year or two. From what I know of Cora, she wouldn't want to linger."

"I agree. Did she sign a DNR?"

"No," Krista said with a sigh. "So, legally, we will continue to resuscitate. Unfortunately, her daughter hasn't returned our calls or responded to our attempts to contact her."

"Do you know anything about Beatrice?" I'd only met her a couple of times through all the years I've known Cora, and one of those times was at my father's funeral.

"Only that she's a high-powered executive with some software firm in Minneapolis. She's divorced with two grown kids. I don't think Cora has any great-grandchildren." Krista shrugged. "I don't really know."

How sad. I'd never seen cards from grandchildren or anyone else.

"Ellie, in many ways, *you* are Cora's family. I'm sure—somehow, in some way—she knows you're here and that you talk to her. That you love her."

I nodded and wiped away a tear. "Thanks, Krista. You have my phone number, right? Call me if anything happens. Day or night."

Krista nodded. "I will. For the record, and I'm sorry if the timing is wrong to ask, but did Ryan propose that day or did he wait?"

"Well, Ryan knows I love lighthouses, and he took me to the Marblehead Lighthouse. They have tours on select Saturdays, and we were able to join one of them. We climbed the steps to the top to view South Bass, the Middle Bass Islands, and the Sandusky Bay area. And then we spent some time at the beach, walking along the shore, playing in the waves."

"So, is that where Ryan asked you to marry him?"

My lips upturned. "He waited until we went back home that evening. I told him I didn't want to go to a restaurant. I fixed fried egg sandwiches with mayo and cheese—his favorite—and we ate them by candlelight. It turned out to be very romantic. After our meal, Ryan helped me with the dishes, and then he escorted me to the sofa. At some point, he'd placed a red velvet ring box on the coffee table. Ryan slid to one knee, opened the lid of the box, and held it up for me to see the beautiful round diamond inside. Then he said, 'Eleanor Rose Franklin, I love you with all my heart and always have. Will you please grace me with the honor of loving you for the rest of my life?'"

I lifted my hand for Krista to see my engagement ring.

"Let me guess. You said no?" Krista smiled and took my hand to see the ring from a closer angle. "It's gorgeous, Ellie. Even though I haven't met Ryan yet, he sounds like a great guy. And he's marrying a lovely girl. I know you're going to be very happy together."

An idea popped into my mind. "Come to the wedding, Krista. I want you there if you're not going to be busy with your own family. It's on Christmas Day at Cade's Corner Community Church."

Krista's eyes lit at my invitation. "I'd love to come! If you're sure."

"I insist. It won't be the same without you. The wedding's at two o'clock."

"Count on it. Thanks so much, Ellie."

I retrieved my coat and bid Cora good night. Then I began my walk home. With my boots, I kicked up the light, fresh snowfall. Seemed like it'd been snowing most every day in the past couple of weeks.

I thought about when Ryan left for his first deployment. It was at the end of his sophomore year in college. He came home one day with excitement written in every part of his body and in his expression. And announced he'd signed up with the Army. It'd come out of the blue, and I had no idea he'd harbored any interest in joining the military.

"They need more military personnel in Afghanistan," he told me. "How can I resist the call? I can always go back to school later on."

"God and country first," I said under my breath as I turned the corner onto Dream Street. Because of his schooling, he was able to enter the Army with a slightly higher rank, not that it mattered. Maybe it did to Ryan.

How could I beg him not to go without sounding selfish? I respect and admire his loyalty and courage. But, in the back of my mind, I worry for him, for his safety. And try not to feel like third best. I know Ryan would hate it if he suspected I'd *ever* felt that way.

So, I hide my insecurities and pretend to be a grown-up, especially during this second deployment. Ryan promised this would be the last. Then we can get on with our lives.

I don't know how the wives of public servants—firefighters and policemen, especially—can handle the constant stress. If they don't have assurances from the Lord, where do they get their hope? Their strength? How do they come to terms with the constant fear? Do they jump every time the phone rings in the middle of the night, and their husband is out on a call?

Lord, I can't do this without you. Help keep me strong.

I've prayed every day for the Lord to keep Ryan and all our servicemen and women safe. I miss him like crazy. I'm independent to a degree, but without Ryan, part of me is missing. The *best* part. I work better when we're together. We share everything, our personalities complement one another, and we bring out the best in one another. Friends can fill the void to a certain degree, but it's not the same thing.

Through it all, my faith has been strengthened by our separation, and I'm putting my trust in God that He'll bring Ryan home safely to me.

I can't believe anything else.

Chapter 17

~~♥~~

Wednesday Morning, December 20

Glory, hallelujah!

The day I've waited for, prayed for, and hoped for, has finally arrived.

As soon as I spied Nick through the picture window, heading across the street toward the Perchance to Dream office, a feeling of unease coursed through me.

You're supposed to be on your way to Dayton to pick up Ryan!

Had Ryan's plane been delayed? What else could it possibly be? I bit my lower lip to still its trembling.

My first glimpse of Nick's face made it clear something was wrong. *Very* wrong. The slump of his shoulders revealed something weighed heavily on his mind. He opened the front door—the jingle bell ringing merrily—and stepped inside. Brushing snow from his wool coat, Nick's worried expression became cause for heightened alarm as he headed straight for my office.

I told myself that although he appeared worried, he didn't look like a man burdened with grief.

Stop it, Ellie! Listen to what he has to say. My brain wanted to scream, and my heart hurt already. This couldn't be good.

"Hey, Ellie." Nick stood in the doorway and avoided my gaze. That was unusual.

"Hi, Nick. Please. Come in. If you're going to get after me for leaving the front door unlocked while I'm working alone, you needn't bother."

Without answering or removing his coat, Nick fell heavily into the chair on the other side of my desk. I've never seen him like this. Not once. My pulse began to race, and I swallowed hard.

Something was wrong. I could feel it in my *bones*.

"I thought you'd be on your way to Dayton by now. Did Ryan call you? I haven't heard anything. Is his plane delayed?" The questions tumbled out of me.

"That's why I'm here. Um, Mom and Dad got some news last night." Clue number three. Nick never said *um*.

"I'm not sure the best way to tell you this, Ellie, but it seems that Ryan's team is—"

"They're what?" I sat back in my chair, holding my breath, afraid to hear his answer.

Nick's gaze met mine. "They're missing."

"Missing?"

Please Lord, no. No!

I stared at Ryan's brother, trying to form the next question as my mind swirled. Nick explained that the helicopter with Ryan and his team of seven men had disappeared from radar.

"How long ago?" I was afraid to cry, afraid *not* to cry. Giving into crying was as good as admitting Ryan was dead. I refused to go there. I needed to be strong. For me, for Nick, but especially for Ryan.

"Sometime in the early afternoon yesterday, their time. They were on a short, final mission—something unexpected, I guess. It was only supposed to be a couple of hours and then they were headed to the plane that would bring them back to the States."

Oh, the irony. I couldn't even begin to fathom the injustice.

Stay calm, Ellie. I forced myself to take a few deep breaths.

God, you are in control.

Rising from my chair, I moved around my desk and sat in the chair across from Nick. I took his hand in mine and waited until he met my gaze.

"Nick, why didn't you call me?"

Nick's expression softened as he looked at me. I could see the anguish in his chestnut-colored eyes as he slowly shook his head. "Forgive me, Ellie. I just couldn't. Until we had more details, I didn't even want to tell you. I couldn't do that to you. Not now."

I swallowed hard. I couldn't lash out at my friend. He's as stunned as I am. He loves Ryan fiercely, just as I do. We need to keep a united front, our families need to cling to one another, and together we'll get through whatever might come in the days ahead.

"And you still haven't heard anything more, so you felt the need to come and tell me now." It wasn't a question but more a statement of fact. No accusations, no anger.

Nick nodded silently.

"Do they know what happened?" That would explain why I haven't received any text messages or phone calls from Ryan. I also knew Ryan didn't take his cell phone on his missions.

"They believe the chopper went down in an area with a very rough, rugged terrain. There was a mayday signal, so that indicates a system or equipment malfunction as opposed to enemy fire. So, it's entirely possible they parachuted out."

"Is there a chance...?" I couldn't even finish the sentence.

"POW? Yes, unfortunately, there's always the chance they've been captured." Nick breathed out a long sigh and rubbed one hand over his forehead, back and forth. "Honestly, Ellie, I don't know which is the better option."

I couldn't dwell on that statement. Swallowing hard, I needed to push on. "I think, for now, we need to focus on the positive. Do they have any evidence of a crash?"

"No. The Army assured us they're doing everything they can to find them. So far they've come up empty-handed. I guess it's a tricky area to try and search without drawing undue attention. That's hampering their efforts."

"How are your parents handling it?" This must be torturous for them.

"As well as can be expected. There's no rule book for something like this. Kind of hard to know what to do, what to think, what to do next. So, we're going through the motions. Mom was going to come and tell you, but I offered."

"I'm glad you did." I smacked my hand on the arm of my chair with such force that Nick visibly jumped, and my hand stung. "I'm going to put this request on the prayer chain immediately, and I think we should get our friends and neighbors together tonight for a special prayer circle. That's the first thing we need to do."

Nick gave me a slow nod. "Sure. I think that's a great idea, Ellie. Ryan would like it, I'm sure."

"You and I both know the power of prayer, Nick." What I wouldn't say is that we both also knew that prayer couldn't always bring people back who'd been lost to us for one reason or another. Prayer didn't guarantee relationships would be reconciled, or that bodies would be mended. But prayer is the *best* thing we have. Always. I know God hears our prayers. Sometimes He chooses not to answer them in our time, but in His own perfect timing. Or in a way we can never expect.

Nick rose from the chair. "I'll have Mom make a few calls. Come to the house at seven tonight and we'll have that prayer circle. If you want me to come get you, I will."

I shook my head. "Thanks, but I'm sure I can make it on my own."

"You're a strong woman, Ellie. I know that's one of the many qualities my little brother loves most about you. You might consider going home until..."

Tears stung my eyes as I rose to my feet. "I need to stay in the house I'm going to share with Ryan. *That's* my home. And you'd better get out of here now before I bawl all over the place and spoil your image of me. I can promise you, it won't be pretty."

Nick opened his arms and pulled me into his comforting embrace. "Ellie, I'm here if you need me. So is Maura, Mom, and everyone else." He patted my back a few times like I imagined a big brother would do.

Sniffling, I nodded and pulled out of the hug. "Same here for you. We're in this together. I just need time to absorb this information. Ryan's got to be okay. I can't believe anything differently."

Nick tilted his head, surveying me, compassion brimming in his expression. "Did you drive? I can drive you home if you'd like."

"No, thanks. You know how I love to walk, and I've never minded the cold." Something about the brisk air and the snow energizes me.

"You sure you're going to be okay until tonight?"

I forced my chin into the air with more courage than I felt. "No, but I have to be."

"If I hear anything, I'll call you right away. Keep the faith," Nick said, his voice quiet.

"I plan on it. You, too." My voice caught and a tear streaked down my face. "If he were gone, I'd know it in my heart, Nick. Ryan's out there somewhere, and you don't know how much I hate it that I can't jump on a plane and go find him myself."

Nick nodded. "I'm sure you would if you could, Ellie. I would, too."

"I know." We shared a nod of understanding.

"I'll see you at seven tonight." With a small salute, Nick turned to go. Then he looked back at me.

"Get out of here," I whispered. "Please just go."

With the saddest expression I've ever seen, he nodded. Nick hurt as much as I did, but I simply didn't know what else I could say.

I'd left the puppy dog Ellie had given me in the office. I reached for him behind my desk and rested my head on his plush fur, allowing my tears to flow freely. I sobbed, and it brought back the pain of losing my father. But this was a fresh pain, a *new* kind of pain. It hurt every bit as much, but in a different way.

Be still, child, and know that I am God.

The ladies at the nursing facility believe I'm strong. Nick believes I'm strong. My dad thought I was strong. My mom has always called me strong. Ryan knows I'm strong.

So, I was outnumbered. I needed to be…strong. I closed my eyes. "Lord, help me. I'm not sure I know how to be strong right now."

Lay your burdens at my feet, child. I will carry you.

I lowered my head and prayed. Prayed as hard and as long as I'd ever done in my entire life.

Maybe it was a good thing that Maura was out doing her Christmas shopping or she might have been in the office with me, wrapping up the accounting work for this year. Part of me wished she were here. The other part of me was thankful for the solitude. I wouldn't be good company right now. I was numb, and I didn't know what to feel.

All I know is that I felt better after my good cry and then my time of prayer. I'd needed both for my heart, my mind, and my soul.

An hour later, I wasn't sure where to go. I didn't want to go home yet.

I walked through the streets of town and my steps, seemingly of their own accord, took me to the nursing home. I barely acknowledged the greetings of the staffers as they passed by me in the hallway. I caught some of the looks they exchanged, but I had a one-track mind as I made my way straight to Cora's room. No way could I explain my mood (if they hadn't already heard), and I'd break down if anyone expressed sympathy.

After closing the door (something I never did), I stumbled and collapsed into a chair. Without removing my coat, I scooted the chair to the side of the bed.

"Ryan's helicopter has gone missing." I heard myself saying the words as thought I were in a fog or a bubble hovering above Cora's bed. I've never experienced such a weird sensation—like I was present but also *not* there.

Taking Cora's hand in my own, I held on tight. Then I realized I was squeezing too tight and lessened my grip. "Oh, Cora. I'm so sorry."

I smoothed the top of her soft blanket with my other hand. "Is this blanket new? Did your daughter bring it for you?" That was highly doubtful, sadly enough. I needed to keep talking. Anything to numb my brain from worrying about Ryan and dissolving into a puddle of tears.

"I've always loved this shade of pink in your blanket. My mom has a Murano glass conch shell she brought home from her trip to Venice before she married Dad. It's this same color. So pretty."

I blew out a long breath, feeling the urge to talk. "I might as well continue my story from last week."

And so, I began.

Chapter 18

~~♥~~

For a couple of weeks after my father died, I moped around the house and cried a lot. My sisters cried on their boyfriends' shoulders, and I cried all over Ryan. He must have thought I was disgusting because I slobbered all over his shirt on at least three occasions, but he took it like a man.

Ryan's house had a circular driveway which my mother considered the height of sophistication. She'd asked my dad a few times if we could have one made in front of our house. I never understood what was so great about it, but Mom never got her circular driveway. After Dad died, she bought a new BMW convertible in a gorgeous baby blue color with gray leather seats. In my opinion, that car was much better than a circular driveway any old day of the week. Who wouldn't want a car with a heater that warmed up your seat in the winter?

Kara told me some of the ladies in church whispered behind Mom's back that she'd squandered some of Dad's life insurance money to buy the BMW, but it was her money to spend however she wanted. Sometimes people could be incredibly insensitive. If I were Mom, I'd have driven up and down the street in that shiny new car, waving like the queen, smiling like I hadn't a care in the world with the top of the car down, and my hair flying in the wind. More power to her. She was only 47, and she'd lost her husband. She deserved everything life had to offer.

"Isn't that taking it a bit far?" Ryan said when I made the mistake of telling him my revenge fantasy. He'd looked up the price of the car and made me mad when he made it sound like he didn't approve. It wasn't his business, and it was no one's business but Mom's.

"Stop being so goody-goody all the time," I'd said to him. "Not to mention cheap." In a huff, I walked away and didn't speak to him for an entire week. Childish yes, but I had a point to prove.

Our house was always in need of repairs to the roof, the appliances, back porch, the patio, and any number of things. Maybe I noticed them because I didn't have a father to fix the things that were broken anymore. Or maybe it was more that Mom ignored them and didn't address the issues. About a month after Dad's death, the Sullivan men, Ryan and Nick's dad included, volunteered to help us around the house.

So, in the name of friendship and Christian charity, the Sullivan men dutifully traipsed over to our house every other Saturday afternoon to see what needed to be done. In my opinion, Mom lapped up the attention and created things for them to do. She'd never admit it, but I suspected she was lonely. And to their credit, I never heard them complain.

Without wanting to be an obvious tagalong, I sometimes helped Ryan when he was working at our house. I missed his company, and I sensed we were growing apart in some ways. He treated me the same as ever, teased me like always. Even though only a year separated us in terms of age, I felt as though Ryan was somehow leaving me behind.

In addition to being a star athlete at school, Ryan held down a part-time job at Cade's Corner Hardware a couple of nights a week. How the guy earned stellar grades was beyond me with all he did.

I knew Ryan had started dating (and going to proms and maybe other dances) even though he never said anything to me about it. I didn't want to think about it. Brandon Harrison started dropping broad hints that he wanted to date me, but I told him my Mom wouldn't allow me to date until I was older—like 30—and that took care of that. If I were honest with myself, I didn't want to date anyone. Not that Ryan was perfect, but for better or worse, all of my teenage daydreams involved Ryan.

One afternoon, I walked home from a drugstore on the outskirts of town, my twice-a-week, one-mile walk when I'd buy a roll of Sweet Tarts and one of those silly teen fan magazines ("mags" as those in the know call them). My route home took me past Ryan's house. As I walked closer, I spied Ryan leaning against his red Ford F-150 truck, his pride and joy. He wasn't alone.

Slowing my steps, I tried not to stare, but my curiosity was killing me.

Great. Carli Jenkins. I thought I'd be sick right then and there.

Carli was gorgeous, and every guy in school wanted to date her—curvy cheerleader with pretty, long blonde hair who wore her sweaters two sizes too small and had "legs that wouldn't quit" according to the boys. I hated that expression, especially since I'm vertically challenged. Honestly, Carli was too sweet for me to hate, but I detested how she stared adoringly at Ryan with big google eyes. Gag me. As if he could do no wrong. As if he was the most handsome boy on the face of the planet.

He kind of was, actually. Senior. Star athlete. Great student. Perfect guy.

"Sass, what's your problem?" Ryan said the next Saturday afternoon. He'd come over to the house to repair something or other. I can't remember what it was, but Mom always had a running list. Sometimes I think she took advantage of their generosity. It's not like Dad didn't leave us financially secure, at least from what I knew. Unless that BMW cost way more than I realized.

"I don't know what you're talking about." For once, I walked away and ignored him until he cornered me a few minutes later on the back porch.

"I think you have a problem." Ryan's grin was too smug for my liking. "Admit it. You're jealous that I was talking to Carli." Crossing his arms, Ryan blocked my way when I tried to get past him.

"Do you mind?" I gestured for him to move.

"Yeah, I kind of do. We need to talk about this."

"Fine. Talk." Mirroring him, I crossed my arms and pushed my long hair (I'd been growing it out, and it reached almost to my waist) behind my shoulders. "I am not jealous. But I know you can do better than date a girl who has zero ambition."

"Yeah, right. Carli's the prettiest girl in school, and that's the dumbest thing I've ever heard you say. Besides, you can't know whether or not she has ambition. Don't go making judgments." He stepped closer, making me back up a few steps. "I hate to break it to you, but not every girl wants to be Amelia Earhart."

"I never said I wanted to *be* Amelia Earhart." I raised my chin in defiance. "I said I wanted to make a difference."

"Whatever." Ryan shrugged in that annoying way he had of doing. He knew that was a word that riled me as much, if not more, than any other. It signified apathy and indifference, which I hated with a passion. We'd had an entire discussion about that word.

"Okay, I can admit Carli's pretty." Could he possibly understand how magnanimous I was to acknowledge that much? "I'm not judging, but is she a Christian? As I remember, you gave me the big speech about how you'd only date Christians."

He frowned. "I'm working on that."

"Ah, so now you're missionary dating?"

He narrowed his eyes. "Don't start with me, Ellie. That's between me and God."

"Shouldn't it be between God and me?"

"What are you talking about?" His eyes sparked with fire and his agitation was obvious.

"You put yourself first. And grammatically—"

Ryan's lips thinned. "Ellie, get off your high horse and leave me alone."

"You disappoint me, Ryan."

"Yeah? Well, you'll get over it."

I pushed past him, and he let me go.

That wasn't the first time I'd cried over Ryan Joseph Sullivan, and I knew it wouldn't be the last. More than anything, I hated being mad at him.

That night, I made a pact with God. Well, not really a pact. More like a promise. I told the Almighty that I'd settle for friendship with Ryan if that's all He wanted for us. "Please help me not to push Ryan away with my pettiness, Lord," I prayed. "We both have tempers and say things we don't mean sometimes. I'm sorry, and please forgive me." I hesitated. "And be with Ryan. Help him to know I care about him, and I don't like it when we're not speaking."

Two weeks later, we'd still barely spoken to one another except in passing at both school and church. I was miserable, but I figured by his silence that Ryan couldn't care less. He'd obviously moved on. I was just that jealous little girl from the other side of the street.

I'd found raking to be therapeutic. Heaven knows, we have a lot of tall trees in our backyard. Enough to keep me busy for a long time. The only downside was that my thoughts always seemed to focus on Ryan while I was working.

Ryan marched up to me one evening after dinner when I was raking leaves in our backyard. The crunching of the leaves warned me of his approach. In his official letterman jacket and jeans, he made quite a handsome picture.

Be still my heart.

"Give me that." Yanking the rake from my hands, Ryan started his task with determined strokes. Ryan was a hard worker, but this was ridiculous.

"Hello to you, too. What's gotten into you?" I tugged off my gloves and offered them to him. "Here, take these. I wouldn't want those gifted hands to get blisters, or it might affect your ability to catch a pass. A football pass that is," I added. What a snit. Why couldn't I learn to control my tongue around Ryan?

"Thanks for thinking of my welfare." Taking the gloves from me, he pulled them on. Then he started raking again with even more fervor. When Ryan seemed unwilling to talk, I set off for the garage to grab the box of leaf bags and another pair of work gloves.

We worked together in silence for at least 15 minutes. Smoke curled from the chimney of the house next door, and I breathed in deeply. I've always loved the scents of the fall season.

"Just so you know, I'm not dating her."

"Who?" I continued to gather leaves and avoided glancing his way.

"You know very well who. Carli Jenkins." I could hear the smirk in his voice.

"Doesn't matter to me." I shrugged my shoulders and refused to look at him although my heart was doing a little dance. Where this conversation would lead was anyone's guess.

"Oh, yeah, I think it does." Tossing down the rake, Ryan stomped over to me. As he started to yank off the gloves, he frowned when he had trouble with the right one.

"Need a little help?"

"Very funny. I'll get it." With a grunt, he pulled off the offending glove.

I stopped my leaf-gathering, and my heart pounded so loud I knew Ryan must surely hear it. "What's *your* problem? And why bother asking me when you seem to know all the answers?" My sarcasm was going to get the best of me, something Staci liked to remind me of quite often.

"You."

I gave him a look of wide-eyed innocence. "Me? How do you figure that? Are you still mad at me for braiding your hair when you were napping during the youth group movie?" I'd never seen Ryan's hair so long, and I'd been unable to resist the temptation. Of course, it gave me the opportunity to touch his hair when he was sleeping. And, yes, it *might* have made me seem somewhat like a stalker, but that was neither here nor there.

Shaking his head, he ran his hand through his hair, a sure sign of his continued aggravation with me. He took another step closer to me, but I stood my ground. "Answer a question for me, Ellie." Ryan had a glint in his eyes I'd never seen before.

What was on his mind? I swallowed hard and moistened my lips with my tongue. "Shoot."

"You ever been kissed? By a guy?" He glanced into the distance and then back at me. "You know, romantically?"

"No, not that it's any of your business."

"I'm glad to hear it." About this time, my pulse took flight, curling up into the sky like the smoke from the chimney next door. I could barely breathe, and it's as though the air between us crackled with electricity. Crazy, yes, but true.

"Where's this coming from, Ryan?" With the setting sun in the background, a blazing ball of orange-red glory, I dared to meet Ryan's blue-eyed gaze. He moved another inch closer. Unless I was out of my mind, his expression revealed that he cared about me as more than a friend. His features softened, and he appeared less angry.

"I want to be the first guy to kiss you, Ellie."

"Is that an order?" That question was not uttered in a sarcastic tone, it should be noted.

"Pretty much," he said, his voice tinged with a huskiness I'd never heard before. "Not that I'd ever try to tell you what to do."

"Sure you would."

"Nah. They're only suggestions." He reached for me and pulled me to him, planting his hands on my waist. I thought I might be ticklish, but oddly enough, I wasn't.

"I shouldn't ask this, but have you ever kissed a girl?" Maybe it wasn't a fair question, but I had a burning need to know.

"No," he murmured. "Carli wanted to, though."

I cringed. "I didn't need to know that."

"Then you shouldn't ask."

"So, this is the first kiss for both of us?" I could hardly believe it, but Ryan wouldn't lie to me about something so important.

"Yep."

"But you went to dances, a couple of proms…"

Ryan cupped my face between his hands in a gentle but firm hold. "Look at me, Eleanor."

"Don't call me Eleanor and maybe I will."

He blew out a sigh of exasperation. "Work with me here, please. I could have kissed a few girls by now if I wanted. But I didn't."

"Why didn't you?" I searched his face, barely able to comprehend such a thing. How was that possible? I splayed the fingers of my right hand on Ryan's chest. In spite of my racing pulse, I managed to sound somewhat calm. "If we do this, you realize it's either going to be the start of something or we'll know we're destined to be friends forever and nothing more."

"Good grief. I'm not asking you to marry me, Sass." He made an indefinable sound of frustration and seemed at a loss. "You don't have to be so clinical about it. Let's do this. Just kiss me, okay?"

"You're bossy." By this time, I was more than ready. I wasn't nervous, only curious what it'd be like to kiss him. Not just any boy. Ryan Joseph Sullivan.

"I want to be your first kiss," he said. "And I want you to be mine."

"This isn't a stupid idea to see if we're compatible or an experi—?"

"For once in your life, please be quiet, woman."

He called me *woman*. Huh.

I raised my chin and slipped my hands around his neck. I had no idea what I was doing but figured we'd fumble our way through it together.

"I didn't kiss any other girls, Ellie, because they're not *you*."

He'd done it now. He'd stunned me speechless. *Wow.*

Ryan's eyes sparkled and he lowered his head. And then his mouth, warm and tender, covered mine. His hands tightened on my waist, and he drew me closer.

For a first kiss—and considering I had nothing with which to compare it—I'd have to say it was...spectacular. Absolutely.

Kissing Ryan felt like coming *home*.

Chapter 19

~~♥~~

Wednesday Late Afternoon

I escaped to my office at Perchance to Dream after my visit with Cora. If I'd gone home, I'd sit and dwell on things. I'd have to go home at some point tonight, but for now, the office offered comfort and solace. I could continue my end-of-the-project reports for the year. If I felt even more ambitious, I could do some advance planning for the next year. Keeping my mind busy was the most important thing.

A few of the volunteers came in to clean out their desks. They hadn't said anything about Ryan, so I assumed they didn't know…yet. If they *had* known, they'd probably avoid eye contact. A couple of the workers waved and said they'd see me at the wedding. I pasted on a smile and mumbled a generic response.

Seeing the others pack up their desks reminded me that I needed to call the rental company to pick up the furniture and computer equipment before the end of the year. Then I needed to remind Nick he'd be in charge of making sure it was done since Ryan and I would be basking in the Hawaiian sun.

I retrieved my cell phone and clicked on the list of contacts. Ten minutes later, I'd taken care of that task and left a voice mail for Nick. I was relieved when he didn't answer. For once, I wasn't up to conversation. I hadn't even called Mom yet, but I'd need to call her and my sisters.

A knock sounded on my office door. After the last volunteer left, I'd closed it. I never closed that door, and now I wasn't sure I wanted to open it.

I could only pray it wasn't a reporter looking for a story about the poor bride who hadn't a clue whether or not she'd have a wedding in five days. Whether or not she had a groom. Whether or not she'd be helping his parents to plan his funeral.

No! I could *not* think that way.

I'd already had a couple of phone calls from the local news media. Vultures.

I had to be positive. Ryan will be fine.

A second knock sounded on the door, slightly louder than the first.

"Who is it?" I blew out a breath and braced myself.

The door opened. *Mom.*

"Hi, honey. I thought you might want some company. Mary Sullivan called me a short time ago."

"Mom!" I rose from the desk and ran to her. Throwing my arms around her neck, I cried. Oh, how I cried. Like my heart was breaking. Like I hadn't cried with my mother since we lost Dad. She was there then. She was here now.

"Here, sweetie." Mom pushed a wad of tissues into my hand. "When you're ready, dry those tears and let's talk. Take your time." She held me close as I clung to her and cried on her shoulder.

"O…o…kay," I said a minute later. I gulped and then inhaled a huge breath.

Mom guided me by the arm to the two chairs. I dropped into one, still wiping my eyes, and she sat in the other, scooting it closer to mine. At least the flow of my tears had finally begun to ebb. She waited patiently and held my hand.

"Ellie, do you know what your father used to say about Ryan?"

I dabbed beneath my eyes and looked at her with wide eyes. Shaking my head, I gave her a confused look. "You mean what he said to you…or to me?"

"To me."

"If Dad said it, it probably had something to do with the Cavaliers." I half-laughed, half-sobbed.

The corners of Mom's mouth upturned. For the first time, I noticed the newer lines in the corners of her eyes. Not deep lines, but lines caused by the passage of time. She used to smile a lot, but not as much in recent years. Maybe Dr.

Bernard would help bring back her lovely smile. That would be nice.

"It was about a week after Ryan broke his leg, and you'd called for the ambulance," Mom said. "Your dad watched you from the front window one day as you walked down the street to the Sullivan house. He said, 'Ellie feels something special for that boy. And I think Ryan feels the same way. Mark my words, Janet, those two are going to end up together one day.'"

"Really?" I shook my head. "I had no idea. Why didn't Dad ever tell me?" Her words gave me comfort. I liked to believe that my father knew I was marrying Ryan.

"Because you were so young when he died. You might not know it, but Ryan has always had a sparkle in his eyes when he looks at you, honey. For as long as I can remember. Your father saw it even before I did. He was always so attuned to you."

I wiped my eyes. "Did you know Ryan dropped a frog down my shirt when I was five?"

"I heard a little something about that."

"Staci?"

Mom shook her head. "Doesn't matter."

I twisted a few of the tissues between my fingers. "I didn't tell you because I thought you'd say I couldn't play with Ryan anymore." I glanced up at her. "I didn't want to risk that happening. As much as he irritated me sometimes, I liked him. Even if I told him I didn't. Ryan makes me laugh, he's smart, and he challenges me."

"You turned down a lot of dates with other boys."

I nodded. It was true. Brandon Harrison wasn't the only one who'd asked. "I did. Why go out with someone else when I'd already found the best?"

Tears shone in Mom's eyes. "I felt the same way about your father."

"Mom," I said, taking a deep breath, "I've decided I want to stay on schedule with the wedding plans. Until we know otherwise, I have to operate on the assumption that

Ryan will be found safe. I realize it'll be cutting the time short even if they find him in the next day or so, but maybe we can push back the time of the wedding by a few hours. If Ryan's up to it, that is, and—"

"I understand." Mom squeezed my hand. "You know, in my Bible reading this morning, I came across a very familiar verse. I think it's appropriate to what's happening in your life right now."

"Which verse is that?"

"Jeremiah 29:11: 'For I know the plans that I have for you,' declares the Lord, 'plans for welfare and not for calamity to give you a future and a hope.'"

"That's always a verse I've associated with good things," I said.

"Yes, that's when we see the verse most often, but it applies every bit as much to your future. Ellie, do you remember how Mark Sullivan and the boys used to come help around the house on Saturdays after your father died?"

"Yes." I had to wonder why she'd brought that up now.

"Sweetie, I didn't need half of those things done," Mom said. "Did you notice how I usually sent Mark and Nick on their way after a couple of hours?"

Wow. I *hadn't* noticed. "You did that so Ryan would stay longer?" That must be why she also asked me to constantly take him tools, a glass of water or iced tea, a recipe for his mother—anything.

Mom lifted her shoulders with a small smile. "A mother does what she can to encourage a friendship between her daughter and the boy down the street she hopes she'll marry one day."

"Oh, Mom." I rose out of the chair and tugged Mom to her feet. "Thank you."

"Welcome." She hugged me and then pulled back. "I guess what I want to tell you is that you'll be okay. You're smart, you're brave, you're strong, and you're better for having Ryan in your life. I've prayed for you two since the time I saw him kiss you in the backyard when you were raking leaves."

I felt my cheeks warm. "You knew about that, too?" I slid a hand to my hip. "Kara?"

She shook her head.

"I know, I know. It doesn't matter," I said. "You always were diplomatic in these issues."

"God will take care of you." Mom put a gentle hand on the side of my face, and I leaned into it. "Just as He's watching over Ryan. He knows, and He has everything under control. Remember that."

I sniffled. "I'm trying my best."

"It's times like this when I wish your dad were here. You two shared such a close bond, and he always had a way with words."

"Oh, Mom, I never meant to exclude you." A tear rolled down my cheek. "You're here *now*, and that's what I need most of all."

"I love you, Ellie. You're going to make a beautiful bride in a few days. Now, I have an idea."

"Thanks. I love you, too. What's that?" I sniffled and dabbed at my eyes. I appreciated her positivity and her gentle smile.

"We still have that small artificial tree you've always loved. The one that used to sit in the corner of the kitchen. We can decorate it with the white lights and the Murano glass ornaments from Italy that my parents gave us. You haven't put up a Christmas tree in the house yet, have you?"

I shook my head. "I haven't thought much about decorating for Christmas other than to hang a wreath on the door and string up a few lights. I've been focused on getting everything else ready. And I didn't want to get a real tree since we'd be gone, and it could be a fire hazard."

"Then this is what we'll do," Mom said. "Let's go get the tree and go back to your house. I can cook us a nice dinner and then we can decorate the tree together. Sing some Christmas carols. Have some quality mother-daughter time."

"I'd like that." I checked my watch. "We're having a time of prayer at the Sullivan's house tonight. Starts at seven. Come with me."

"That sounds like one of the best things we can do." I heard the catch in Mom's throat.

"Will you stay with me tonight, Mom? I'd love your company. We can save decorating the tree for when we get home if we're not too tired. If we are, we can do it in the morning."

"I'd love nothing better. Let's get your coat, lock up, and go."

When we stepped outside the office, I looked up and down the street, surprised that I didn't see Mom's car. "You didn't drive?"

"No. I thought we'd walk."

Mom linked her arm through mine.

In many ways, I knew Dad was right beside us.

Chapter 20

~~♥~~

Wednesday Evening—The Sullivan Home

Both Pastor Derek and Pastor Jon arrived early to share a private time of prayer with the family.

"I think the best verse to meditate on is Romans 8:28," Pastor Derek said. "'And we know that God causes all things to work together for good to those who love God, to those who are called according to His purpose.'"

Since my sisters lived on the other side of Cleveland, I'd told them not to worry about coming. They'd both offered and told me they'd be praying, and that alone meant so much.

Maura gave me a hug and whispered assurances and then sat beside Nick, holding his hand. The sight of the two of them together warmed my heart. Nick seemed especially quiet, and I ached for him.

Mary, the perennial hostess, flitted about the living room with her serving tray overflowing with finger foods and cookies as if this were a social occasion. I couldn't fault her. Being a proper hostess was what she knew how to do best, and it served to keep her thoughts from dwelling on the fact that her second son—her baby—was now classified as missing in action.

MIA. Ryan was classified as something with the worst three initials possible. Strike that. POW was equally bad. However, DOA would be the worst. I shuddered at that morbid thought. I couldn't allow my mind to go to such dark places.

So many people attended the prayer circle that it was standing room only in the Sullivan's living room. Someone proposed walking down to the church, but that idea was outvoted. A few misguided souls called it a vigil. Oh, how I detested that word. When I heard it, I bit my lip and turned away. These people were good enough to come, and I loved them for their faithfulness to Ryan and his family.

Once we began the time of prayer, the only time we paused was when the home phone rang. For some reason, I figured that was the number the Army would call. I snapped my gaze to Mary's, and she motioned for me, Mom, Mark, and Nick to follow. Mary encouraged Kim Higgins to continue praying as we all hurried into the kitchen.

False alarm. The call was from a sales rep trying to sell them Cavaliers season tickets for next year. Go figure. Wishful thinking aside, could the call be a sign from the Lord that Ryan and his team were safe? With a collective sigh, we returned to the living room.

An hour later, I closed the time of prayer. Maybe it was more that I was the last one to speak. Surprisingly, my voice didn't waver, although inside I quaked something fierce. I've never minded praying out loud, but my nerves seemed precariously close to snapping.

Going through the motions as the others departed, I murmured my thanks. In an odd sort of impromptu receiving line, I exchanged hugs and shook hands with members of the church and community. If asked, I wouldn't have been able to recall one thing I'd said.

Mary and Mark moved into the kitchen to clean up. I offered to help, but Mom told me she'd help them. She insisted I stay in the living room and talk with Nick, and Maura had already departed. Maybe I should just go home, but I *couldn't* leave just yet.

In the back of my mind, being in Ryan's house somehow kept me more closely connected to him. The presence of Ryan's family—their warmth and their love—gave me comfort. If it didn't seem inappropriate, I might have asked to curl up in Ryan's bed. Then I remembered that Mom was staying at the house with me tonight. Most likely, I'd wrap myself in one of Ryan's shirts, one that might still carry his scent.

"Ryan defended me at school when I was eight," I said to Nick as we sat across from one another in the living room—me on the sofa and Nick in the recliner. After that

136

random observation, I rubbed a hand across my brow. My head hurt from emotional overload.

Nick leaned forward, elbows on his knees. "Tell me."

"Lori Dingleback teased me about my long pigtails on the playground. Apparently everyone but me was aware that a girl should *never* wear pigtails past the age of five. I ran home, tugged the hairbands out of my hair with a vengeance, and then brushed my scalp so hard it hurt. It even bled a little bit. I vowed never to wear little girl pigtails again."

Nick grinned and, somewhat encouraged, I continued my story. In my mind, the events were as clear as if they'd happened yesterday.

"How come you're wearing your hair like that?" Ryan asked me a couple of days later.

"Because I'm not a little girl anymore."

"Oh. I thought it was because Lori teased you."

"Yeah. That too." Was my humiliation on the school playground public knowledge?

"You tell me if she says anything else. Or if anyone picks on you," Ryan said. "I'll take care of them and make sure they don't say anything ever again."

That was surprising to me. "You'd beat up somebody, Ryan? For teasing me?"

"Yeah, I would. But I'd try to talk them down first before resorting to violence." Ryan rubbed his hand over my still tender scalp, and it took everything in me not to wince. Ouch. "You're like my little sister, Sass. We take care of our own."

"Thanks." I punched his arm. "You could be like my personal bodyguard."

"Right." He laughed. "Don't push it."

Snapping back to the present, I stopped when an odd expression covered Nick's face.

"What?"

"You probably don't know this, but Ryan *did* beat up someone on your behalf."

"Really?" I shook my head. "Who? When? Although maybe the question should be…why?"

"Do you remember when I had that fat lip? Ryan was about eleven, I think."

"Maybe. I think so, now that you mention it." I retrieved my water bottle from a nearby table and plopped back on the sofa, curling my feet beneath me. I took a long drink of water, wondering what Nick's fat lip had to do with me.

Nick's grin grew broader. "Believe it or not, I told Ryan that *I* wanted to marry you one day."

I coughed and almost choked. "Excuse me?" I wiped both sides of my mouth with the back of my hand and stared at Nick. "This is new information."

"Maybe this will jog your memory. Do you remember when Ryan announced he wanted to build a log cabin in the driveway? And that he wanted you to live with him in that log cabin?"

"Sure. That was during his Abe Lincoln phase. Ryan never said anything to me directly, but your mother told my mom about it. To be honest, I thought the idea of living in a home constructed of logs sounded like a cool thing to do."

"I challenged Ryan and made a smart aleck remark," Nick said. "I mouthed off and said some stupid things about how he needed to marry you first before he could live with you. We were just kids, and I didn't have the first clue what I was saying."

My lips curled. "That doesn't sound so stupid to me."

Nick nodded. "He couldn't believe I'd imply that *you'd* ever do such a thing. And that I'd dare to suggest such a thing. Even back then, Ryan was incredibly honorable. So, he hauled off and popped me in the mouth. Knocked a tooth loose. My little brother's got a fierce right hook. He's tough. The Army definitely knew what they were doing in recruiting Ryan."

"Oh, my. I'm sorry, Nick."

"Don't be. You understand why he was mad, don't you?"

"I think I do, but why don't you tell me so we're both on the same page?"

"He didn't want to believe that I could marry you one day. He didn't want to believe that *anyone* else would ever marry you. Ryan's always wanted you. Only you, Ellie. Don't ever forget that."

A tear streaked down my face. "I won't."

Chapter 21

~~♥~~

Thursday, December 21

After pulling the front door of the house closed and locking it, I carefully made my way down the walkway toward my blue Prius in the driveway. Mom had already left to get to the medical office for her last day of work until the New Year.

I halted my steps when I caught sight of a bright yellow ribbon wrapped around the thick trunk of the large, bare oak tree in the front yard.

The bitterly cold wind caught a few loose strands of my hair not fully tucked beneath my wool cap and whipped them about my face. I stared at the tree for a few long moments before I moved my gaze to the left. Then to the right. Then across the street. I pivoted in a slow circle, being careful not to slip. I felt rock salt under my feet.

Nick. Either he or Mark Sullivan must have come over last night or, more likely, early this morning, to coat the ground for me. They'd known Mom was staying with me overnight. Fresh tears stung my eyes, and I blinked hard to keep them at bay.

"Lord, bless those Sullivan men for watching over me."

At least one tree in each yard up and down the street had an identical yellow ribbon tied around its trunk. If I hadn't applied mascara this morning, I would rub my eyes like a kid to make sure I was focusing clearly. Who had done this? From what I knew, tying a yellow ribbon around a tree represented best wishes, hopes, and prayers for the safe return of a missing person, often someone in the military.

A small cry escaped, and I stuffed mitten-covered fingers in my mouth. Fibers from the glove stuck to my tongue. With a frown, I pulled my fingers from my mouth. *Eww.*

A blast of wind hit me, so strong it threatened to knock me off my feet. Tugging my purse strap tighter over my shoulder, I lowered my chin into my scarf and hurried to the car. One thing Ryan had done before leaving on this last tour of duty was install one of those wonderful systems to heat up my car while I was still inside the house. Such a wonderful invention.

After stopping my Prius at the end of the street, and then making another left onto Main Street, I caught sight of a small white car in my rearview mirror.

Wait a minute. That same car had been behind me for several minutes. Must be a coincidence. I pushed the thought aside until I pulled up in front of Nelson's Flower Shop a few minutes later. The shop was on the outskirts of town, which necessitated the need to drive in the first place.

I pushed open my car door and spied the other car parked on the opposite curb. Was I being followed? If so, I couldn't fathom why. After a moment's hesitation, I closed my car door and headed for the shop.

"Miss Franklin! Could we have a word with you, please?"

My brows lifted as I turned around. From across the street, a tall, lanky young man hurried toward me with a microphone in his hand. My eyes widened when I saw another man, this one older, burly, and wearing a heavy parka with a fur-trimmed hood that concealed most of his face. He carried a portable video camera, anchored on his right shoulder by one hand.

Should I run? Should I stay? I paused outside the front door of the flower shop. I could see Luther Nelson inside by the front window, hands on his hips.

My brain vaguely registered what the man with the microphone was saying. I think he mumbled the call letters for a Cleveland television station. "Would you mind if I ask you a few questions on camera?"

"About what, exactly?" I glanced from one man to the next, trying to comprehend what was happening.

"Your MIA boyfriend," the reporter said. "Sorry. I mean your fiancé."

I swallowed hard. He'd invaded my privacy, and yet he apologized for using the wrong word?

"I have no comment." In spite of the frigid temperatures, I felt my cheeks growing warm. Wrapping my hand around the brass knob on the front door, I prepared to bolt inside. Luther and Nancy Nelson have known me since I was a kid. I'd also tutored their daughter, Meredith, in high school English. Considering she'd aced her final exams, I felt reasonably confident they'd offer me asylum.

"You've heard nothing further about Private Sullivan's status?"

Status? That invasive question didn't deserve the decency of a reply. Although the reporter was only doing his job, I felt like I'd been ambushed. Ducking my head, I pushed open the door.

"Any idea what you're going to do now?"

Emotion clogged my throat, and my jaw muscles tightened. How *dare* he? I pulled the front door closed again while I gathered my thoughts. The man might not deserve a response, but for some reason, I felt compelled to give him one.

Lord, give me your strength.

In the event I'd be on the evening news, I needed to conduct myself with dignity although I'd rather spit in the guy's face. Stomp on his foot. Something that would convincingly convey my disgust. But no, that wouldn't be mature.

Squaring my shoulders, I looked straight at the blinking light on the camera. "I'm moving forward with my plans. If you'll please excuse me."

"What will you do if Ryan doesn't return before your wedding on Christmas Day?"

Without flinching, I moved my gaze to the reporter and drew upon what I remembered from every press conference I'd ever seen on television. Remain cool under pressure, give quick, succinct answers, and then depart.

Lord, give me your words.

"That's not a consideration at this point. I have every confidence that Ryan will return." I turned the brass knob and then hesitated. "Whether or not it's before or after Christmas doesn't matter. His safe return is all that matters."

I escaped into the store. Releasing my breath in a whoosh, my heart still pounding, I moved to stand beside Luther at the front window.

"They're fixin' to leave with their tails between their legs," Luther said, his eyes still trained on what was happening outside the front window.

"Are you okay, honey?"

I turned to see Nancy lumbering toward me as best she could with her bad knee. Putting one arm around my shoulders, she hugged me. "What was that all about?"

Luther grunted. "Nosy reporters."

"They wanted to know my plans if Ryan…" I couldn't finish the sentence. Starting to tremble, I wrapped my arms across my upper body. "I guess everybody in town knows about Ryan?"

"You know how word flies around Cade's Corner," Nancy said. "We love Ryan, and we love you. We're all praying. Now don't you pay any mind to those reporters." Nancy increased her hold on me. "They've got no business poking into your private life." She made a *tsk tsk* sound. "People don't respect others anymore. Way of the world."

"I hope you told them where they could put their camera," Luther said with a snort.

Nancy shook her head. "Luther…"

"Should have mentioned the name of Jesus," Luther continued, not skipping a beat. "Held up one hand and rebuked them." He chuckled. "That's a surefire way to get them runnin' in the opposite direction."

Nancy laughed. "Maybe you should have done that. Leave the girl alone."

"It's okay. I gave them a couple of statements, and I hope that'll be the end of it," I assured them. Time to focus on the reason I'd come to the flower shop. "Mom told me last night that Grandma Franklin is making the trip from Florida for the wedding after all. I'd like to order a corsage for her. Is it too late?"

"Of course not," Nancy said. "You come on over to the counter with me, Ellie. We'll get right on it and have the corsage ready at the same time as the other flowers."

"Thanks so much."

"You want a cup of coffee?" Luther passed by me and headed for the coffeemaker.

The percolating coffee's rich aroma filled the small shop. "It smells wonderful, but I'd better not." I focused on Nancy again as she opened a book on the counter. She flipped through the pages and stopped on a page with FRANKLIN-SULLIVAN WEDDING handwritten at the top. My eyes misted, and I turned my gaze away from the book.

Nancy's hand covered mine. "Sweetie, keep the faith. God brought you and Ryan together for a reason. Remember that. He's got His purpose."

"I know," I murmured. "I'm not mad at God." My shoulders heaved with the force of my sigh. "I'm mad by the idea of a war that calls our men overseas in the first place."

"The Good Book says there's always gonna be wars," Luther said.

"That's true," Nancy said, acknowledging her husband's comment. "People always want what belongs to somebody else. Always wantin' to start a fight." She patted my hand. "If they were all good people like you and Ryan, the world would be a whole lot better place."

"Thank you," I murmured. "Nancy, did you schedule your knee replacement surgery yet? Mom wanted me to ask so the ladies in the church can get a sign-up started to deliver meals to you and Luther whenever you say the word."

The older woman nodded. "Sure did. February 20th. I'll be at Shady Oaks for therapy for a few weeks, but that should give me enough time to heal before we go out to California for the big celebration for my sister's 50th wedding anniversary."

Luther shook his head. "Shady Oaks. I hate that name. Sounds like a cemetery."

Nancy waved her hand at him. "Drink your coffee, Luther. I'm not planning on kicking off anytime soon."

I hid my smile at their lively banter.

In the middle of discussing the corsage with Nancy a short time later, I darted a quick glance over my shoulder.

"Don't you worry none, Ellie." Luther gave me a smile above the rim of his coffee mug. "They're gone."

True enough, but for how long?

Chapter 22
~~♥~~

Maura and Nick sat across the table from me at Miss Charlotte's Tea House. When the small, quaint establishment first opened its doors for business six years ago, some of the men in town refused to be seen going into "that frilly place for ladies." With its eyelet curtains and linen tablecloths, it *did* look girly. Once word spread that they had some of the best food in town, the male citizens of Cade's Corner arrived in droves.

"All it takes is good food and the men will come." That's a direct quote (the owner, Charlotte Mayfield, is a close friend of Mom's).

Excellent food or not, I eyed my soup and sandwich with no appetite whatsoever. My stomach had been unsettled. Unlike a lot of people, I don't eat when I'm stressed. What little food I've managed to ingest since the news about Ryan broke has been tasteless, anyway, so what would be the point?

I fiddled with my spoon. "When I came out of the house this morning, I noticed a lot of the trees on our street had yellow ribbons tied around them."

Maura's eyes widened. "Really? I've heard about doing that for missing military men. That's sweet, don't you think?"

"Yes, but it was unexpected. It does my heart good to know that people care. Of course, that's based on the assumption the ribbons are actually *for* Ryan. And me, too, I suppose, to a lesser extent."

"Of course they are." Maura squeezed my hand on top of the table.

"There was a song about tying yellow ribbons around oak trees back in the 70s," Nick said. His appetite clearly wasn't affected as he chewed off a huge bite of his Reuben sandwich. After swallowing it down, he continued. "I heard the song was based on a true story. It was originally about a white handkerchief tied around the tree, but it was changed to a yellow ribbon because it made the song better. Resonated more with listeners."

Maura and I exchanged a knowing glance. Nick has always been a trivia guy.

Finishing her bite of Caesar salad, Maura blotted her mouth with her napkin. "That doesn't make sense. A handkerchief's not long enough to go around a tree."

Nick shrugged. "Maybe they were tied together, end-to-end. From what I know, the song was about a convict after his release from jail. He's on a bus and headed home. If the girl still wants him, she's supposed to tie a yellow ribbon around the old oak tree as a sign." Seeing our skeptical expressions, he raised his hand. "True story."

I cleared my throat. "Well, they *are* oak trees in our front yard. And, no offense, but I'd rather see a pretty yellow ribbon tied around them any day than a bunch of dirty old snot rags."

Maura almost spit out a bite of salad. "Sorry." She wiped her mouth again. "Wasn't expecting that."

"My dad had a hankie," I told them, fiddling with my spoon again. "So did Grandpa Franklin. I hated that thing. Without fail, he'd always pull it out at the dinner table and blow like I've never heard before or since. It was extremely disgusting." I smirked at Nick. "So, yeah. Yellow ribbons are much better all the way around. So to speak."

He managed a small grin. "Point taken."

"Glad to see you're maintaining your sense of humor," Maura said.

I pushed myself up in the chair. "Now that I think of it, I remember from my American History class that the yellow ribbon became a national symbol of freedom when the hostages were being held in Iran. So the practice *does* have a strong connection to the military."

Maura snapped her fingers. "That's right! I love sentimental traditions like that. After the Iran hostage situation, ribbons for all kinds of causes started popping up right and left." She focused on me. "Ellie, you need to eat.

Your soup's getting cold, and I know how much you love it. Come on now. Taste it."

My friend was right—the pumpkin squash soup was a late fall specialty at Miss Charlotte's Tea House, so popular they planned on extending it until after the New Year.

"I'm not sure I can." I picked up the package of saltines and tore off the cellophane wrapper. While Maura and Nick watched, I bit into the corner of a cracker. "Satisfied?"

Maura and Nick exchanged a glance. Why couldn't they just let me be?

"Okay, look at it this way," Maura said. I sensed an impending mini-lecture. "If you don't eat, you'll lose weight. You don't need to lose weight. If you do, your wedding dress will hang on you."

"As if *that's* the biggest problem I'm facing right now." We stared at one another for a long moment and then I picked up the spoon. "For the record, I'm not wallowing." Scooting the bowl closer, I took a sip. Oh, it tasted rich and scrumptious as it slid down my throat. Thankfully, it was still warm.

"We know," Nick said. "You're not the type to wallow."

"Neither will you see me gnashing my teeth and wailing. Totally not my style."

"Here. Have a bite of my grilled chicken." Maura pushed her bowl closer to me. "I love the seasoning Charlotte adds to the Caesar salad."

Obliging Maura, I stabbed a forkful of chicken and put it in my mouth while I pondered Nick's statement. I chewed the chicken, but it hardly registered on my taste buds. "What type am I, exactly?"

"For one thing, you're incredibly strong," Maura said.

"I'm not so sure about that." I frowned.

"At least you're getting a little sleep. That's something." Not that Nick would lie, but I'm well aware I have circles beneath my eyes and my skin is even paler than usual.

"Ellie, no one can tell you how you're supposed to act or what to say," Maura said. "We just have to take this thing one step at a time."

"Right." Nick nodded. "You're not alone. We're right beside you."

"Thanks. He's your brother, and forgive me for sounding selfish in my...*not* wallowing." I felt the need to divert the focus of our current conversation. "In other news from the morning, I was followed by a reporter and his cameraman. All the way from the house to Nelson's."

Both Nick and Maura sat up straighter at that comment.

"We've had a few calls at the house. Did he approach you?" Nick said, assuming his lawyer tone. In a strange way, I found it rather amusing.

"Yes." I took another slow sip of the soup. "He asked me some pointed questions before I escaped into the flower shop. I doubt I gave him anything worthy of a television spot."

"You're a celebrity now. I suppose it comes with the territory."

My frown deepened at Maura's observation. "I sure hope not. That's the last thing I need now—to share my angst with the public watching."

"I imagine your story with Ryan has captured the imagination of everyone."

I stared at Nick and returned my spoon to my bowl, my stomach suddenly sour. "I should think they'd come to your family first before they'd come looking for me. Explain your reasoning."

"Why come to us when they've got a potentially huge human interest story hanging in the balance?" Nick said. "Think about it, Ellie. It has all the makings of the kind of sentimental story people love, especially at this time of the year. Emotions are high, and people are home decorating the tree, making cookies, listening to the news..."

"Right." Maura's eyes lit. "Not to be insensitive, Ellie, but I doubt the reporters are going to go away anytime soon.

I'm not saying to embrace them, but you might have to lay low if you don't want to subject yourself to the intrusion." She nodded to Nick. "We'll be by your side as much as possible to provide a buffer zone."

Nick nodded his affirmation of Maura's words. "Of course we will."

I relaxed a bit. "I appreciate that. Thank you."

Seemingly undaunted, Maura continued. "The thing is, your story with Ryan has the childhood friendship that turned into love. Then you have the military man and separated sweetheart angle, the longing, the romance, the anticipation of the wedding, the—"

"The *will he or won't he come home* element? Come on, we all know it's true," I said when both Nick and Maura said nothing for a long moment. "Admit it. That's the real draw here, isn't it? My story with Ryan has all the makings of a happily-ever-after love story or a tragedy. A tragic love story that is." My lower lip trembled. "Star-crossed lovers without actually being lovers"—I wiped my eyes—"in the physical sense."

A tear escaped, and I wiped it with the back of my hand. As I looked over the lunch crowd with tear-blurred eyes, I tried to block out the expressions of pity on the faces of the other patrons. I know most of them. A few people have come to our table to tell me how sorry they are and to say they're praying for Ryan. Others simply give me "the look." I can't blame them, really. What can you say when something like this happens? It's awkward and uncomfortable.

"I think the Perchance to Dream aspect is another factor that could take this story even wider," Nick said. "The charity will appeal to a lot of people. It could bring you some more publicity."

"You and Ryan are very attractive, photogenic, and charismatic people. Together, you're an adorable couple. No wonder the media is all over this." Maura took another bite of her salad.

"It was only one guy following me. I hardly think this story is big enough to attract much more attention than here locally and in Cleveland." I crossed my arms and sat back in the chair, silently counting to ten. I needed to be dignified and put on a brave face even though my heart was cracking. Not breaking, mind you.

Lord, keep me calm.

"Guaranteed the newspapers in Ohio will pick up the story. Maybe even across the country," Nick said. "Anything's possible, and it's been a pretty slow news week otherwise."

I looked from Maura to Nick and back again. "I can't believe we're sitting here discussing Ryan's disappearance like this is some kind of public relations or marketing opportunity. I never wanted to be in the limelight, you know, and especially not for something like this." More tears sprang into my eyes. "I wish Ryan were here. He'd know what to do. You don't really think they'll run that so-called interview on the evening news, do you?"

"I'm sure they will." Nick leaned closer. "Do you remember which television station it was? Or what number was on the side of the camera?"

"No, but I'm sure Luther Nelson took note of it."

"Then I'll check with him," Nick said.

Maura brightened, apparently unfazed by my chastising words. "Here's an idea. How about we go over to the gym tonight? Physical exertion is always a good way to work out frustrations."

"That always works for me," Nick said. When he scrunched his napkin into the palm of his hand, that action reminded me of Ryan. At the moment, some random person could cough, and that would remind me of Ryan. It didn't take much. Human beings reminded me of Ryan. Any human would do.

But they weren't my Ryan, and they never would be Ryan. Only Ryan is Ryan. That statement might not be profound, but it was the truth.

I considered the idea of going to the gym. "Working out is a good idea. I think they're closing an hour earlier these days, so we should get there no later than seven."

"It's a date then." Maura sounded pleased. "Nick, you want to come?"

"I might be persuaded." He gave me a pointed look. "If you eat some more soup."

"Taskmaster." But I picked up my spoon and did as he asked.

Chapter 23

~~♥~~

After two hours of the most strenuous workout of my life, I collapsed on my sofa later that evening. I propped my bare feet on the coffee table, and in so doing, violated my personal rule against committing such a heinous act. Glancing at the chipped polish on my toes, I remembered my long-standing appointment tomorrow morning for a full manicure and pedicure. I'm supposed to meet Kara and Staci at the salon promptly at 10 a.m.

"Here you go." Maura handed me a bowl of microwave popcorn and then plopped down beside me. "This occasion definitely calls for decadent movie theater butter flavor."

"Wonderful. Perfect for the pony show. Or the circus. Bring on the clowns." I didn't like the sarcasm in my tone, but I couldn't help it. "I can't believe all the people who left me voice mail messages about this two-minute segment on the news tonight."

"How'd they know? Was it on the earlier newscast?'

"Bingo. I'm not sure I can even watch it. After all"—I made air quotes with my fingers—"I was there. Not sure I want, or need, to go through it again."

"Stop worrying. I'm sure you did great," Maura said, patting my arm, an action that made me irrationally mad although she had the best of intentions. "You're very good under pressure, Ellie. From what I've heard, you always have been."

I snorted. "That's what *you* think. You haven't seen my hidden rubber room."

Maura shook her head and gave me a quick hug.

"You can say that again." Nick came into the room and took the armchair, Ryan's favorite chair. "I heard those last comments. Maura's right. You're holding up great."

I shot him a skeptical glance.

"What?" He gestured to the popcorn bowl and grabbed a handful when Maura passed it to him. "It's true. Not many people would be as calm as you. Mom and Dad told me you've called them at least five or six times today. I know you ran over to see Cora Brown. You and Maura are helping to keep me calm. You've exhibited true grace under pressure. That's a rare gift."

"Maybe you should be the reporter since you seem to know what I've been doing all day." I stared at Nick. "And are you on meds? In my entire life, I don't think I've heard that much come out of your mouth in one sitting."

He and Maura both grinned. "Stick around," Nick said, popping more popcorn into his mouth. "I figure God's got this one, Sass."

"That does it." I shifted my position. "You're on meds. You've never *ever* called me Sass. That privilege is reserved for your little brother."

"Duly noted. My apologies."

"You're fine." I gave him a hint of a grin. It felt good.

"Nick, you're right that God has this one," I said. "I know He's carrying me through this storm. I hope your high opinion of me still holds after you see this news segment, though. Human interest feature or whatever they're calling it," I groused. "Like I said, I never asked for this media thing, and I hope and pray this will be the end of it."

I started to rise from the sofa, but Maura caught me by the arm and pulled me back down beside her. "Sit," she ordered.

"This whole thing is so weird." I popped a few kernels in my mouth just to have something to do. "I'm in limbo here days before my wedding. *Our* wedding," I corrected. "Thanks for being here with me." I glanced from Maura to Nick and then back again with tears in my eyes.

Nick got up from the armchair and came to sit on the other side of me. "We're here for you, honey."

"Don't call me…honey," I sputtered. "I mean, I like it, but"—I waved one hand in the air—"it gets me all emotional. More than I already am. I feel like a basket case, as it is."

I sniffled and reached for my ever-present tissue tucked into the pocket of my workout pants. Opening out the tissue, I dabbed it beneath my eyes. "Mom offered to come and stay the night or to have me stay at the house. But I wanted to stay here. This is my home now."

I glanced around the small living room. Photographs and a few paintings Ryan and I had picked out together leaned against one wall, ready to be hung. "I want Ryan to help choose where to hang the pictures. I want him to feel the awesome thread count on the sheets. I want to kiss him under the mistletoe." I gestured to the evergreen hanging above the doorway to the kitchen.

On either side of me, my two best friends put their arms around me.

"We love you, Ellie." Maura tightened her hold and gave me a quick hug.

"Always." Nick kissed the top of my head.

"Wait, the news is starting," Maura said. "Where's that remote? I need to turn up the volume."

"Got it." Nick adjusted the sound and then took another handful of popcorn before putting the remote on the side table out of my reach. Whether that was intentional or not, I'd adopted a quiet resignation about the whole thing.

Feeling somewhat abandoned, I sniffled again and prepared to listen. Maura and Nick both kept one arm around me as the newscast began. "You're holding hands behind me on the back of the sofa, aren't you?"

"Well, yeah," Nick admitted.

"For crying out loud." I jumped off the sofa and moved to Ryan's armchair. "It's all yours. Move closer together, you two. I'm not your chaperone. I'm all for your relationship. You know that." I laughed a little and wiped the tissue under my runny nose. Might as well stuff it in a nostril and leave it there. "Fair warning: if you don't obey, I'm going to turn on some Barry White and make you slow dance."

Maura laughed and Nick shook his head. If I wasn't mistaken, I made the esteemed Nicolas Randall Sullivan, Esquire blush. That didn't happen often.

"All right. If you insist," Nick said. He moved closer to Maura, and she cast a wary glance in my direction.

"I'm done. It's up to the two of you from this point on." I popped more popcorn kernels in my mouth. "You kids have fun." Apparently flippancy is my defense mechanism against breaking down in a crying fit.

"Stay tuned for our next story tonight," the male anchor announced ten minutes into the newscast. "A bride-to-be in Cade's Corner got the shock of her life a few days ago when word came from the U.S. Army that her fiancé is missing after the helicopter he was in with six other members of his team disappeared from radar while on a specialized mission in Afghanistan. That's our next story after the commercial break. You won't want to miss this one, folks. We'll be back in two minutes."

I groaned. "I felt sure they'd stick the segment at the end of the broadcast when a lot of people would have already gone to bed."

"This is good," Nick said. "The more people who know about your story, the more people you'll have praying for you and Ryan."

"That's a very good point you make, Counselor. I hadn't thought of it that way."

Another ten minutes later, I breathed a sigh of relief. The segment wasn't as bad as I'd feared. I couldn't care less how I looked or came across on camera (although I'd sounded surprisingly articulate and my cheeks were flushed from the cold so I didn't have a horrible pallor). It was more the whole sensationalized aspect that bothered me considering the man I love is missing.

"Well, I guess that's that," I said. "I'm glad they mentioned Perchance to Dream, anyway. Ryan will be gratified when he hears his chopper's disappearance has focused more attention on our project."

"That's the spirit!" Nick said. He rose from the sofa. "Well, I need to take off. I'm meeting the groomsmen tomorrow morning at the tux shop for the final fitting."

"What about..." My voice trailed. I blinked away more tears. I'd somehow managed to avoid blubbering like an idiot this long, and I was determined not to do so now.

"Pastor Jon is the same size as Ryan and nearly the same height, give or take an inch. He can stand in, if needed, although I don't think that'll be necessary." Nick grabbed his coat where he'd left it draped over a dining room chair. "Unless we hear otherwise, I say we keep doing everything as planned."

"I agree." I rose from the sofa and crossed the room. "Nick, you're the best man Ryan could ever have. The best man *we* could ever have. The best brother. Just...thank you." My voice broke, and I moved my arms around him. "I love you."

"You're going to get through this, Ellie." I couldn't miss how his strong voice wavered. "We'll all keep praying, and you know where to reach me if you need me. Call anytime."

"I will. Thanks again. Call if you hear anything at all. I doubt I'll be sleeping."

"You've got it. Promise." Nick crossed the room and gave Maura a quick kiss on the cheek.

"If that quick peck was for my benefit, I can go into the kitchen so you can give each other a proper good night," I suggested. "I won't be offended, and I'd much rather you not hide your affection."

I headed into the kitchen. "Wait a second." When I turned around, Maura was already in Nick's arms. "You know what? I'll be fine. Nick, take her home now. Please. That's an order."

"Are you sure that's what you want?" Maura said. "I'll stay however long you need."

"Yes, it's what I want. Just don't ask me again or I might cave." I gave her a tremulous smile. "Not that you're not a great support system, but I need to spend quality time with the Lord tonight. I feel as though I've neglected Him, and He's the one I need to lean on the most right now."

Five minutes later, after I'd given them repeated assurances that I'd be okay, Nick put his arm around Maura, and they departed. Shivering from the brisk night air, I quickly closed the front door and leaned against it.

The idea of my two closest friends falling in love gives me reassurance that life goes on. We all have our separate lives to live. Each person, each day, each special moment, should be treasured. Perhaps I've turned more philosophical because of recent events. I've known these things all along, but those truths suddenly resonate with much more poignancy.

And now, the man I love is missing, and I'm faced with the reality that I may never see him again this side of Heaven.

I shook my head to clear those thoughts and marched straight down the hall to the bedroom.

"Here I come, Lord. It's time to pray."

Chapter 24

~~♥~~

I picked up my well-worn Bible from the nightstand and crawled under the covers. I smiled as I ran my finger over the front, my embossed name now so faint I could barely see it anymore. This Bible, full of hope and promises from the Lord, is one of the most precious possessions I own.

My mind traveled back in time to that summer day when I'd been given this Bible. Ryan found me on our back patio, reading selections from the list for Honors English my senior year of high school.

"Hi, Sass. What are you reading?"

I laid the book aside and tried to disguise the fact that Ryan's appearance sent a thousand butterflies fluttering about in my belly. "Poetry that's so depressing I can understand why the poet stuck her head in an oven."

Ryan's brow creased as he settled beside me on the cushioned bench. "Seriously? That bad?"

"Well, something in her life must have been that bad. Her poetry's good, but it's so sad it makes me want to weep buckets. It's on the required list for English, or I wouldn't be reading it. Trust me."

"Here. I got something for you." Ryan handed over a square package wrapped in sailboat paper. It was obviously a book of some kind. A rather heavy book.

"That's the only wrapping paper I could find in the house," he said. "Mom used it for my dad's Father's Day gift. Sorry it doesn't have flowers and stuff all over it."

"That doesn't matter. What's the occasion?" I found it incredibly sweet that Ryan had brought me a gift, much less wrapped it himself.

"I didn't get you anything for your birthday this year. Sorry about that."

"Not a problem. I didn't get one for you either."

When his gaze skimmed over me, lingering on my tanned legs, I felt my cheeks flush. Until that moment, it hadn't occurred to me that I was dressed in ratty old shorts and a faded tank top. I moved my fingers to the hem of the shorts and started to pull them down. "Maybe I should go change."

"You're fine. You look really…pretty."

"Thanks, but maybe you shouldn't say something like that considering you broke up with me three weeks ago. And now you're staring at my legs." I turned my head so he couldn't see how much I'd been hurting since that miserable day when he'd approached me at my locker. He made sure to do the dirty deed in a public place. It was good Ryan didn't hear the things I spouted about him during my rant once the shock wore off. By the grace of God, I was home alone with only the four walls of my bedroom to absorb my nasty comments and to hear me cry.

"That's kind of why I'm here. I hope you're still my friend." Ryan's comment brought me back to the present. "You always have been and always will be. Ellie, would you at least look at me?" Those incredible blue eyes of his zoomed in on me, pinning me down so that I could barely breathe.

He waited until I did as he asked, and then he gestured to the gift in my lap. "First things first. Open it, please."

"Okay." My interest piqued by his comment, I began to purposely remove the wrapping from one end of the package with painstaking care.

"Just rip it already." Ryan laughed. "I know I did a horrible job, and you can't tell me you're going to save that paper. You're just trying to torture me."

"Why wouldn't I keep the paper? Maybe I will." I pointed to the paper. "The sailboats are pretty, and you know how I've always loved lighthouses." I shot him a grin. "I'm not trying to torture you, but I'm glad to know it's working."

In one quick action, Ryan reached across me and tore the paper off the top. His movements carried the combined scent of freshly mown grass, sweat, and masculine-scented soap—an oddly intoxicating combination.

I stared at the Bible peeking out at me beneath the shredded paper. "You got me a Bible?"

"I know you already have one, but you're getting a little old for it, don't you think?"

I knew what he meant. I'd been carrying my tattered pink Bible with daisies since the eighth grade. Ryan didn't need to know that I'd doodled Ellie ♥ Ryan in some of the Old Testament chapters during moments of boredom in Sunday school. A few New Testament books, too.

"I read my Bible and take it to heart, and that's the main—"

"You know what I mean. Time to grow up, Ellie."

I balked. "Excuse me? You give me a Bible and then insult me?"

"Sorry. I'm not doing this right." Rubbing his hand over his forehead, Ryan rose to his feet and started to pace in front of me.

For once, I held my tongue, knowing he'd tell me when he was good and ready. If I had to sit here all day, I would. Mom wouldn't allow me to starve. She'd eventually take pity on me and bring some food.

"Look, here's the thing." He stopped his pacing and crouched in front of me. "Give me your hands, please."

I gave them to him. I couldn't wait to hear what would come out of his mouth next.

His eyes held mine captive all over again. "Ellie, I want us to sit in church every Sunday. Together." He tore the remainder of the paper away from the Bible and watched as I thumbed through it with a certain measure of awe and reverence.

"You bought a...study Bible for couples?" Things were starting to make sense in spite of the fact I sounded somewhat like an imbecile with my questions.

"Yes. I want us to study this Bible together. God knows what's in our hearts. I should never have told you we should break up. I thought I wanted to go out with Amber. I made a stupid mistake, and I hope you can forgive me."

"You're young and misguided, so yes, I can forgive you, Ryan. But I *should* make you sweat a little." When Ryan's eyes widened, and he looked stricken, I grinned to soften my words. Boys could be so clueless sometimes. At other times, they could be surprisingly insightful. The problem was, I never could tell with Ryan. In some ways, that made him fascinating. I'm sure he'd say the same about me.

"You wanted to go out with Amber," I said. "I know that. You can at least be honest with me." Amber had been after Ryan for months. Last I heard, she was going to Ohio State, too. The Cleveland extension of the university, same as Ryan. When I'd heard that, it sent the stake deeper into my heart. I'd had visions of Ryan's wedding to Amber. In a few years, all their adorable kiddos would fill an entire pew in church. Of course, by that time I'd be off in Africa, living in a hut and teaching missionary kids.

"Ellie, listen to me." With gentle fingers, Ryan guided my chin back toward him. He waited until I lifted my gaze to meet his. My stomach was doing somersaults, but I inhaled a deep breath and prepared to listen.

"The last couple of times I've gone out with Amber, all I could think about was that time our families went sailing on the lake together."

My eyes widened with surprise. "You were on a date with Amber thinking about something that happened a few years ago? I'm surprised you even remember. You said like twenty words to me that day and then ignored me."

"You were fourteen," he said. "We were swimming in the lake, and I noticed for the first time that you weren't a little girl anymore. And I wasn't a little boy. I didn't mean to ignore you that day, but I couldn't stop staring at you. It's like it hit me full force—*bam!*—that you'd grown up. And you weren't the little girl down the street I used to tease." His eyes softened. "You were this gorgeous girl that I suddenly couldn't get out of my mind. But you were way too young to date. My parents wouldn't even let *me* date yet."

"Wow," I murmured. "I had no idea. Ryan, I know I'm not as pretty as Carli or Amber or half the girls in school."

"No, you're not." When he heard my small gasp, Ryan cupped his warm hands on either side of my face, cradling it. "Ellie, you're more beautiful than all of them put together."

"You're just saying that because you want to get back together." I pulled back, and he released his hold on me. "Did you break up with Amber?"

I caught his quick grin before Ryan dropped onto the patio, crossed his legs, and then propped his chin on his hands. "What's my favorite color?"

"Fire engine red. Is this a test?"

"Maybe." He smiled. "Favorite food?"

"Rodeo Burger at The Soda Shoppe. With extra barbecue sauce and two onion rings on top."

"You're batting a thousand," he said. "Let's move to the next category. Favorite shirt?"

It was my turn to laugh. "Too easy. Your old Cavaliers T-shirt that's a size too small and emphasizes your muscles." My cheeks grew heated with that admission. "And it has a fairly good-sized hole right...here." I pointed to a spot just below my right arm.

Ryan stared at me for a long moment.

"What?" I squirmed on the bench. "I kid you not. Check your T-shirt."

He grinned. "I know about the hole. You're right, but I can't throw it away."

"I'll do it for you." I giggled when he raised one brow. "Matter of fact, I'll get you a brand new T-shirt as a belated birthday gift."

"That might work. In answer to your question, I broke up with Amber a couple of days ago. When we were going out, we never talked about anything important. She goes to church, but Amber doesn't know Jesus the way you do. She doesn't know what I like to eat, my favorite restaurant, things like that. I know practically nothing about her. All she cares about is how she looks and that what her date wears doesn't clash with her outfit."

"Well, fashion *is* a big deal to some girls." My nerves had started to take over, but I could tell he was working up to something important.

Surprising me, Ryan jumped to his feet. Hauling me off the bench, he easily circled his arms around me as if it was second nature. Then he tightened his hold on my waist like he'd never let me go. I knew he had to feel how fast my pulse was racing.

"The thing is, when I was out with Amber, all I could think about was you, Ellie. You might only be seventeen, but you want to know what I see when I look at you?"

"I'm not sure I—?"

"That was a rhetorical question," he said. "I see the girl I've known my whole life. The girl I teased and probably made miserable more than a few times."

I nodded. Miserable might be pushing it, although mad would be accurate.

"The girl I've tried to protect."

Again, I nodded. He'd protected me on several occasions. Sometimes it was as simple as making sure I arrived home safely. Or giving me his umbrella so I wouldn't get wet at the risk of getting soaked. Ryan is my hero even though I've never told him as much. Never said it out loud in his presence.

"The girl who makes me laugh." Ryan moved his hand to the side of my face, lightly caressing the line of my jaw. "You watched over me and called for help when I had the bike accident and broke my leg."

"Anyone would have done the same thing."

"That's not true. The lady who hit me didn't know what to do, Ellie. You'd barely turned thirteen, but you took charge. You're one of the smartest people I know. You make me laugh. You're fiery and passionate, especially when you care about someone. You're the only girl who knows me well enough to say things that hurt me because deep down, I know you're right."

I swallowed. "You'll meet other girls. You might get tired of me. I'm familiar, I'm comfortable, and I'm your friend." I tried to pull away, but Ryan captured both my hands.

I lifted my chin to meet his gaze directly. "I won't let you break my heart."

He took my hand and positioned it over his heart. "Feel that?"

Oh, I did. Solid and steady. "Yes. You're very healthy."

"That's for you, baby. Ellie, my pulse is racing right now, and I feel a little crazy because I want to kiss you so bad it hurts. Look, I can't promise never to make you cry, but I promise I'll never break your heart."

My jaw went slack. "You called me *baby.*"

"I did. Does it bother you?"

"No." I smiled. "I kind of like it, coming from you."

He tucked a long dark strand of hair behind my ear. "Your favorite color is purple. Buttercup yellow is a close second. You love the pepperoni and mushroom pizza at Martinelli's with an ice cold root beer in a glass mug. Your favorite shirt is that pretty pink one that makes your eyes look incredible with little gold flecks dancing in them." He chuckled. "I'm not very good at saying romantic things."

"You're doing fine. Keep going."

"I don't want to kiss someone just because she's pretty, or it feels good, and I like it. I want to kiss someone who means the world to me. The girl I've loved all these years."

I gasped and planted my hands on Ryan's chest. "You *love* me?" If only that question hadn't come out as an embarrassingly high-pitched squeak.

In answer, Ryan Joseph Sullivan lowered his head and caressed my lips with his. "I do, Ellie." Those blue eyes—clear and pure as the summer day—wouldn't lie.

His kiss proved we weren't fourteen and fifteen anymore. The boy has been blessed with an amazing talent for kissing. I'm certain our lips were made for each other.

"I'm saving all my kisses for you," he whispered.

I swooned and lost my footing for a moment, but Ryan steadied me. "As long as you don't put any more frogs down my shirt."

He laughed. "I'm sorry for that and all the other things I've done to make you mad."

I sighed with contentment. "Yeah, well, you already apologized, so get over it. And that frog was pretty slimy, but I survived. For the record, I haven't gone nuts and kissed any other guys during your period of temporary insanity. Not that you asked, and not that I feel compelled to tell you. I just thought you should know. So"—I smiled and winked—"I guess that means that I've saved all my kisses for you."

"Thanks." Ryan's smile reached his eyes. "And why is that?"

"Because I kind of love you back."

He kissed me then. And, all over again, I knew I'd found my home.

Chapter 25

~~♥~~

A tear fell on the pages of my Bible on my lap. Propping myself higher in my bed, I focused on the page turned to the third chapter of Ecclesiastes.

There is an appointed time for everything.
And there is a time for every event under heaven—
A time to give birth and a time to die;
A time to plant and a time to uproot what is planted.
A time to kill and a time to heal;
A time to tear down and a time to build up.
A time to weep and a time to laugh;
A time to mourn and a time to dance.
A time to throw stones and a time to gather stones;
A time to embrace and a time to shun embracing.
A time to search and a time to give up as lost;
A time to keep and a time to throw away.
A time to tear apart and a time to sew together;
A time to be silent and a time to speak.

"A time to love and a time to hate; A time for war and a time for peace." I pondered the verse as I read it aloud in the quiet of the bedroom. I moved my finger down a few verses. "He has made everything appropriate in its time."

"Lord, I know you'll always take care of me"—I swallowed a sob—"but you know how much I love Ryan. Thank you for the time you've given me with him all these years. Call me selfish, but I want to have babies with him, sit next to him on our pew at church every Sunday, cook him anniversary dinners, go on fabulous vacations together, watch our kids grow old."

I stopped and wiped away my tears. "So many things I want to share with him. The intimacy of a physical relationship, bringing our babies into the world—Ryan beside me, holding my hand, telling me it's worth it—and all the things a husband and wife are supposed to experience together. I know it won't be easy, Lord, but I just want to do them with Ryan."

Closing my Bible with another small sob, I placed the Bible on the nightstand. "In the end, I know Ryan belongs to you more than he belongs to me."

This wouldn't do. I shoved back the covers and slid down to my knees by the side of the bed. Clasping my hands together as I used to do as a small child, I lowered my head and closed my eyes.

"Heavenly Father, I know you hear my prayer. You know my heart. You know my motivations are pure. In faith, I'm asking for a sign from you that Ryan's okay. Or that he's not. That's all I need."

More tears slipped down my cheeks. "If you need him for your purpose in Heaven, then so be it. You know best, and I'm sure"—I sniffled and blinked away more tears—"you need Ryan for a very good reason." I wiped the moisture from my cheeks with my palms, shifted on my knees, and then resumed my prayer.

"Lord, if you *do* have Ryan in Heaven with you now, please put your arms around him. Tell him how much I miss him. Most importantly, please tell Ryan how very much I *love* him. I always have," I whispered. "And I always will."

Chapter 26

~~♥~~

Friday, December 22

"You need to scoot your pale self into the tanning booth," Staci scolded me in her best schoolteacher voice late the next morning. She waved her freshly manicured hand toward the back of Joelle's Spa and Salon.

When I stared at Staci with a blank expression, Kara took over with the big sister patronizing. "Ellie, I think you should consider going to Hawaii anyway. But with your fair skin, if you go without preparing for that hot sun, you're going to fry."

Lovely image. I prayed for the grace not to snap at my oldest sister. Kara has always been blunt, a fact I have appreciated and disliked in equal measure through the years.

I narrowed my eyes. "Maybe you're right, but I have my 1,000 SPF sunblock and a ridiculously oversized sun hat."

Staci winked. "I doubt you and Ryan will see much of the outdoors."

I ignored that comment from the sister who'd given me lingerie for a shower gift that defined the meaning of *unmentionables*. The mere thought of that flimsy little piece of fabric made my cheeks flame, especially since Ryan's mom had been seated next to me when I'd pulled it out of the box.

"Keep Ryan happy in the *boudoir*, and all will be well," Staci said loud enough for everyone at the shower—held at the church, no less—to hear. The whispers and twittering had zoomed around the room at warp speed after that statement. I heard Mom trying to explain Staci's comment to hard-of-hearing Paulette King as I opened the next gift of a flannel, button-up-to-the neck nightgown from a never-married woman who lived with her parents and a collection of porcelain cats.

"Kara, what do you mean by saying I should go to Hawaii 'anyway?'"

My eldest sister cleared her throat. "Honey, a tropical island can soothe your heart in a way not much else can, considering the circumstances. What's the difference in whether or not you think about things either here or there?"

"No," I said. "I need to be here for whatever happens." I would not under any circumstances mention the thought of planning a funeral, but the longer Ryan was missing, the more those thoughts would loom as an eventual possibility.

While I silently thanked my sisters for not using words like sulk, mope, stew, or—Heaven forbid—grieve, I wasn't in the best frame of mind. These two women had a unique talent for setting my nerves on edge without the added circumstances of Ryan's *situation*, for lack of a better word. It was difficult to know what to call it. Only the Lord held the answers at the moment. I just had to try and be patient and wait for His timing. Mom used to have a sign hanging above the kitchen sink that read, GOD GRANT ME PATIENCE, BUT HURRY! I could identify.

"I asked God to give me a sign."

Staci snapped her gaze to mine. "What do you mean? Like a burning bush or something?" She shook her head. "God doesn't give people signs anymore, does He?"

"Why not?" I couldn't help my smile. "Relax, Staci. I've never asked Him for a sign before." Why did I feel the need to defend myself? "I'm not testing Him, or demanding anything of Him. It's more reassurance that Ryan's okay."

"'And all things you ask in prayer, believing, you will receive,'" Kara quoted from the Book of Matthew.

"I think the key word in that verse is *believing*." I watched as the salon technician lifted my right foot from where it'd been soaking in paraffin wax.

"Agreed," Staci said. "I admire your optimism, Ellie."

Kara spoke again. "Remember when Karen Hicks saw that hummingbird land right outside her kitchen window? She interpreted it as a sign that her daughter would be okay."

"Karen is also one egg short of a dozen." Staci grunted. "Better make that a couple of eggs."

Kara half-laughed, half-scoffed. "That's an unkind thing to say. Poor Karen was in that car accident a few years ago…"

I tuned out my sisters' chatter and willed the phone in the pocket of my jeans to ring.

"Why isn't Maura here? Wasn't she supposed to join us?" Kara eyed her fresh nail polish, a muted shade of cranberry that would coordinate nicely with the gowns she, Staci, and Maura would wear in the wedding.

"She was planning on it," I said. "She's helping Nick file a new probate with the court today. After that, she'll be freed up until after the wedding."

Staci arched her brows. "Speaking of Maura and Nick, I hear they were getting pretty cozy in the corner booth at that new deli in town the other day." She snapped her fingers. "What's the name? It's right on the tip of my tongue."

"Petrowich's Deli. And they're dating." My announcement made both my sisters sit up straighter. The woman working on Kara's feet shot her a frown. "If she can get away, Maura's meeting us for lunch at The Soda Shoppe. You can ask her your questions then." Maybe it would take the attention away from me and give me another welcome focus.

I handed the bottle of pale blue polish to the nail technician. The color might be a bit untraditional, especially for a Christmas wedding, but I'd decided that's what I wanted. The shade was soft and classy with a hint of silver sparkles. Call it my personal stamp of individuality. In the back of my mind, I remembered that Ryan told me once he thought the pastel blue color was sexy, especially on my toes. Given what was happening now, not even my outspoken siblings would dare to defy me. As I watched her start to paint my nails, I thought how gorgeous the color would look with Hawaiian sand sifting through my toes.

A bright flash outside the large front window startled me. I turned my head toward the sidewalk outside and was almost blinded by another flash. I shielded my face with my forearm. Too late. They'd already snapped their photos. I could see the headlines now: BRIDE WHO WON'T GIVE UP GETS PRE-WEDDING PEDICURE. No, that would be too boring, not sensational enough. Something like BRAVE BRIDE SPITS IN THE FACE OF DESPAIR. Wow. I'm in advertising, and even *I* wouldn't read an article with a headline like that. Times are tough, and I'm obviously off my game.

"Reporters." Marcella, the manager of the spa, flew across the room and pulled down the window shade with an emphatic tug. "Nosy people! Why can't they mind their own business?"

"I'm sorry, Marcella."

Marcella waved her hand as if dismissing my comment. "I don't care. It's you I'm worried about, sweetie."

"Why would reporters want to—?" When Staci gave her a knowing look, Kara stared at me. "They're following you around, Ellie?"

I breathed out a sigh. "That would seem to be the case."

Staci perked up again. "It's like you're a real celebrity or something. That's pretty awesome."

Kara grunted. "Staci, a little more sensitivity might be nice. Need I remind you that poor Ellie's fiancé is missing? Her misfortune is no reason to get excited."

"Your story has captured the imagination of everyone in the Cleveland area, that's for sure," Marcella said. She'd moved across the room and stood over the shoulder of the woman painting my nails. I silently willed Marcella to back off since the nail technician's hand shook, no doubt from nerves.

"Marcella, can I please get a bottle of flavored mineral water? Any flavor. I'll pay you."

"Sure, but I won't take payment from the bride-to-be." When Marcella walked into the other room, the woman at my feet gave me a grateful smile.

"How did things go this season with Perchance to Dream?" Kara asked next.

Grateful for the change of topic, I told them some of the highlights. Both Kara and Staci told me they were proud of me. Maybe they were being extra nice to me because of circumstances, but I enjoyed the camaraderie. When they weren't busy being bossy, my sisters could be quite caring and compassionate. Marriage and motherhood have softened them both in some ways.

My tension eased as we talked quietly together while waiting for our manicures and pedicures to dry. They told me about the latest adventures of my nieces and nephew.

"We're still getting together in January, right?" I took a sip of the mineral water Marcella brought to me.

Staci laughed. "Of course, we'll be there. But we also insist on cooking."

"Hey, I'm getting a lot better at this cooking thing," I protested. "Ryan is going to be amazed by how domestic I am."

Kara gave me a nod of approval. "Mom said you're becoming a master with the chicken dishes. Thanks for watching over her, by the way. I know the holidays are especially rough for her."

"Welcome, but I think Mom can take care of herself." Best not to share that Mom is now more or less dating her boss (she's also specifically mentioned she hasn't yet told Kara and Staci). Unless Mom shocks me in the next day or so and announces her intentions to bring Dr. Phillip to the wedding. I don't believe she will; she confided that she didn't want to upstage my special day. I told her to do whatever her heart desires, but she said she'd prefer to honor Dad's memory and not bring someone else. I guess there are several ways to look at it, but I respect her decision either way. She needed time after Dad's death, but it's been six years. I've seen a hint of a twinkle in her eye, and it's quite nice.

"I can help you with the beef recipes, if you want," Kara said, interrupting my thoughts.

Where was Kara when I was struggling with beef bourguignon a few weeks ago? Didn't matter. She was a great cook. I gave her my best smile. "You're on. I would appreciate your expertise."

"I thought Mom would join us here at the spa." Staci lifted her foot and turned it first one way and then the other to admire her fresh pedicure.

"She told me she wanted us to have this time together. She's coming in later with Maura."

Kara blew on her fingernails as if that would speed the drying time. "We're here for you. Ryan's coming back. We're moving forward with all the plans, including the rehearsal on Sunday night at the church and…everything else."

"Thank you," I said. I appreciated Kara's words more than she could know. "I know it might seem like a pipe dream, especially now, and the more time that passes—"

"The more time that passes, then the closer it is to Ryan's return," Staci said.

I looked over at Staci. If we didn't have freshly painted nails, I would have clasped her hand in mine. Kara's, as well.

I've never loved my sisters more.

"I'm glad you're my family," I told them. I might not always feel that way, but deep down, we share a deep, abiding love.

We'd get through this together.

You are not alone, child.

I love those sweet whispers in my heart, giving me incredible comfort.

I am with you always.

Oh, how glad I am about that.

Chapter 27

~~♥~~

Maura made a welcome appearance at The Soda Shoppe an hour later as I sat with Kara and Staci. Not that it had been awkward. Both of my sisters could talk to a wall and be perfectly okay with the lack of response. Today I appreciated that particular quality.

"Hey," I said as Maura slid into the chair beside me. "Did you get the probate filed?"

"Sure did. By the way, Marion Sanders wanted me to tell you she's got her whole prayer circle, knitting circle, and every other circle she's involved with, praying for you and Ryan."

"Thanks. That's a whole lot of circles."

Lisa, one of The Soda Shoppe's long-standing servers, came over to take Maura's order and asked me if I wanted something else to eat. "I'll take a carryout box, please." I caught Maura's look. "I'll eat when I hear that Ryan's okay. Until then, I can't."

Thankfully, neither of my sisters nor Maura said anything. Maura slipped her hand over mine and squeezed.

"You should have seen the reporters who followed us from Joelle's on the way here," Staci told Maura. The latter's brows raised, and she bumped my knee beneath the table.

I waved my hand. "Nothing worth discussing, and I didn't talk to them."

To keep up appearances as much as anything else, I joined in the discussion of final wedding details. That odd sensation came over me again—as though I was peering in from the outside, a physical participant without being fully involved in what was happening around me. I'm quite sure a lack of sleep had a bit to do with that odd feeling.

Maura asked for the ketchup and then discovered the bottle on the table was empty. The sound when she squeezed the bottle made a little boy laugh. He sat with a woman,

175

whom I assumed was his mother, at a table close to the front counter. I knew the family was new in town, but I hadn't met them yet.

Needing something to do—and to escape Staci's not-so-subtle suggestions for my wedding night etiquette—I hopped up from my chair so fast the chair grated against the tile floor. I took my sweet time walking to the counter with the empty ketchup bottle. As I waited for the bottle to be refilled, I drummed my fingers on the counter before remembering I shouldn't do that. I needed to protect my fresh manicure.

Behind me, I heard Lisa taking the lunch order from the little boy and the woman with him.

"Honey, what sounds good to you today? They have hot dogs, grilled cheese, chicken tenders."

After a short pause, I heard a sweet little voice ask, "Do you have fried egg sandwiches?"

I froze. Blood rushed to my head. Blinking hard a few times, I focused on the illuminated retro clock behind the counter while I listened to what was being said at the table behind me. My pulse started to race, and my palms suddenly felt clammy.

Eavesdropping or not, I *had* to know.

"You know, we used to have a little boy come in and ask for those all the time, too. I'm sure I can convince the cook to make one for you. How do you like the eggs cooked?"

"So the inside's not all gross and runny."

"Over hard, then. Anything else on it?"

"Cheese. American and not that stinky Swiss stuff with holes." Hearing that comment, I slapped my hand over my mouth. Ryan hates Swiss cheese.

"Maybe a little mayonnaise, too?" That question came from the woman.

I hope I thanked Tom Larkin, the owner of The Soda Shoppe, after he handed me the full ketchup bottle. I think I did. I gave the little boy a big smile as I passed by their table and stumbled back to my chair. Dropping into it, I sat as though in a daze.

"What's up? Are you okay?" Maura asked while Staci and Kara gave me curious looks.

I burst into tears.

Maura grabbed a handful of napkins from the dispenser on the table and handed them to me.

"Honey, it'll be okay," Kara said as both she and Staci got up and came behind my chair, one on either side of me. They put their arms around me, hugging me tight while Maura put her hand on my arm.

"Did you get a phone call or something?" Maura asked.

"No," I said, through more tears. I blew my nose—honked was more like it—and then sniffled some more. "The little boy over there by the counter… Please don't stare at him, but he said…"

Kara grunted. "Did he say something to upset you?"

"No, no." I gulped and tried to say more but couldn't.

"Then what is it?" That question came from Staci. "Tell us, Ellie. We're here for you, sweetie. Whatever you need."

I drew in a deep breath. "I just got my sign." I looked up at my sisters and then at Maura. "Ryan is okay. I know he is. God just gave me His sign. Clear as a bell."

"That little boy?" Kara glanced over at him, clearly puzzled.

"He doesn't look like Ryan," Staci observed. "What happened?"

Nick burst through the front doors of The Soda Shoppe. He glanced over the lunchtime crowd as if searching for someone. Maura waved to him. "Nick! We're over here."

A huge grin spread over his face when Nick's gaze rested on me. "They found them, Ellie! They found them!" Nick pumped both fists in the air. "All of Ryan's team is accounted for and safe."

Tears streamed down his face. "Ryan's okay, and he's coming home!"

Chapter 28

~~♥~~

Cheers broke out across the restaurant as I cried tears of joy. The servers wiped away their tears and called out congratulations. Everyone clapped and the place erupted in a buzz of talking, laughing, hugging, and back-slapping. Maura and Nick hugged and kissed. Staci and Kara cried and hugged me again. Many of the patrons rose to their feet and rushed over to me like a gloriously crazed flash mob.

All I could do was close my eyes and absorb the best news of my life. As always, Nick had great timing. I wanted to laugh and cry at the same time. I thought my head might explode if my heart didn't burst first.

Nick pulled up a chair at our table to give us the details. The chopper had developed mechanical problems, and the team parachuted out with seconds to spare. Ryan had twisted his ankle and sprained his arm, but otherwise, he was fine. They'd been surrounded by enemy fire, and they'd escaped into a cave for almost 18 hours before it was safe to be rescued.

I listened and nodded, overcome with such a sense of gratefulness like none I'd ever felt in my entire life.

My cell phone rang with a number I didn't recognize. Should I answer?

"Answer it, Ellie. Might be Ryan," Nick said. Now that he mentioned it, the international area code preceded the telephone number.

"This is Ellie Franklin." From the corner of my eye, I saw Nick waving his arms and demanding that everyone be quiet. When Nick Sullivan speaks, people listen.

I heard a crackling sound on the line and static. "Ellie? It's me, baby."

Putting my hand over my mouth, I cried out. The voice of my love. The voice I'd hoped to hear. The voice I'd *prayed* to hear once more, even if only for a heartbeat.

"Ryan? Where are you?" Tears ran down my face. All the ladies at the table shed tears, and Nick's eyes were wet. People clapped again, but softly this time. More tears were shed all around The Soda Shoppe. Some embraced their loved ones. The little boy happily ignored us all and devoured that precious fried egg sandwich. With American cheese and mayo.

"At the hospital currently. Sorry, Sass, but this was the first time I could call you."

Alarm shot through me. I gasped. "Are you okay?" That question seemed rather silly, in a way, but it was my first reaction.

"Just a twisted foot and arm and some minor cuts and bruises. Otherwise, I'm fine except for a little worse for wear." I heard faint sounds on the other end of the line that made me suspect Ryan was shedding a few tears, too. In the midst of my joy, my heart ached for him. Will he be traumatized after his harrowing brush with death? He sounded fine but exhausted, as was to be expected.

"God saved us, Ellie. There's no other explanation. I'm sure Nick told you what happened, but God led us straight to a cave, and we stayed there until we could be rescued. While we were there, we prayed, and one of the team members accepted Christ. Nothing like death staring a man in the face to make him acknowledge his mortality."

"Praise God," I said, wiping away more tears. Happy tears. The *best* kind of tears. I'm tired of crying. From now on, I would only shed tears of joy and happiness.

"They're transporting us to Frankfurt as soon as they can. Hold on, Ellie. I'm going to do everything I can to get back to Cade's Corner on schedule for the wedding. I wouldn't miss marrying you for anything."

"Just come back to me, Ryan. I'll be waiting. As long as it takes."

"I'll be there. Love you, Ellie. See you soon."

The line went dead. I looked up to see Nick and Maura sharing a sweet moment, their heads close together as they talked quietly.

Ryan was alive. And he was coming home. That's all that mattered.

I bowed my head.

Thank you, Jesus.

Chapter 29

~~♥~~

Saturday, December 23

The next morning, I put in a call to the Editor-in-Chief of the *Cleveland Plain Dealer*. Being Saturday, and only two days before Christmas, I understood the chances were slim I'd get a response until after Christmas, if not in the New Year.

"*Cleveland Plain Dealer.* How may I help you?"

Startled, I hesitated a moment, unsure whether a "live" person was behind the voice or whether it was a recorded message.

"My name is Eleanor Franklin, and I'd like to leave a message for the Editor-in-Chief."

As soon as I said my name, I could tell the call was patched through to another number from what must be an answering service.

"Hello, Miss Franklin. This is Aubrey Markham. I'm the Managing Editor of the *Cleveland Plain Dealer.* I've heard the good news about your fiancé. Congratulations to you and Private Sullivan from all the staff here at the paper."

"Thank you." I inhaled a quick breath. "Ms. Markham, I have an idea to propose to you."

"I'm listening."

"I've received several messages from one of your staff reporters, Jonathan Bell, asking for an exclusive story. I'll give you that story," I told her, "*if* you will agree to make prominent mention of Perchance to Dream. I'm not offering our story to anyone else. I'd prefer to keep it local."

"Certainly, Miss Franklin. When do you have in mind?"

"I realize it's very close to Christmas, but are you available to meet in two hours? I'm willing to come to your offices."

"We can come to you—"

"I know where you are."

Ms. Markham didn't hesitate. "We'd love to get your story. Will you grant permission to syndicate?"

Even better. "That won't be a problem."

"Thank you, Miss Franklin. I'll meet you in my office in two hours. Check in with the security guard at the desk on the ground floor. He'll send you up to our floor, and I'll meet you at the elevator doors."

I smiled. "I'll see you in two hours."

Late in the afternoon, I pulled open the heavy wooden door and stepped inside Cade's Corner Community Church. The sanctuary was open most of the time during the season of Advent and until midnight the week leading up to Christmas. The doors in the front vestibule leading into the chapel were open. I smiled at the sight of the beautiful rows of poinsettias lining either side of the raised platform. The festive and elegant holiday wreaths that Mom, Mary, Nick, Maura and I had helped to hang decorated the side walls.

"Fairest Lord Jesus," I began to sing under my breath as I slowly made my way down the aisle. I don't know why that hymn popped into my mind, but I'm not going to resist the inner prompting from the Holy Spirit. I've learned to listen.

Removing my coat, I unwound the scarf from my neck and then yanked my gloves from my near-frozen hands. I could hear the popping of static cling as I removed my knit cap. Ugh. With a frown, I slid the ponytail holder from my hair and shook my hair around my shoulders, smoothing my hands over it.

This is the church where I've grown up—dedicated when I was six months old, baptized when I was eight. The same church where Ryan and I will be married in two days.

"Thee will I cherish," I sang. "Thee will I honor." My voice faded as I dropped onto the same pew I'd occupied nearly every Sunday morning through the years. Sunday evenings when we still had an evening service (they discontinued it a number of years ago) and Wednesday prayer meetings. Blessed with good health, I rarely missed a Sunday, and neither had Ryan. His family sat across from us on the left side of the sanctuary. My gaze wandered to where he'd sit and make goofy faces at me as we rose for a hymn.

As I sat there on that pew, a vision of Hayley Kellerman came into my mind. A quiet girl, Hayley was in my class at school. Her family started coming to the church one September, not long after her diagnosis of leukemia—cancer of the blood, my dad explained. I didn't know Hayley well, but her parents never allowed her to come to Sunday school. I never understood why. From what I knew, a person couldn't "catch" cancer by sitting next to someone who suffered from it.

Unfortunately, Hayley's cancer spread quickly. After she died late in the spring of the following year, I asked Jesus for the second time to come and dwell in my heart. Full of doubts, I wanted to be positive I'd be in Heaven for eternity in the event my "conversion experience" (Grandma Franklin's term) didn't really "take" the first time around.

All I know is that Hayley's death scared me. How could we be absolutely *sure* we'd go to Heaven? I don't think it was so much that I doubted God, but that I was afraid of the unknown. I definitely had a lot of questions.

Ryan caught wind of my doubts after I let it slip in one of our many conversations. We were waiting for our parents in the church parking lot, leaning against the Sullivan Big Red Monster, their fire engine red minivan.

"Sass, if you confessed to Jesus the bad things you've done"—a whole other topic, but really, how bad can you be when you're a kid?—"asked Him for forgiveness, and asked Him to come live in your heart, you can't lose your salvation. Ever."

"Really?"

He gave me a look that clearly conveyed I was a silly girl with frivolous thoughts.

"But how do you *know*?" I said. "Does God talk to you directly?"

"Sort of." His brow scrunched in the way it did when he was deep in thought. "I mean, it's not like I hear this booming voice from Heaven or anything. It's more like a whisper inside me or something." He shrugged his shoulders. "It's kind of hard to explain, but I think that's what faith is all about. We believe that Jesus watches over us and takes care of us."

A week later, Ryan came to our house with his Bible under his arm. I'd barely let him in the front door when he opened the Bible and started reading me verses of scripture.

"Whoa." I held up one hand. "Hello to you, too."

"Sorry." Ryan's cheeks flushed a light red color. "The answers to your questions are in your Bible, Sass. Can we go sit down in the kitchen or something?"

I gestured for him to follow and led the way. He started in again as he walked behind me. "There's a lot of verses that talk about how if you believe in Jesus Christ as the substitute for your sins and received Him as your personal Savior, that's the only requirement for salvation. Free and easy." He made it sound as easy as picking up the one free sample item Keeley's Market offered every week.

"Not everybody thinks it's so easy," I said with all the wisdom of an eight-year-old kid.

"Yeah, maybe." Ryan plopped down on a chair and put the Bible in front of him on the table. "Can I have a glass of milk?"

"Sure. Want a fried egg sandwich?"

He frowned. "Depends. Who's making it?"

"You're looking at her. I can try, anyway."

"That's okay. Milk sounds good, though." When I poured the milk and put the glass on the table in front of him, he thanked me. "Got any chocolate syrup?"

With a sigh, I returned to the refrigerator, pulled out the bottle, and then presented it to him. "Your chocolate flavoring, sir." I sat on the chair beside him. "So which verse about eternity and salvation do you think is the most important?"

Ryan choked on a sip of milk. How he managed to do that, I'll never know. "Sass, *all* of the verses are important."

"I know that." Shaking my head, I scooted my chair closer to his, prepared to learn. "I'm just asking your opinion. Don't get mad at me for the way I asked a simple question. That's carrying this little Bible lesson a bit too far, don't you think? I go to church, too, you know."

Ignoring that comment, Ryan thumbed through his Bible. "John has several verses. The most famous one is John 3:16."

"That's the verse people print on those big signs and wave at the ballgames, right?"

"Right." Zealous in his effort to prove his point, Ryan pointed out several verses from John—1:12, 3:36, and 5:24. Then he flipped over a few books to Ephesians. "This one. I think it's one of the most important verses about how we know we're going to Heaven." He stabbed his index finger on the page. "Ephesians 2, verses 8 and 9. Read those."

"Out loud?"

"If you don't mind." He sat back, prepared to listen as I dutifully read the passage.

"'For by grace you have been saved through faith; and that not of yourselves, it is the gift of God; not as a result of works, so that no one may boast.'"

Sitting at my kitchen table, Ryan and I had a discussion about what it meant to be a believer in Christ. Taking my hand, he prayed with me. Afterwards, he asked me if I knew I was secure in my salvation.

I'd nodded. "I think the word 'salvation' is what threw me off. It confused me."

Ryan bumped my shoulder with his fist. Only a little so that it didn't hurt.

As Ryan left the house that day, he turned at the door and said, "We need to trust in the Lord, Sass. If we become missionaries and get killed or something, we'll still know we're going to Heaven. Don't doubt your salvation."

"Yes, we do need to trust in Him, but I'm not sure about the missionary idea."

He grinned and tucked his Bible under his arm. "You can do that right here in Cade's Corner. See you later."

Chapter 30
~~♥~~

"Yes, Ryan," I said into the silence of the empty church, "I *do* trust in the Lord. He takes care of us. He always has, and He always will, no matter what may come." That sentiment means so much more to me now than ever before in my life. Another chopper carrying Army service personnel had gone down in the last few days. In that crash, however, there had been no survivors. Tears squeezed from my eyes and trailed a path down my cheeks.

"God, please be with those soldiers and their families."

I lifted my eyes to the wooden cross behind the pulpit. Rather crude, it had been hand-carved out of maple by one of the now-deceased elders in the church. "Thank you, Lord Jesus," I whispered. "Thou, my soul's glory, joy, and crown." I sang quietly in my slightly off-key voice.

Thank you.

Wiping the tears from my face, I started to rise from the pew. The hour was growing late, and I needed to go home and try to get a few hours of rest, if not sleep. I felt so mentally, physically, and emotionally exhausted, even my *bones* were tired.

My cell phone rang, the sound jarred me as it echoed around the silent sanctuary. I retrieved it from my purse and stared at the display. NICK SULLIVAN.

"Hi, Nick." I don't know why I lowered my voice since no one else was around to hear.

"Ellie, where are you?"

"At the church, but I'm getting ready to head home. Why?"

"Can you stay put a few more minutes? I'll be there shortly."

A pulse of alarm shot through me, alerting all my senses. "Ryan's still coming home soon, right?" I started to tremble and moved my arm over my middle as I began to rock back and forth on the pew. I stared blindly at the card sandwiched between a Bible and a hymnal in the rack in front of me. Closing my eyes, I prayed under my breath there had been no new developments.

"Nothing to worry about, Ellie. I have a message for you from Ryan, and I'd prefer to give it to you in person," Nick said. "Considering the sun is going down now, I'll come to the church. Then I can make sure you get home safely."

"I'll be fine walking home. This is Cade's Corner," I reminded him.

"I insist. Stay put, and I'll be there in ten minutes tops."

"All right, Nick. As you wish." No sense protesting.

Disconnecting the call, I twisted around and glanced at the pews behind me. Specifically, the pew five rows back. After Ryan and I became an official couple, we sat together on that pew. Some of the other kids even dubbed it "Ryan and Ellie's Pew." The only weeks we hadn't sat together was during the time he dated Amber.

I'd once seen Kendall Lange chase away a new young couple by telling them that pew was reserved. Appalled that Kendall would say such a thing to visitors, I ran over to them with an overly enthusiastic welcome and practically pushed them down onto the pew. Not surprisingly, they'd never returned to the Church of Crazy People.

When I was eighteen, something Pastor Jon—seemingly the church's youth pastor for all time—told us in our small group Bible study caught our attention.

"In First Timothy, the first chapter, verse 5," Pastor Jon said, "it says this: 'But the goal of our instruction is love from a pure heart and a good conscience and a sincere faith.'"

Ryan and I had been growing closer physically—not anything dangerous—but we acknowledged the need to be careful when we were alone. Even sitting on a pew next to one another in church, we'd taken the arm and hand stroking a bit too far on occasion, prompting chastising glares from a few of the more prim and proper older ladies. I'd confessed my uncharitable thoughts to the Lord, but had they forgotten what it was like to be young and in love before they married? Did the passage of time erase that part of their memory?

Later that night, sitting on opposite ends of the sofa in his family room, Ryan and I discussed that verse of scripture. We agreed we both wanted those three things: a pure heart, a good conscience, a sincere faith.

"Are you saying we shouldn't even kiss?" I said to Ryan. "Is that even possible?" I wasn't pouting, really, but I wanted to hear how he'd respond.

With all the love in the world shining in those gorgeous blue eyes, Ryan shook his head. "No, I'm not saying that at all. We just can't take it to the level we did last Saturday night. I'm sorry for getting too carried away."

"Oh. That's okay. You weren't alone on that couch." My cheeks colored at his honesty, but I fully understood his meaning even though his idea of getting carried away was nothing more than some serious deep kisses. "Ryan, I'll admit I've sinned, at least a little bit, in my thought life about you and me. Does that make me a bad person? I don't think God loves me any less for having those thoughts."

Ryan shook his head. "He just wants you to talk with Him about it. Don't act on those thoughts, but give them over to Him. I know He'll bless us in the long run for being faithful to Him and each other." Then he grinned. "When we're married, feel free to act on those thoughts all you want."

I'd half-laughed and half-groaned at the same time. I'm pretty sure my cheeks were flaming red. "Not sure that helps."

From that point on, we'd been more careful. Of course, there were times when one of us would get a little carried away. Then we'd take a deep breath and pull apart. Somehow, by God's grace, we managed to control ourselves. I can't lie and say it hasn't been difficult at times.

I smiled as I recalled the one time when Ryan whispered that he wished we could run away and get married that same night. "I can't believe how much I want to be married to you, Ellie. Like right this minute."

"That's just your hormones talking," I said, pushing against his chest with a firm but gentle hand. He'd been a little irritated by that comment, mainly because he knew that I was right. For one thing, sitting in his truck wasn't the safest place.

"Nothing wrong with hormones, but I'm glad the Lord gave me you to keep me in check," he'd said, raking the fingers of one hand through his hair.

"Glad I can oblige. Right back at ya."

Before leaving for his second tour of duty, Ryan sat beside me under the big sycamore tree in our backyard. I'd been going on and on about details for the wedding, mostly about flowers and table settings, and flipping through magazines. At one point, I stopped and caught his look of amused indulgence. "You don't care about any of this, do you?"

"It means a lot to you, so I care. But now it's time to take a little break."

With a sigh, I allowed him to take the materials from my hands and put them on the ground. Then he pulled me in his arms. "You are my beautiful girl," he'd whispered. Cradling my face between his hands, Ryan's gaze swept across my face, back and forth.

"What are you doing?" I bit my lower lip, feeling uncharacteristically shy under his scrutiny.

"Shh." He ran his fingers with a gentle touch over my forehead, in a slow trail down my temples, over my cheeks, my jawline, lips, and chin. Like I'd seen blind people do in the movies. "I'm memorizing your face. To carry you with me when I'm gone."

"You have my photo, Ryan. Several of them."

He kissed my nose.

"And please don't say things like 'when I'm gone.' You won't be gone, Ryan. You'll just be…absent. Temporarily."

He shook his head with a smile that appeared rather sad although not melancholy. "Not the same thing. What I can tell you is that the Ellie sitting here now, smiling at me with her beautiful hazel eyes"—he brushed his thumbs over my cheeks—"*this* is the girl I will hold in my heart."

With a deep sigh, I glanced at my watch and shifted on the pew. What was keeping Nick? He should have been here by now. Crossing my arms over my chest, I leaned my head back on the pew and closed my eyes.

"Ryan, wherever you are, I love you and can't wait to see you." I glanced at my watch. Since I hadn't heard more from him, I could only assume he was somewhere in the air between Frankfurt, Germany and Cleveland, Ohio.

"Ellie."

I laughed under my breath. Great. Now I'm hallucinating.

With my eyes still closed, I twirled a strand of my long hair around one finger.

"You're doing that twirly thing with your hair again."

"You know it. I always do that when I'm talking with you—even in my overly active imagination, apparently—and sooo wishing you were here." My shoulders heaved with my deep sigh, and my eyes fluttered open.

"Is that a new sweater you're wearing? I like it when you wear light blue, Sass. Brings out the color of your gorgeous hazel eyes."

"Is that a fact?" I smiled and released the strand of hair. "Good thing, since I bought it with you..."

I wasn't hallucinating. *I'm not crazy!*

My mind screamed, and my pulse pounded.

Ryan! A strangled cry crept into my throat. I moved my hand over my mouth and tears sprang into my eyes.

Inhaling a deep breath, I twisted around on the pew.

Chapter 31

~~♥~~

Nick stood at the back of the sanctuary.

My eyes widened, and my body trembled from twisted nerves combined with excitement.

"Nick?" I whispered, my voice raspy.

What's going on here?

He gave me a nod and a reassuring smile. "I've brought someone to see you."

Seconds later, with Nick's support, Ryan hopped into view. And I do mean *hopped*. His right ankle was wrapped, and he wore a heavy snow boot on his left foot. A crutch was propped beneath his right arm, his left forearm rested in a sling. He wore jeans, a navy blue sweater, and a red down vest. He gave me a slightly crooked smile, that smile I loved so much. The smile I'd pictured in my mind so many times each day since he'd been gone.

"Thank you, Jesus!" My words caught on a sob that came from the deepest part of me.

Ryan shifted on the crutch and winced. His handsome face was miraculously untouched. God, in His infinite grace and mercy, had spared him from much more serious injuries that could have been devastating and life-threatening. I'll love this man with everything in me. I want nothing more than to take care of him the rest of my life.

Jumping off the pew, tears streaming down both cheeks, I sprinted down the aisle. Reaching him, I threw my arms around Ryan's neck, whispering his name over and over.

"You can't even know how great you look to me right now," he said.

"Oh, I think I have a good idea." Smiling, I put my hands on either side of his face and feathered light kisses over his cheeks, his jaw, his nose, his forehead. Then I stopped and stared at him for a long moment, finding it difficult to believe he was truly home.

Seeing Nick over Ryan's shoulder, I mouthed *Thank you.* With a silent nod and a salute, he turned and exited through the front door.

Ryan leaned against the wall. I felt his smile as his mouth met mine.

"I can't believe you're really here." I gulped, and my nose began to run in a most unladylike way. I didn't care, couldn't care, couldn't think of anything but how eternally grateful I'd be to the Lord for keeping my Ryan safe. Bringing Ryan back to me, to his parents and Nick, to all of us. For sparing his life.

I lightly pinched his cheeks. "You don't know how many times I've thought about this moment. Dreamt about it. I thought you weren't coming in until tomorrow. If you were going for the big surprise, you accomplished it."

"I wasn't supposed to come until tomorrow, but God had another plan." Moving his good arm around me, pulling me as close as possible to him, Ryan buried his face in my neck.

I felt his tears dampening my skin, felt his shoulders shaking, and his thick lashes tickled my neck. As long as I've known him, I've only seen Ryan cry a couple of times—when his grandfather died and when we said good-bye at the airport before this last deployment.

"I've missed you so much. I love you, Ellie."

"Oh, Ryan, I love you, too. So much." My hands moved to his hair, and I ran my fingers through his thick, dark waves. "They didn't cut your hair," I murmured.

"I told them I had the most beautiful woman on the planet waiting for me back home, and she'd probably kill me if I had a buzz cut when I married her."

"That doesn't matter," I said, half-laughing. "But thanks for thinking of me." In my daze, I managed to pull a tissue from the pocket of my jeans, thankful I'd had the foresight to tuck one away. I dabbed the tissue over Ryan's face and then used it to mop mine.

"They seemed to take pity on me and granted me that last wish, so to speak," Ryan said. "Probably because they knew I was being shipped home. Or maybe they felt sorry for the groom who might not be as agile as he hoped to be on his honeymoon."

Blushing down to my toes, laughing, I put my arms around him again as best I could around his sling. He leaned his forehead on mine. "God's given me more days to spend with you, and I intend to take full advantage of the time He's granted me."

I nodded. "I've always loved you, Ryan. I always have, and I always will."

His lips met mine again in a longer kiss, filled with the same want and need I'd experienced so intensely. "I was careful, Ellie," he whispered as he angled his head in the opposite direction and kissed me again. "I want you to know that."

"I know," I whispered back. "You always are." I smiled against his lips. "Most of the time."

After another very lengthy kiss—one of the best ever, and that was saying something—Ryan pulled away. "I think we both need a tissue now," he said. "As much as I'm enjoying this, baby, I need to sit down before I fall over and take you with me. That's not something I want to do."

"Oh, I'm sorry! I left you standing all this time. I'm so selfish. Please forgive me."

He chuckled. "You are not selfish in any sense of the word."

"Here. Let me help you." I started to reach for him but stopped, faltering, giving him a helpless look. "Tell me what to do. When you broke your leg before, you wouldn't allow me to help other than to read to you or beat you soundly at Monopoly."

His grin emerged. "I still say you cheated."

"Did not. Keep that up and I'll push you down on that pew, injured or not."

"Yeah, why don't you try?" Ryan waggled his brows as if challenging me. "Hey, bro?"

"Here." Nick stepped inside the front door of the church.

I stared at Nick. "Have you been standing outside in the cold this whole time?"

"Affirmative." Nick's lips looked almost blue, and he rocked back and forth and gave me a rather sheepish, half-frozen smile. "I didn't want to interrupt the moment."

"Nick's going to take us back to our house," Ryan told me.

Ten minutes later, Ryan sat on the sofa and glanced around our living room. "The place looks great. You've done a terrific job, baby. I can't wait to get the grand tour."

Nick smiled and headed for the front door. "My job is done. I'll let myself out."

"Nick." I ran to him and hugged him close. "Thank you again for everything."

"Always." Nick kissed my cheek. "See you soon."

I turned back to Ryan. "Can I get anything for you? Want some water? An egg sandwich with mayo and cheese? Christmas treats?"

"Just you," he said with a tired smile. "Hurry up, please. My arms are already empty again."

My pulse flew off the radar. I grabbed a tissue from a box on the kitchen counter and hurried back to the living room and gingerly seated myself next to Ryan. He moved his arm around me. After kicking off my shoes, I curled into him and snuggled as close as possible to his side.

Taking my hand, Ryan kissed each finger, one by one. "I like the light blue polish." He raised his brows and grinned. "Do your toes match?"

"You'll have to wait and see."

"Ah, you're playing coy with me now?"

"No," I said, laughing. "I just want you to have something to look forward to on the honeymoon."

His gorgeous smile surfaced again and his eyes lit. "I don't think that'll be a problem."

Finally, Ryan began to tell me as much as he could remember about the helicopter crash and the ensuing events.

"We all shared about the people waiting for us back home," Ryan said. "It helped pass the time, but it served to remind us why we needed to stay strong and have faith we'd get out of our circumstances alive."

"And then you shared your faith in Christ." I squeezed Ryan's hand and ran my finger over his hand. "I admire how bold you are."

Ryan pressed his lips to my hair. "I didn't have a choice, Sass. It's like the Holy Spirit took over and gave me the words. You know I had trouble memorizing some of the Old Testament verses in Sunday school"—we shared a grin— "but the one that immediately popped into my mind was the one from Deuteronomy 20, verse 4: 'for the Lord your God is the one who goes with you, to fight for you against your enemies, to save you.'"

"How did the guys react?" I said.

"We all prayed, even the one team member who always gave me constant grief. He told me later he'd never forget those words. He said he'd never been to church, and he's never heard anyone recite a Bible verse from memory."

I shook my head. "Yet another reason to be thankful we're sharing the Bibles with the Perchance to Dream kids."

"Exactly," Ryan said. "I'll never forget those guys and what we shared together. We all know how blessed we are."

He gave me a kiss and then shifted on the sofa. "It's getting late, and I need to go soon, but I need to tell you about something else that happened."

When I nodded, he continued. "Like I told you, the Army transported me to Frankfurt. Then the strangest thing happened. A lieutenant general I'd never met before and two guys walked over to where I waited in the holding area to board the plane at the airport. When he called me by name, I scrambled to my feet as best I could and saluted. Then the lieutenant general informed me the two men would be escorting me home."

"Escorting you? What do you mean?"

Ryan smiled. "By private jet, believe it or not. Like I was an important bigwig or something."

"You are to me," I told him, giving him another kiss. I couldn't get enough of his kisses. In some ways, I never wanted to let him go even though I knew I must. "My forever hero."

"I figured I'd be stuck in the cargo hold or something. Not really," Ryan said when I nudged his arm. "The lieutenant general assured me I was in the best hands possible to get me back to Cleveland before Christmas."

I kissed Ryan's cheek, and he squeezed my hand.

"Baby, I can't tell you why, but I got the strong impression those guys came to Germany *specifically* to get me and bring me home. All they said was it takes teamwork, but they were determined to make sure I got home for the wedding."

"Such a miracle," I murmured. "I don't know if Nick told you, but our story made the national news." International, most likely. I still found it surreal.

I sat up straighter, still holding onto Ryan's hand. "Who were these guys? Army, I'm assuming?"

Ryan shook his head. "They were in civilian dress, but they had military stamped all over them even without the uniforms." I knew what he meant. Military men carry themselves, and conduct themselves, in a distinctive, authoritative manner that embodies confidence and commands respect. I could tell by their posture alone.

"I should have asked for their names, but I didn't. I was so tired, Ellie. I've never been that exhausted. The one guy was seriously buff, and he did something awesome."

I ran my thumb back and forth in a light, caressing motion over Ryan's hand. "Tell me."

"He bumped his fist with mine and said, 'Everything according to His purpose.' There wasn't a doubt in my mind he was talking about God. I took it as a sign from the Lord that I'd be okay."

I smiled, filled with deep contentment. "I know a little something about a sign from God. Let's just say there was a little boy at The Soda Shoppe the other day who ordered a fried egg sandwich with mayo and American cheese."

Ryan grinned. "See? He's got very good taste. I'm not the only one who likes those sandwiches."

"No, but I'd prayed to the Lord that He'd give me a sign to let me know you were...all right." My voice caught on the last two words and a few tears fell onto my cheeks.

"Oh, baby. Don't cry. I'm here." Ryan bundled me in his arms. We sat that way for an extended moment, holding one another—clinging, really—our fingers laced together.

"The guys also prayed with me before we took off. They mentioned you, too, without asking your name."

I wiped away my tears and pushed myself up straighter on the pew. "What do you know about the other guy?" I was so curious to know about Ryan's rescuers. Who were they? Would we ever see them again?

"Hard to say where the fist-bumping guy was from, but he was about 6' 4"." The pilot was almost as tall, and I detected a bit of a drawl. If I had to guess, I'd say he's from Texas or Louisiana. They were both great. We had some pretty bad turbulence, but the pilot handled it like a pro. I hardly felt a bump. I think I heard the other guy call him Louis." Ryan scratched his head. "Or maybe Will. Sorry, I can't remember. They seemed to know each other fairly well. They sat together in the cockpit and, although I heard them talking, they kept it down, probably for my benefit. I guess they figured I was tired and needed to sleep. I slept some, anyway."

"Well, whoever they were, I'll be grateful to them for the rest of my life for bringing my love back home. The way I see it, they were God's messengers. Earthly Angels, in a sense."

"Amen," Ryan said.

Shortly after midnight, I drove Ryan back to his parents' house.

"I'm going to ditch the crutch and the sling before the wedding. Promise," he said as I helped him into the house.

"Ryan, I don't care if you're in a wheelchair. Or if you limp. All I ever want is you."

"Not a problem. You've got me forever." His smile filled all the places in my heart remaining to be filled. Healed them and made them whole again.

Chapter 32

~~♥~~

Sunday Afternoon, December 24

I heard someone grunt and then a knock on my office door. "Go away," I mumbled.

With a small groan of protest, Ryan removed his lips from mine. We both turned as the office door opened.

Nick stood in the doorway. "Sorry to interrupt, but I knew you were both in here. I could see the steam seeping through the bottom of the door."

Ryan dropped his arms from around my waist while I tried not to laugh. It wouldn't be the first time Nick caught us in a passionate embrace.

"I'm glad you're both here, actually. You need to see something."

"This had better be good," Ryan muttered under his breath.

"May I?" Nick gestured to my computer on the desk.

"Be our guest," Ryan said.

Nick sat in front of the computer. "Come around and take a look at this."

Hands joined, Ryan and I walked behind my desk and peered over Nick's shoulder.

"A specific website for the two of you was set up during the time Ryan was missing."

"What do you mean? What kind of website?" I looked at Ryan and lifted my shoulders. "This is the first I've heard of it."

"It's a site set up by some big sports advertising guru named Marcus Thompson in Boston. I did a little digging. His dad was a huge NBA star for the Celtics years ago."

"Why would he do something like this?" Ryan voiced the same question I'd been pondering.

"Beats me, but he's a guy with a lot of power and friends in high places. Went to Yale. He's also heavily involved with a worldwide Christian missions organization." Nick clicked on a page. "Here it is. The slogan here at the top of the website says it all."

I moved my gaze to where he pointed. *When God's People Pray.*

Releasing my hand, Ryan planted both palms on the desk and leaned close to Nick. "Sorry to invade your personal space, bro."

"Not a problem. Invade away. It's my honor."

I smiled at their familiar, easy banter.

On the other side of Nick, I mirrored Ryan's stance as the three of us read through the first page of the website. When I glanced over at Ryan, he seemed as surprised as me. "So, Mr. Thompson set up a website for people to pray for your safety?"

Ryan nodded. "That's what it looks like. And to pray for you while I was gone."

I moved my hand over my heart. "Ryan, can you believe this?"

"In some ways, no." Ryan's gaze met mine. "In other ways, yes."

"Hang on," Nick said. "People left messages and prayers for Ryan's safe return and for your wedding." He clicked on another page. "Here's the visitor page and a list of names. As you can see, it's a long list." Nick began to read the names aloud as we looked over his shoulder.

"Wait. Stop scrolling a second." I pointed to a name on the screen. "H.L. Joseph? She's a new Christian romance writer. I read her first book last month, and it was really fun. Who else?"

Nick moved the cursor farther down the page. "People all over the country—Houston, Louisiana, New York, San Antonio, Boston. The list of names goes on for like five pages. I think the names are listed in the order they visited the page since they're listed by date and not in alphabetical order."

Nick looked at Ryan and then at me. "Any of these last names ring a bell?"

"No," Ryan and I said simultaneously.

"Stop there a second." Ryan smiled and nodded to the screen. "Beckett and Babs are on the list."

"Seriously?" A small cry caught in my throat as I moved my hand over my mouth.

Nick frowned. "Didn't Babs die a long time ago?"

"Yes, but she'll live in Beckett's heart forever," I said. "It's very sweet." Earlier that morning, I'd told Ryan about the letter from Beckett and the possibility of my assuming the leadership at The Beckett Agency. He was proud and supportive, and we'd briefly discussed how my priorities wouldn't change—my husband, family, and Perchance to Dream would always come first. We'd figure it out, and no definitive decisions needed to be made now.

"Whatever you say," Nick said, shaking his head.

As Nick scrolled down the page, I noted the names of more familiar Cade's Corner citizens. "So, let me get this straight. Our local friends knew about this website, and they've never said a word?" I nudged Nick's shoulder. "Including you?"

Nick lifted his hands in the air. "I didn't know a thing. Honest truth. In fact, Mom just heard about it from someone after the church service this morning. I guess they figured we had enough going on, which is true. Maybe they wanted to surprise you. Dad said there were a number of similar websites set up for Ryan and the other missing members of his team. This one was set up *specifically* for both Ryan and you, Ellie."

A large majority of the service this morning—our Christmas service—had been dedicated to praise and worship. I felt somewhat bad for Pastor Derek, but he'd been the one to spearhead the time of testimonies interspersed with Christmas hymns and the message about the birth of the Christ child. My mom and Maura sat on the other side of me, and Nick and his parents sat on the other side of Ryan. My sisters and their families sat on the pew directly behind us. I noticed Dr. Phillip on the pew behind them. If he hadn't come in late, I would have marched over to him and asked him to join Mom on our pew.

After the service, Ryan was surprised by an impromptu parade down Main Street. I rode beside Ryan in his red truck as the townspeople lined the streets, smiling and braving the cold, as we drove to Martinelli's for lunch. While we were having lunch, family after family, and person after person, came over to our table. They hugged us both, told us how thankful they were that Ryan made it back safely, and they wished us well in our upcoming nuptials. Several small boys hung onto Ryan's every word and begged to hear more about his Army adventures.

"Ellie?"

I started and looked over at Ryan through watery eyes. "I'm sorry. I was thinking about everything that's happened. I'm so overwhelmed, I'm not even sure what to say. For once."

"Nick, stop again." Ryan seemed fixated on the computer screen. "Scroll back up a few names." He leaned even closer and pointed to the screen. "There. Commander William Jordan Lewis."

Ryan's voice sounded a bit odd. "Look him up, Nick."

Nick minimized the current screen and then typed WILLIAM JORDAN LEWIS in the search bar.

I snapped my gaze to Ryan's as we waited a few seconds to bring up the results. "The guy who flew you out of Frankfurt?"

"That's what I'm thinking." Ryan rubbed his hand over his chin without moving his gaze away from the computer screen. When Nick brought up the search results, he pointed to a link for a website. "That one right there." Was his finger actually shaking?

Nick pulled up the link, and we all strained forward to read.

JoAnn Durgin

The screen changed and brought up the man's full biography.

"Ryan," I said, "it mentions he's part of a Christian missions organization called TeamWork." I pointed to the computer screen. "Didn't you say one of the guys mentioned how it takes teamwork or something? Do you think this is what he meant?"

Ryan nodded. "Maybe. I need to see a photo."

Nick quickly brought up a photo of William Lewis in an Air Force uniform. When he scrolled down, I gasped. "He's an *astronaut?*"

"Whoa!" Nick said with unrestrained excitement. "This guy's with NASA all right." As a kid, he'd talked about wanting to be an astronaut, and he'd attended space camp one summer.

"That's definitely him." I haven't heard that kind of awe in Ryan's voice often, but I heard it now.

"*That's* the guy who flew the private jet?" Nick looked at Ryan.

"Yes," Ryan confirmed. "Along with another guy I could tell was military. But William Jordan Lewis was my pilot."

Nick sat back in the chair, clearly astonished. "Dude, you were flown home by the next NASA shuttle commander! Not too shabby, bro. Wow! They pulled out the big guns for you."

"That also explains why he told me to reach for the stars and saluted me when we landed in Cleveland. I think I need to sit down." Ryan half-stumbled back to the window ledge behind my desk and perched himself on it. He crossed his arms and shook his head as if in disbelief.

"Praise God for working out the details in such a unique way," I breathed. Moving over to Ryan, I wrapped my arms around him. "I've always believed in the power of prayer. This is another example of how God's people rally around each other. And then how God provided His best to bring you home."

"There's something else you two need to know."

"Is it good?" Ryan's voice sounded thick with emotion.

204

"Oh, yeah," Nick said. "It says here they collected donations. Not to bring you home," he said quickly when Ryan started to protest. "Trust me, it's all good. They didn't solicit them, but it says here that enough people asked, so they've set up a fund."

"Then what are the donations for? Our wedding? Honeymoon?" I couldn't fathom why anyone had collected money other than to cover the costs of bringing Ryan home. The funds for our wedding and honeymoon had been allocated a long time ago.

Nick twisted in the chair. "Your mutual pet project."

"Perchance to Dream?" Ryan and I both croaked out the question at the same time.

"None other," Nick said. "Looks like they've collected a very sizable sum. Enough to keep you in business for a whole lot of years. From what it says here, they're going to leave the website up for a few more months. When you get a chance, check it out. There's all kinds of prayers, best wishes, and blessings from people all over the world."

"We'll take a look and try to answer them," Ryan said.

"There's a lot of messages, Ryan. It'd keep you busy for a long time."

I glanced at Ryan. "Then at the very least, we need to make a statement of some kind on the website and thank everyone for their prayers."

Ryan nodded. "I agree."

"You two should come and see me, professionally speaking, when you get back from the honeymoon and we can get it all set up."

"There's really that much?" Ryan appeared as dazed as I felt at this new turn of events.

"Yes, it's *that* much," Nick confirmed. "A very substantial sum. You might even want to think about hiring staff. If I have your authorization, I'll send an email to Marcus Thompson in Boston and get the wheels turning. I'll give you an update when you get back from Hawaii. All nice and tan."

"Fine by me," Ryan said. "Ellie?"

"Sure. I still can't believe it." I rubbed my hand over my brow. "How else can you explain this whole thing other than to say it's a miracle from God?"

"Believe it, Ellie. Merry Christmas." Nick lifted from the chair and leaned over to drop a light peck on my cheek. "See you kids at the church in a few hours for the rehearsal."

Nick gave me a wink, gave Ryan a brotherly slap on the shoulder, and then departed.

Sometimes words aren't necessary. Not at all.

For a long time, Ryan and I simply held one another, sharing the moment and God's grace.

Chapter 33

~~♥~~

As Ryan and I left the Perchance to Dream office for the last time this year, my cell phone rang.

"Aren't you going to see who it is?" Ryan asked when I didn't reach for it right away.

"I'm tempted not to check. Everything I need is right here with me now."

He chuckled. "Thanks, but maybe you should check."

"Okay. To humor you." I reached into my pocket and pulled out my phone. "It's from Krista at the nursing home." I darted a worried gaze at Ryan and bit my lower lip. "I hope nothing's happened with Cora."

"Ellie, hi. It's Krista. Cora's fine, but I thought you might want to stop by with Ryan for just a few minutes if you can. I understand how busy you are, so if not, I'll understand."

Twenty minutes later, a tall, slender woman who resembled young Cora in the photograph on her bureau turned as Ryan and I appeared in the doorway of Room 365.

"You must be Beatrice." I walked toward her and held out one hand. "I'm Ellie Franklin, and this is my fiancé, Ryan Sullivan."

"Nice to meet you both." She smiled. "My mother has always spoken so highly of both of you. I understand congratulations are in order and that you're getting married tomorrow."

"That's right," Ryan said, squeezing my hand.

"Thank you." I squeezed back.

Krista wasn't in sight, and I wondered why she'd called us to come. Maybe to see that Cora's daughter had finally come to visit. The holidays were always a sentimental time, so perhaps it had prompted Beatrice to make the trip. For whatever reason, I was thankful.

"I asked Krista to call you," Beatrice said as if she could read my thoughts. "She's told me how faithful you've been to come and see my mother. I wanted to thank you in person." She lowered her gaze from mine and stepped closer to her mother's side.

"I've always loved Cora. She's a very special person in my life." I tried my best not to allow any sarcasm or anger to seep into my voice. It wasn't anger I felt toward this woman, but sadness.

"Thank you for your faithfulness to her. After my father died, I'm the first to admit that I haven't been as good about visiting Mom. That's to my shame, but I've made a decision recently." Beatrice raised her head and looked at me. "I'm moving Mom to Minneapolis."

Part of me hated to hear this news. I'd miss my dear friend, and the staff here in Cade's Corner also loved this precious soul. But, as much as we loved her, we weren't Cora's family.

I swallowed hard. "I'm sure you're doing what you feel is best, but this has been Cora's home most of her life." Whether or not she'd ever regain consciousness, Cora's friends were here. She had a plot reserved in the church cemetery.

"I know that." Beatrice's tone sounded rather snappish, and I could tell the decision weighed heavily on her mind. "But I'm her only child, and I've built a life in Minneapolis. I have a career there and, with Mom nearby, I can better watch over her."

"I understand," I said, lowering my voice. "I know you're only doing what you need to do."

"Stay."

My eyes widened, and I looked around the room. Who had said that?

Ryan angled his head to Cora in the bed.

"Stay." There it was again!

I moved to the opposite side of Cora's bed from Beatrice. "Cora? Cora, it's me—Ellie. Ryan's here with me, and your daughter Beatrice has come to see you. Isn't that wonderful?"

The older woman's eyes fluttered open, and she stared at me, glassy-eyed, for a long moment. A smile touched her lips. "Ellie."

"Yes, Cora. It's me." I took her hand in mine as I'd done so many times before.

On the other side of the bed, Beatrice took her other hand. "Mom? It's Beatrice. I'm here. Is that what you want? To stay here in Cade's Corner instead of coming to Minneapolis with me?"

Cora's nod was barely perceptible, but the three of us in the room witnessed her acknowledgment of Beatrice's question. We'd all heard her say the word *Stay*. Twice.

The older woman's eyes opened once more and she moved her gaze to Ryan. "Love her well."

"I will, Cora." Ryan's blue eyes met mine. "The rest of my life."

"Cora, we love you," I said.

Her smile stayed in place. Although she said nothing, Cora squeezed my hand.

Beatrice glanced across the bed at me. "Well, I guess that's the answer."

"If you feel the need to take her home with you, Beatrice, everyone here will understand. You're her family, so it's completely your call."

"No, it's not." Beatrice wiped away tears, smoothing one hand over Cora's hair. "It's *Mom's* decision, and she's made her wishes known. In many ways, you're every bit as much Mom's family as much I am. This is where she's meant to be. Who am I to take that away from her?"

Beatrice patted her mother's hand. "I'm going to come and see you more often, Mom. I promise you that much. And I'm going to give Ellie my contact information and hope she'll let me know how you're doing." She looked up at me. "I hope you won't mind."

"Of course not. It would be my honor."

I walked around the bed and enveloped Beatrice in a warm hug. "Thank you."

Chapter 34

~~♥~~

December 25, 2006

The sun awakened me as it streamed through the open blinds of my childhood bedroom the next morning. I'd enjoyed the best sleep I'd had in weeks.

"Thank you, Jesus." I sat up straight in the bed.

Today is my wedding day!

A huge smile crossed my face. The rehearsal at the church had gone off without a hitch. I had been in such a euphoric mood—and so had Ryan—that nothing could have diminished our joyful anticipation. My sisters' kids acted up a bit by crawling beneath the pews and sliding on the floor while we were going through the motions, but I just smiled while Kara and Staci called for their husbands to corral them. As kids, Ryan and I had done the same thing. That slippery floor was difficult to resist.

Afterwards, the group—including Grandma Franklin and a few assorted relatives—all went to the Sullivan house where his mother had prepared a feast of Sullivan family holiday favorites.

"Ellie has learned how to make Ryan's preferred dishes now," Mary announced to the group crowded around their dining room table.

I held up one hand. "Except for the one with beets," I said, kissing Ryan's cheek. "He can learn to make those recipes himself."

"I'll get you to like them yet," Ryan said, tapping my knee with his beneath the table. "Love me, love my beets," he whispered in my ear. His lips tickled my skin, and I laughed.

As Ryan's best man, Nick rose to his feet and toasted us. "Ryan's been my best friend since we were kids. I figured out that the pesky little kid wouldn't stop following me around," he said, and we all laughed. "Then I finally accepted the fact that he wasn't going anywhere soon. He's always been the first one to step up if I needed a friend. The first one to tell me what needed to be said, even if it was hard to take, and I've done the same for him. I've watched him grow from a reckless kid who drove his bike too fast to the kind of man who's served his country with uncommon loyalty and valor."

Nick paused, and I could see the emotion in his eyes as he continued. "Through the years, I've seen him fall in love with the cute little neighbor girl from down the street."

A chorus of *aww* floated around the table. I dipped my head and smiled.

"And now Ryan and Ellie have created Perchance to Dream, their joint project—their 'baby' for now if you will—that provides more than toys to children. It provides *hope* for kids who desperately need it with Bibles and a personal note. It's a ministry that will continue to flourish and grow and bless hearts not only in the Cleveland area but around the globe. Separately, these two are terrific individuals. But together? They're the *best* example of what can happen when God's people pray. Simply put, Ryan"—Nick turned to his younger brother and raised his glass—"you are the kind of man I hope to be one day. I love you, brother."

Ryan rose from his chair, and my eyes misted as the two brothers embraced.

Kara and Staci delegated the honor of the toast to the bride to Maura. She glanced at Nick and he gave her a smile as she slowly rose to her feet. "I'm not as eloquent as the good counselor here," she said, and everyone smiled.

Maura swallowed and met my gaze. "I haven't known Ellie as long as the rest of you here tonight, but Ellie makes it so easy to know *her*. She's one of the first people I met here in Cade's Corner. Ellie showed up in Nick's law office and welcomed me with a smile and a homemade blueberry pie." Her lips curled. "I'd been told to stay away from anything with vegetables, but that her baked goods are excellent."

Ryan kissed my cheek while I rolled my eyes and the others laughed quietly.

"I don't have a sister," Maura said, "but *Ellie's* my sister." Okay, that one made me tear up again. I'd already told Ryan there would be a "No Tears" clause for the honeymoon although the wedding would be pretty much a given.

Maura paused to gather her thoughts, her gaze never leaving mine. "Her love for Ryan is an inspiration to many here in town and, after recent events, around the country and the world. She never gave up hope that Ryan and his team would be found safe. She believes in the precious promises of her Lord and Savior, Jesus Christ. Ellie pours her all into everything she does for her family, for Perchance to Dream, and for her friends. She has more energy than ten people, she has the kind of compassion that's remarkable and memorable. When Ellie Franklin—soon to be Ellie Sullivan—moves into your life, even from the first meeting, you'll know your life will *never* be the same. Ellie,"—Maura lifted her glass and raised it in my direction—"here's to you and a lifetime of love with Ryan and continuing to bless everyone you meet. I love you, my friend."

With tears streaming down their faces, Staci and Kara hugged Maura and then all three women came over to me for a group hug. Mom and Mary joined us. I'm glad they came prepared with a box of tissues. My goodness. But it's all wonderful.

After dinner, Grandma Franklin took me into Mark Sullivan's study for a private chat. She shared a few tidbits of advice with me about marriage. "Don't stress over the little stuff," she said. "Focus on building up Ryan and he'll honor you in return. If you burn a dish, don't cry and fret. Shrug off the things you can't fix, and accept and take care of the things you *can* fix. Try to speak in a soft tone, especially when you're aggravated. Hold your tongue. Instead of lashing out when you're angry, take Ryan by the hand, and fall on your knees together. Give over any struggles to the Lord."

"Thank you, Grandma. I might need you to remind me of a few of those things."

"In that case, ask your mother. I wrote them all down in a journal and gave it to her before she married your father."

"You did?" That made me smile.

She nodded. "I sure did. And then when the kids come along, it's a whole different way of life." Grandma patted my hand. "I have no doubt you'll do fine."

Then she presented me with the beautiful antique pearl necklace, matching bracelet, and teardrop earrings she'd worn on her wedding day more than 60 years before. "I'd love it if you'd wear them in your wedding tomorrow, but only if you want, Ellie. In any case, I want you to keep them."

"I'll be honored to wear them." I ran a finger over the lovely pearls. "I'll treasure them."

She squeezed my hand. "I've been praying for you and Ryan for a long time, honey."

My eyes widened. "You have?" She'd lived in Cade's Corner until Grandpa died three years ago, and then she'd moved to Florida. Mom's parents were both in a nursing home in Columbus.

Grandma touched my cheek and gave me the sweet smile I loved so much. "You smashed cake in Ryan's face at his fourth birthday party, and he repaid the favor the following year. I've watched the two of you tease each other and grow to love one another over the years. But when I saw Ryan put his hand over yours at your father's gravesite"— Grandma's eyes shone with emotion—"I knew he was the boy for you. Ryan has *passion* for you, Ellie. He'll be a very attentive husband. And you will be his perfect helpmate. God's choice for my dear granddaughter."

"Thank you, Grandma." I kissed her soft, sweet cheek. "I love you."

"Can't wait to see you married tomorrow, dear girl."

Ryan and I outlasted everyone as the festive evening drew to a close.

"I'll meet you at the church tomorrow afternoon," Ryan whispered after he walked me home to Mom's house, and we stood outside the front door. I was sleeping in my old bedroom for the last time as a single woman.

"I have our travel documents ready to go," Ryan said. "I double checked with the limo company. They'll pick us up at the church at 5:00 to take us to the airport."

"Can't wait." I smiled and gave him a kiss he wouldn't soon forget. "I'll be there."

My gaze rested on my gorgeous wedding gown hanging on the closet door. My dream dress—cap sleeves, scooped neckline, fitted bodice made from imported white lace with seed pearls and iridescent sequins which tapered to a natural waistline before billowing into a gloriously full, pale blush-colored skirt that made me feel like a beautiful princess. My simple but elegant veil hung in a bag behind the gown.

My packed suitcase for the honeymoon sat in the back of Mom's new car, a Toyota Camry. I went through my mental "to do" list. Satisfied that everything was in order, I jumped out of bed. Retrieving my cell phone from the night table, I sent Ryan a text. Now that he was home, I could freely initiate our texting.

THIS IS THE DAY THE LORD HAS MADE. GOOD MORNING, MY HUSBAND-TO-BE.

Carrying my cellphone with me, I stopped in the upstairs bathroom and then headed downstairs to prepare a light breakfast. Ryan sent a response while I sat eating at the table.

LET US REJOICE AND BE GLAD IN IT. WELCOME TO THE REST OF OUR LIVES TOGETHER, MRS. SULLIVAN-TO-BE. COUNTING THE HOURS. MERRY CHRISTMAS, BABY.

Three hours later, dressed in my wedding gown, I tucked the voluminous skirt beneath me as I sat on a chair at the small desk in the living room. Glancing over my shoulder, I smiled at the lit Christmas tree behind me.

I pulled out the specially made, embossed Perchance to Dream notecards we use for writing the personal notes to the children. Bright colors, pink for the girls and blue for the boys. Not original, but it works well. Then I opened my desk drawer and pulled out my best writing pen.

Since I only have a few minutes before going to the church, I need to make my words count.

I have in mind what I want to say and set my pen first to the pink card.

God's miracles are real, my precious daughter. You are loved and living proof of His greatness. Trust in Him always. Love abounds.

I wrote the identical message on the blue card (substituting "son" for "daughter"). Then I signed them Eleanor Rose Franklin Sullivan and wrote the date immediately beneath my signature. As a last touch, I added the reference for Jeremiah 29:11.

With a smile, I placed the cards in envelopes marked FOR OUR DAUGHTER and FOR OUR SON in my Dream Box. I closed the box and smoothed one hand over the top. I slowly made my way back up the stairs and stored the Dream Box in my closet. I'd take it to the new house when we returned from our honeymoon.

The idea to write the notes and place them in the box had come to me shortly before I'd drifted to sleep the night before. I'd asked Ryan to do the same. Many years later, we'd share these envelopes with our own children. If we couldn't have children of our own, we'd adopt several. God has given us so much, and we need to share His love. We can't know if we'll have a son, or a daughter (hopefully one or more of each), but we share those dreams, hopes, and wishes.

More importantly, Ryan and I share our faith and our prayers.

Lifting the skirt of the gown, I carefully made my way back down the front stairs. Kara had arranged for her friend to come to the house and do my hair (Maura was pleased since it was an elaborate updo, one I'd chosen since it flattered the neckline of my gown). I'd insisted on doing my own makeup using a sheer foundation that allowed my

JoAnn Durgin

freckles to shine through in all their glory. Ryan loved my freckles, so I've decided to embrace, not hide, them.

Another hour later, in my snow boots and with my white silk high heels in a satin bag, I allowed Kara and Staci to help me into my long, white, fake fur coat.

Kara shook her head with a small smile. "Are you sure you want to do this, Ellie?"

"Yes, I do. I want to take a walk with Dad on my wedding day."

Staci's eyes filled with tears and Mom moved her hand over her heart.

Kara nodded. "Just be careful."

I smiled. "I will. I'll see you at the church shortly."

The day was glorious, and I squinted as I stepped outside on the front step. The church bells began to chime, making me smile.

I breathed in deeply, filling my lungs with the fresh, crisp air as I began my short walk.

Dad, this is it. I'm marrying Ryan today. He's the boy Mom told me you always hoped I'd marry. He's a good man. The best. The man of God's choosing for me. He's been my protector since I was a little girl, and he's watched over me in your absence. He can't take your place. No one can ever do that. But I know Ryan will love me and do everything he can to protect me for as many years as the Lord gives us together. Whether that's 10 years or 60 years, I'll be thankful.

A few of the neighbors smiled and called out greetings as I passed by their houses. None of them seemed surprised to see me walking down the street in my bridal gown. That's because they know me so well. Most of them have lived on this street as long as I've been alive. They know I walked this sidewalk with my father in every season of the year, and in all kinds of weather. They might even understand that's what I was doing now.

Not that I'm saying good-bye to Dad, but I'm sharing my special day with him in a private way. The way we would have done if he were walking beside me, my hand in his. He might not be here physically to walk me up the center aisle of the church to meet my groom, but he'd forever be in my thoughts, my prayers, and in my heart.

I had the comfort of knowing I'd join him one day in Heaven. I don't know about the streets paved with gold or winged horses, but I know I'll walk again with my father. Share the smiles and the joy. No more pain, and no more tears.

Ryan's experience in Afghanistan has changed me. Taught me some profound truths. Taught me that small-town living may have its aggravations, but there's nothing like knowing my friends and neighbors have been praying for Ryan, for me, and for us as a couple. Nothing like the townspeople coming alongside me in Keeley's Market or The Soda Shoppe, holding me close, putting their arms around me, and giving me the encouragement and support I need. Saying a prayer for me. Sharing my joy and my pain.

Could I find that in a larger city? Maybe, to a lesser degree. Perhaps not.

But then to think what miracles can be accomplished when God's people pray. Ah, such joy that fills my soul. Good people are everywhere, small town or big city. But this is *home*.

I breathed in and then watched the small puffs of air escape my warm lips as Cade's Corner Community Church comes into view. Such a pretty white church building with its steeple rising majestically in the sky as if to greet the Son. A gathering place for many in town since the 1950s. My parents married in this church. We've buried countless family members, neighbors, and friends in the cemetery behind the church, including my father.

Ryan and I will have a rich life together, Dad. I hope the Lord blesses us with children to carry on the Franklin-Sullivan legacy. Even though I won't be able to see you today, I feel your presence, and I know you're happy for me. Thank you for helping to make me a better person.

Lifting the skirt of my gown, smiling, I slowly climbed the front steps of the church.

Most of all, Dad, thank you for teaching me to love.

Teaching me how *to love.*
And for teaching me to love well.

Chapter 35

~~♥~~

"Ellie, there are reporters on the front steps."

"How many are there?" I watched as Maura scooted back inside the bridal party changing room and closed the door.

"At least four or five from both local and national news outlets. I think some of the big magazines are here based on the names they called out when I peeked out the door." She grinned. "I feel like the press secretary for the president."

"What do you mean? What are they saying?" Kara the Protector was in place. She might come in handy today. Not much could bother me today with the exception of reporters.

"I thought once they knew Ryan was home safely they'd leave us alone," I said. I'd thought my exclusive interview granted to the *Cleveland Plain Dealer* would negate our current situation. "I guess that was wishful thinking."

Kara's dress swished as she walked past me. "Let me at them! Is nothing sacred anymore?"

"Kara, we'll handle it." My tone of voice stopped my oldest sister.

"I need to see Ryan," I said. "He'll know what to do. Maura, can Nick keep the reporters at bay for now?"

"Already done," she assured me. All over again, I silently thanked those two wonderful people. The last few days would have been much more stressful without them to pray with me, counsel me, and stay by my side.

"Wait!" Staci called from behind me as Maura opened the door for me to exit the room. "It's bad luck for the groom to see the bride before the ceremony."

I whirled around, and Staci almost ran into me.

"Whoa. Sorry!" Backing away, she held up her hands.

"That's only a silly superstition." I surprised myself by how calm and in-control I sounded. "This is something unexpected, and I need to discuss what to do with the man who will be my husband in less than an hour."

"Of course," Kara said. "Let us know if you need any help. Or need us to rally the troops."

"Thanks." I relaxed as a feeling of calm swept through me. I couldn't allow anything to spoil this beautiful day. Not even pesky reporters.

Maura stepped over to the door again. "I'll go get Ryan. Ellie, wait for him in the church nursery. I'm sure he'll be in shortly."

I nodded my thanks and started down the hallway.

Within a few minutes, Ryan strolled into the church nursery and closed the door behind him. Turning to face me, his bright smile emerged and made me weak in the knees. Standing before me was the most devastatingly *handsome* man I'd ever seen, inside and out. A man of God, a man of faith.

Ryan moved his hand over his heart. "Ellie, you are more beautiful today than yesterday, and I didn't think that could be possible."

"You say the sweetest things, Man of my Dreams. You clean up very well yourself."

Laughing, Ryan turned in a circle, modeling his dashing black tuxedo. "This old thing?"

"You can't begin to know how much I love you," I told him. "I'd come closer, but I honestly don't trust myself with you looking as good as you do right now. Besides that, I can't risk shedding tears and messing up my makeup before the ceremony or my sisters will yell at me."

The corners of Ryan's lips upturned. "I understand. We can't have that. But I'm going to come closer now, hold your hands, and kiss your cheeks."

"I'll try to control myself. It will be difficult." He chuckled, but I was totally serious.

I placed my hands in his, and my eyes misted as Ryan softly kissed one cheek and then the other. When he pulled back, his eyes shone with anticipation of what was to come. The day we thought might never come. With one hand, he gently trailed his fingers over my freckles with the lightest touch.

"I suppose this wouldn't be a good time to ditch our family and friends and run off to the Justice of the Peace?"

I laughed. "Soon enough, my love. How's your ankle? I see you've ditched the crutch and the sling."

"I'm moving a little slow, but I'll be fine." Ryan's blue eyes darkened, his lids appeared heavy. "I can't wait to be married to you, Ellie." He said those words in a deep, smooth tone he had to know got to me every single time. "I'll make you happy, and we're going to have a great life together, baby."

"I've never doubted it for a minute." I looked away for a moment to regain my composure. "You must stop saying sweet things like that before the ceremony." I sniffled. "Not that I don't love them, but first things first." I blinked hard a few times and then shook my head to clear my thoughts. "I understand we have some unexpected guests."

"Yes," he said. "I say we go outside on the front steps of the church for five minutes. Give them a statement and allow them to take their photos."

I tilted my head. "In exchange for leaving us alone during the ceremony and the reception?"

"That's my plan." Ryan shrugged, drawing attention to his broad shoulders. "I hope it works. Are you game?"

A smile covered my face. "Bring it on."

He laughed and kissed my cheek. "That's my gorgeous girl. Do you have a coat?" His gaze skimmed over me in a way that revealed his strong desire and deep love for me.

"I'll be warm enough," I assured him. That was a huge understatement. "Let's go."

With Ryan's hand in mine, we stood on the front steps of the church and faced the reporters together. Bright lights from the cameras nearly blinded me to the point where I could barely see individual faces, only hear the questions being called out to us.

"Ryan, why do you think you were one of the lucky ones who survived?"

"Because God's not done with me yet," Ryan said. "He has a purpose and a mission for me that I have yet to fulfill." Ryan squeezed my hand. "Job number one is marrying my beautiful girl."

"Ellie, your story with Ryan is being called a fairy tale. What do you say to that?"

"I'm just a small-town girl who loves the small-town boy from down the street. And blessed beyond measure that Ryan loves me back. I don't look at our story as a fairy tale. To me, it's a living, breathing example of God's infinite grace."

I glanced up at Ryan and he lowered his lips to mine for another sweet kiss.

Turning to face the small crowd once more, Ryan informed the reporters and photographers that we would not be answering any more questions.

And then he politely and diplomatically told them to leave.

As we waited in the vestibule for Mom to walk me up the aisle to meet Ryan, I noticed light snowflakes dancing outside the frosted windows. Kara and then Staci gave me quick hugs and whispered they loved me before they began their slow walk up the center aisle.

"Don't forget this." Mom handed me the gorgeous wedding bouquet made by Nancy and Luther Nelson. I couldn't begin to name the flowers, but the arrangement consisted of large blooms in deep purple and off-white with baby's breath and a few sprigs of Christmas greenery. I'd never seen anything quite like it, but it was breathtaking and exquisite.

"Ready, Ellie?"

I smiled at my mother. She looked radiant, lovely and elegant in her wine-colored, tea length gown. I'd noticed Dr.

Bernard sitting at the back of the sanctuary. He was quite a distinguished-looking man. Mom must have invited him to come, after all. That made my heart smile, and I was truly happy for her.

"Mom, I was *born* ready to marry Ryan."

She pressed her cheek to mine. "Good answer. I love how God's had His hand in your relationship with Ryan from the time you were babies. Yours is truly a love story for the ages. That kind of love is rare. I know you will cherish one another. As I cherish *you*, my darling daughter."

"Thanks, but we'd better start up the aisle now or I'm going to cry."

Mom smiled. "Then let's take you to your groom."

I wasn't nervous. I only had eyes for Ryan, and he for me, as the prelude began, and I started my slow walk to the front of the church with Mom. A string quartet played a classical piece, and it sounded beautiful in our beloved little church.

I smiled when Mom kissed my cheek and answered the pastor's question about who gave me away in marriage by saying, "Her father and I do."

The service progressed smoothly, and when Pastor Derek pronounced us husband and wife, Ryan brushed his lips over mine. "Think they have any pesky amphibians in Hawaii?"

Laughing, I cupped his jaw with one hand. "I can't wait to find out."

He whispered something else I'll always remember, for my ears only, and then pressed his lips to mine once more for a longer kiss. One for the ages. Ryan's kiss is filled with such precious promise.

Oh, how I love this man. And he loves me right back.

With joined hands, smiling, Ryan and I turned to face our guests. The relatives and friends who've seen us grow up, the ones who've walked this journey with us. The ones who've touched our lives and the lives of those whom we love. The ones we'll never forget. Each one of them has brought us to this day.

This glorious day to rejoice and be glad.

Ryan put his hand over mine and together we started back down the aisle. As we did, the words of that old hymn came back to me again, making my heart smile.

Fairest Lord Jesus.

Thee will I honor.

Thee will I cherish.

Thou, my soul's glory, joy, and crown.

The End

www.ingramcontent.com/pod-product-compliance
Lightning Source LLC
Chambersburg PA
CBHW021234130626
46554CB00004B/1490